C0-AVF-221

HOMETOWN HEARTS

SHIPMENT 1

Stranger in Town by Brenda Novak
Baby's First Homecoming by Cathy McDavid
Her Surprise Hero by Abby Gaines
A Mother's Homecoming by Tanya Michaels
A Firefighter in the Family by Trish Milburn
Tempted by a Texan by Mindy Neff

SHIPMENT 2

It Takes a Family by Victoria Pade
The Sheriff of Heartbreak County by Kathleen Creighton
A Hometown Boy by Janice Kay Johnson
The Renegade Cowboy Returns by Tina Leonard
Unexpected Bride by Lisa Childs
Accidental Hero by Loralee Lillibridge

SHIPMENT 3

An Unlikely Mommy by Tanya Michaels
Single Dad Sheriff by Lisa Childs
In Protective Custody by Beth Cornelison
Cowboy to the Rescue by Trish Milburn
The Ranch She Left Behind by Kathleen O'Brien
Most Wanted Woman by Maggie Price
A Weaver Wedding by Allison Leigh

SHIPMENT 4

A Better Man by Emilie Rose
Daddy Protector by Jacqueline Diamond
The Road to Bayou Bridge by Liz Talley
Fully Engaged by Catherine Mann
The Cowboy's Secret Son by Trish Milburn
A Husband's Watch by Karen Templeton

SHIPMENT 5

His Best Friend's Baby by Molly O'Keefe
Caleb's Bride by Wendy Warren
Her Sister's Secret Life by Pamela Toth
Lori's Little Secret by Christine Rimmer
High-Stakes Bride by Fiona Brand
Hometown Honey by Kara Lennox

SHIPMENT 6

Reining in the Rancher by Karen Templeton
A Man to Rely On by Cindi Myers
Your Ranch or Mine? by Cindy Kirk
Mother in Training by Marie Ferrarella
A Baby for the Bachelor by Victoria Pade
The One She Left Behind by Kristi Gold
Her Son's Hero by Vicki Essex

SHIPMENT 7

Once and Again by Brenda Harlen
Her Sister's Fiancé by Teresa Hill
Family at Stake by Molly O'Keefe
Adding Up to Marriage by Karen Templeton
Bachelor Dad by Roxann Delaney
It's That Time of Year by Christine Wenger

SHIPMENT 8

The Rancher's Christmas Princess by Christine Rimmer
Their Baby Miracle by Lillian Darcy
Mad About Max by Penny McCusker
No Ordinary Joe by Michelle Celmer
The Soldier's Baby Bargain by Beth Kery
A Texan Under the Mistletoe by Leah Vale

HOMETOWN HEARTS

In Protective Custody

BETH CORNELISON

⟨H⟩ HARLEQUIN® HOMETOWN HEARTS

Recycling programs
for this product may
not exist in your area.

ISBN-13: 978-0-373-21465-5

In Protective Custody

Printed in U.S.A.

Beth Cornelison began working in public relations before pursuing her love of writing romance. She has won numerous honors for her work, including an RWA RITA® Award nomination for *The Christmas Stranger*. She enjoys featuring her cats (or friends' pets) in her stories and always has another book in the pipeline! She currently lives in Louisiana with her husband, one son and three spoiled cats. Contact her via her website, bethcornelison.com.

To my parents, who gave me roots and wings.

Chapter One

"Mr. Caldwell, your sister has been shot."

Max Caldwell wiped sooty sweat from his face with the back of his hand and strained to hear the voice on the phone over the ruckus of the fire station. "Can you repeat that? What did Emily do?"

"She's in critical condition from a gunshot wound to the chest."

Max's stomach pitched, and he slumped against the painted concrete wall. *A gunshot wound?*

"Dr. Hoffman needs your permission to perform an emergency C-section and deliver her baby right away." The woman rattled off the name of the New Orleans hospital where Emily had been admitted.

Max plugged one ear with his finger to mute the shouts and laughter of the other firemen. Just back from saving an antebellum home from an electrical fire, his fellow firefighters were pumped with adrenaline. Their boisterous celebrating made it hard to hear, much less grasp the enormity of what the woman said.

"What about her husband, Joe Rialto? Shouldn't he make that decision?"

"I'm afraid Mr. Rialto was pronounced dead on arrival."

"Joe is...dead?" Max plowed his fingers through his sweat-dampened hair and swore under his breath. The sour taste of dread climbed his throat, and his limbs shook. "O-okay, do whatever you have to but...save my sister."

A disturbing silence followed. His chest tightened.

"Hello? Did you hear me?"

"Yes, sir. I... We will naturally do everything we can for her, but...the odds are not in favor of your sister surviving, Mr. Caldwell. It's the baby we're trying to save now."

"Damn it!" Max yelled into the phone, an

uncharacteristic wave of panic raising his voice. "She's all I have! Don't let her die!"

The fire station fell silent, and he glanced up to find all eyes staring at him. He turned his back to the other men and gripped the phone like a lifeline to his sister. The lingering scent of smoke and the stink of sweat and Ben-Gay suffocated him. He needed air. Couldn't breathe.

"We'll do our best, of course."

His fire station was at least twenty minutes from the hospital, and he'd have to fight the New Orleans rush-hour traffic. Max squeezed his eyes closed and silently begged God not to take his sister. Then drawing a deep breath, he murmured, "Save the baby. I'm on my way."

"Joe?" Emily gazed at Max with unfocused eyes. Her voice sounded thready and hoarse.

Max's heart thundered like a rookie's on his first four-alarm call as he leaned forward and gently squeezed her hand. She'd been unresponsive for two days, so even weak, her voice was music to his ears. The doctors had warned him Emily might never regain consciousness.

"No, Em. It's me. Max."

"Where's... Joe?"

"Shh. Don't talk. Save your strength." He fumbled to mash the call button to alert the nurses' station that his sister had awakened.

"What happened?" Emily whispered.

Max grinned slightly, not really surprised that his younger sister ignored his directions. In twenty-one years, she'd never done what he told her. The spoiled brat.

"Don't try to talk. You've lost a lot of blood, and you need to save your strength."

He stroked her fingers with his thumb, and a lump swelled in his throat. God in heaven, how did he tell his sister she was a widow? A single mother? They'd lost so much in their lives already. Both of their parents. Max's unborn child, then his marriage. Now Joe.

Focus on the positive. Emily's baby was doing well.

A nurse in purple scrubs poked her head into the room. "Yes?"

"She's awake."

"Wonderful." The nurse hustled toward the bed and checked the machines hooked to Emily. She took Emily's blood pressure then smiled at Max. "Her vitals have improved. I'll get the doctor."

He nodded in response then turned back to Emily when the nurse exited.

"Hey, congratulations. You're a mama. The doctors delivered your son by C-section a couple of nights ago, and he's doing great. Six pounds, five ounces of future starting quarterback. I'm saving a spot for him on my Pee Wee team." He hoped the cheer in his voice didn't sound as fake to her as it did to him.

Emily's eyes warmed, and a faint smile touched her lips. "He's...okay?"

Her whisper was barely audible now. He could tell even the few words she'd spoken had taxed her limited strength.

"He's perfect. And he needs his mama to rest now. He needs you to get well." Max brushed a wisp of hair, as black as his own, from his sister's forehead then gave her cheek a kiss. "And so do I."

She closed her eyes, probably succumbing to fatigue rather than in acquiescence, since Emily lived to defy him.

Her marriage to a man she barely knew and her immediate pregnancy at the tender age of twenty-one typified her willfulness. *God, please let her live to defy me again.*

The door opened, and Emily's in-laws stepped into the room.

"There's our girl," Joe's father said with a politician's smile.

Mrs. Rialto, whose puffy red eyes and splotchy face bore evidence of her grief over her son's death, cast a watery-eyed glance to Emily.

A nurse in scrubs caught Anthony Rialto's arm. "Excuse me, sir. You'll have to wait outside. Only one visitor at a time."

Joe's father scoffed and, giving the nurse a superior grin, lifted the woman's hand from his suit sleeve. "Nonsense. We're family. We only want a minute with her." His expression grew more ingratiating, though still edged with impatience. "Surely you can bend the rules this once."

Max felt Emily's grip on his fingers tighten slightly. He glanced at her, but Emily's attention was focused on the Rialtos.

"Sir, the rules—" the nurse said.

"Only a minute," Anthony interrupted. He winked at the nurse and placed a hand at his wife's back to escort her farther into the room.

The nurse sighed her exasperation but stepped out of the room without pressing the issue.

Emily's eyes widened as her in-laws approached, and what little color she had in her cheeks paled. Her reaction puzzled Max, put him on alert. Though wary, Max rose to greet the couple, extending a hand to Anthony.

"Well, well, Emily. So glad you're feeling better. We have business to discuss." Ignoring Max's offered handshake, Joe's father swept past Max with the air of a man used to having his way. The wealthy New Orleans business tycoon exuded power and an iron will.

Max was unmoved by the man's credentials in the business world. He'd protect his sister's interests at any cost.

As her father-in-law approached the bedside, Emily shrank into the mattress.

"B-business?" Emily's wary eyes cut to Max in a silent plea for help.

"Not now." Max grabbed the older man's shoulder, and his grip bit into the expensive silk suit Anthony wore.

The man sent him a dark glower and shook off Max's hand. "Now! The baby could be released as early as tomorrow night, after Joe's funeral. Besides, we can't wait around and risk her dying without signing."

Max bit out an earthy obscenity. Of all the heartless...

"Signing?" Emily squeaked. The monitor registering her heartbeat beeped faster.

Max's chest clenched. She'd just regained consciousness, and her condition was still too unstable for them to upset her this way. "This can wait. Emily has to rest."

"Lydia." Anthony snapped his fingers. "Give me the papers."

Joe's mother sidled past Max with an apologetic grimace and a swirl of exotic perfume as she dug some folded sheets from her purse.

Anthony snatched them from her. "Custody papers for our grandson. If you die, he belongs with us. We've lost Joe, but we won't lose Joe's son."

Emily gasped. "Joe's d-dead?"

The man's thoughtlessness roiled like lava in Max's gut, and he squeezed his hands into fists.

"Didn't your brother tell you?" Lydia asked.

His sister's eyes found his and filled with tears. The proof of her grief kicked him in the chest, stealing his breath.

The erratic display on the cardiac monitor verified how news of her husband's death affected Emily. Max didn't need a doctor to tell him this stress would set her recovery back.

Rage for the Rialtos' insensitivity exploded

inside him like a backdraft. "Get out and take your damn custody papers with you! She won't be signing anything. Do you hear me?"

"But my grandson—" Lydia sniffed.

"Excuse me, folks." Emily's doctor stepped into the room, a frown creasing his brow. "Mrs. Rialto is very weak and needs rest. If I have to, I'll call security and ban all visitors from her room." The doctor directed a hard look on Mr. Rialto. "No exceptions. Do I make myself clear?"

Anthony stepped away, glaring a menacing challenge to Max. "Don't think this is over, Caldwell. Whether or not she signs, we *will* have that baby. Make no mistake."

Grabbing his wife's arm, Anthony stormed from the room, but the chill of his parting threat hung in the air.

Max saw Emily shiver, and apprehension shimmied through him, as well. From the first time he'd met the senior Rialtos at Emily's wedding, something about the shipping mogul and his kowtowing wife had rubbed Max the wrong way. Something beyond their ostentatious wealth and the man's condescending attitude. Anthony's disregard for Emily's well-being cemented Max's disdain for his sister's father-in-law.

Cutting a quick glance to the doctor, who wore a mask of concern as he felt for Emily's pulse, Max decided he should give the doctor room to work. Pressing a kiss to Emily's cheek, he excused himself to the corridor.

In the hall, a homicide detective wearing a wrinkled suit and a grim expression sat in a folding chair, waiting for the chance to question Emily about the shooting.

Max's lungs felt leaden. Rubbing eyes as scratchy as his two-day beard, he struggled for a breath. What in God's name had Emily gotten herself into this time?

Ignoring the suspicious look from the cop, Max headed to the cafeteria for coffee. He needed time to collect himself before seeing Emily again and another hit of caffeine to get him through the afternoon.

When he returned to her room several minutes later, Emily was unresponsive again. Damn the Rialtos for upsetting her like that! Max gritted his teeth and fought for his composure. He had to stay in control for Emily's sake.

Even the suggestion that he could lose his baby sister, whom he'd helped raise, knotted his chest and haunted him with sickening dread. She was his only surviving family. He'd do anything, *anything* to better her chances of recovery. For now that meant serving as watchdog, keeping the wolves who would discourage and upset her away.

He bowed his head and clutched her hand. *Please, God, don't take my sister. I'll do anything....*

"You want me to *what?*" Max stared at Emily in disbelief, and a prickle crawled up his spine. She couldn't be serious, could she?

"Take m'baby... Hide 'im." Emily's slurred speech indicated how much talking wore her out. She'd wakened again the next morning after a long, worrisome night. For her health's sake, Max had tried to avoid discussing her in-laws, but Emily would not be swayed. Her pale face and haggard expression showed the degree of her distress.

"Look, nothing's going to happen to your baby," Max crooned, hoping to placate her. After witnessing the ill effects of stress and worry on her condition the day before, he knew he had to calm her somehow. Her weak system couldn't handle the strain.

"I know losing Joe has upset you, but... now is not the time to talk about this. You have to save your energy and get stronger—"

"Max—"

"—so you can take care of your son. Now quiet down and—"

"Lis'n!" Emily winced in pain, and even more color drained from her face.

When she grew eerily quiet, Max's heartbeat stilled. "Emily?" He patted her hand. "Emily!"

The lids of her soulful brown eyes fluttered open. "Rialtos...dangerous."

Max frowned. "Dangerous?"

An ominous tension made the air thick. Emily's face reflected the strain, and her eyes grew dark.

"I...didn't know," Emily whispered. The sadness in her eyes pleaded for her brother's forgiveness and understanding.

A vise-like tightness squeezed his chest. He knew she wouldn't rest until she'd had her say. Arguing would only waste her breath and his, so he sat in the chair beside her bed and squeezed her hand.

Emily whispered something he couldn't understand. Max leaned closer. "Say it again."

"Drugs."

Drugs? A chill burrowed into Max's bones.

"Joe was involved with drugs? You mean he used them?"

"No."

"Then you're saying he sold drugs or smuggled them or—"

She closed her eyes and dropped her chin slightly. *Yes.*

Max sighed. "Em, why didn't you leave Joe when you found out about this?"

Emily raised a misty gaze then looked away.

Because she was pregnant with Joe's child.

"Em, what—" He snapped his mouth closed and swallowed his questions, his rebuke. Now was not the time to get into whatever poor choices Joe had made. Emily needed to stay calm and concentrate on healing.

"All of…them," Emily whispered. "Dang'rous."

"Not now, Em. We'll talk about this later, once you're better."

Whatever she thought her in-laws were involved in could wait. Hadn't he already bitten his tongue regarding the Rialtos for more than a year? While Max had instinctively distrusted Joe from the start, Emily had been blinded by love.

Emily drew an unsteady breath and frowned. "Joe…murder'd."

This much he already knew. The police had

filled Max in on witness accounts of how an armed man had barged into the restaurant where Emily and Joe had been dining and shot her husband in cold blood.

Max choked back the bile that rose in his throat, imagining his sister's fear and pain the night Joe's killer had opened fire on them. The horror. The violence.

"I know, Em. The police are working a few leads to try to find the man—"

"Joe…murder'd."

Acid burned his gut. Was she saying she knew who killed Joe? That his murder was somehow linked to his family and drugs?

Max mentally reviewed what he knew of Joe and his father. Their shipping business was small but enormously lucrative. And could easily have been infiltrated by drug smugglers.

Or did Joe's murder mean the Rialtos' involvement was consensual?

That possibility kicked Max's pulse up a notch, stirred a cold frisson of suspicion in his bones. Either way, living on the fringes of such a volatile business was no life for Emily. Or her son.

"Pr'tect…baby from… Rialtos." Emily's

pleas echoed his own thoughts, and a fore-boding chill washed through him.

"Maybe you could get a restraining order to—"

Emily shook her head, her eyes reflecting the same skepticism that twisted in him. After witnessing Anthony Rialto in action, Max knew she was right. A court order wouldn't stop the Rialtos from taking what they wanted.

He tried to reason out a better option, but Emily nixed every idea, offering cold truths she'd learned about her father-in-law. When he suggested involving the police, she claimed Anthony Rialto had dirty cops on his payroll.

Gasping her beliefs one key word at a time, she argued breathlessly that if the Rialtos got the baby when he was released from the hospital, they'd take him out of the country and fight her custody rights. Her impassioned pleas for her child, even as she fought for her own life, wrenched Max's emotions in knots.

"You're only…one I…trust. Don't…let baby…outta…your sight." She was truly winded now, struggling for air, and Max place his free hand over her lips.

"Easy. Hush now." He clenched his teeth and sighed. "I won't go to the police, and I won't let Joe's family get near your son. I promise."

Her grip loosened, and relief softened the tension in her face. "You'll…take…m'baby? Hide?"

Her breathlessness plucked at his heart as much as her determination. The pleading in her eyes tore him apart. The fear and resignation in her voice tormented him.

What else could he do? The Rialtos didn't negotiate. They had the money, the lawyers, the power and influence to get their way, right or wrong.

"But what about you, Em? I can't leave you like this. And I can't care for a baby and be here for you at the same time."

Tears welled in her eyes, and Max knew he'd lost. He was a sucker for a woman's tears. Especially Emily's.

"I don't know anything about babies," he mumbled, dragging a hand over his stubbled chin.

"You'll…learn. All new…fathers do."

"But I'm not his father."

"If… I die—"

Ice sluiced through his veins. "Don't talk that way! You can't die. You have a baby to raise."

"Raise him…for me."

A cold ball of fear lodged in his throat. He'd tried the family-man thing once.

And failed. Miserably.

He was all wrong for the job of raising a child.

Another tear escaped his sister's eyelashes. *Hell!*

"How am I supposed to get the baby out of the hospital without Joe's family knowing? They've hovered around the nursery like a pack of wolves since he was born."

That news seemed to suck the spirit from Emily. The hope in her eyes dimmed, and pain sliced Max's chest. If she gave up hope and quit fighting for her life…

He had to do *something*. But what she asked of him was daunting. A baby! Memories of his failed marriage rose to haunt him. Emily's need battled the demons of his past.

Finally, Emily's desperate, tormented expression swayed him. He leaned close and whispered fiercely in her ear. "Emily, listen to me. For once in your life, do what I'm telling you. I'll make a deal with you, okay?"

She met his gaze, hope lighting her eyes.

"I'll find a way to get your son out of here, to hide him from Joe's family and keep him safe for you, if..." He wagged a finger in her face to punctuate his point. Already the hurdles of getting the baby past the Rialtos loomed in his mind. "Swear to me, promise me now, you will fight. You *cannot* give up hope. You *have to* get well, so that you can take care of your baby yourself. Like I tell my Pee Wee football kids—no quitters on my team. Understand?"

A flicker of warmth lit her eyes, and Max knew he'd made the only choice he could. If his promise would give Emily the hope she needed to survive, he'd promise her the moon and figure out how to get it. Despite his track record.

Maybe helping Emily would redeem him in some small way for his failures in the past. He refused to let her down.

"I'll keep your son safe for you."

The next afternoon, Max backed out of his sister's hospital room and closed the door. Tucked to his chest, he carried the duffel bag he'd used to bring her clean pajamas and a pillow from home. The police detective, having gotten a few minutes alone with Emily earlier in the day, had finally left the hospital. Only one hurdle remained.

Max cast a wry grin to the beefy-armed thug standing guard at her door. "She's nursing the baby and doesn't want her big brother watching," he lied.

The Rialtos' lackey, obviously assigned as watchdog while the family attended Joe's funeral, shifted his bulky weight and cut a nervous glance toward Emily's door. Max's ploy worked as he'd hoped. The guard seemed uncomfortable with the idea of a breast-feeding mother and didn't enter the room to check on them.

Max aimed a finger at the duffel bag. "I'm gonna drop her dirty clothes at the laundry and get a bite to eat. Want anything from the snack bar?"

The Rialtos' man glowered at Max and shook his head.

"Whatever." Max turned and headed for the elevator, praying that the baby hidden in the duffel continued to sleep until he got out of the hospital. He hoped no one looked too closely through the large gap in the duffel's zipper he'd left open for air.

After he'd promised to take care of her son, Emily's mood and condition had improved enough that her doctor and the baby's pediatrician had both agreed to let her see her son. And Max's sketchy plan began to take shape. He spoke to the pediatrician privately and convinced the man to sign for the baby's discharge while the Rialtos attended Joe's funeral.

During Emily's visit with the discharged baby, they waited for his nephew to fall asleep. Now, careful not to jostle the boy in the vented bag, Max exited the medical center New Orleans natives fondly called Charity Hospital. He made his way across the divided street to the visitors' parking garage.

Phase one of his mission complete, Max buckled his nephew in the car seat he'd bought on the way to the hospital that afternoon. When he slid behind the wheel of his Jeep Cherokee and cranked the engine, the radio blared from the rear speakers. Mick Jagger woke the sleeping baby, who tuned up and added his vocals to the Stones.

Max cringed and turned in the seat to try to comfort the infant. "Hey, easy, little guy."

As he jiggled the baby's seat, he spotted the Rialtos' thug at the front door of the hospital. The man scanned the street then zeroed in on Max's SUV. Reaching under his coat, the henchman started toward the parking garage.

No doubt Mr. Thug kept something besides his wallet tucked inside his jacket.

"Hell!" Max had no time to do anything about the crying child. His first priority was getting out of Dodge. Fast. He might have the child with Emily's permission, but the Rialtos made their own rules.

Max pulled out of the garage and darted into the evening traffic. Emily's son continued to wail like a fire engine siren. The thought of the Rialtos' armed guard on his heels kicked Max's pulse up a notch. He zipped through a yellow light, anxious to put distance between himself and the gorilla at the hospital.

He thought of the wistful expression on Emily's face as she'd kissed her son goodbye, and his throat clogged.

"I've done my part, Em. Now you fight, damn it!" He hated not being at her side. What if she got worse or...?

Don't think that way. Visualize success. Make it happen. Wasn't that what he told the kids he coached in the Pee Wee football league?

Max drew a deep breath and flexed his fingers on the steering wheel.

Focus. Focus.

But the baby's cries reached a fervid pitch, and he couldn't think, much less concentrate on the problems at hand. As he headed away from the hospital, he encountered a road-block where a construction crew was fixing the street. A backlog of cars inched toward the detour.

Frustrated with his slow progress, Max zipped around a bus of tourists and turned down a side street. He crawled a few more blocks until he turned onto Canal Street headed toward the French Quarter. Snarled in traffic, Max flicked a glance to his rear-view mirror. No sign of the armed henchman. But Max knew the thug hadn't given up. He was still hunting him.

When a group of women dashed in front of him to catch one of the city's famous street-cars, he stood on the brakes to avoid hitting them. The near miss sent an extra jolt of adrenaline through his already edgy system. By the time he turned on Baronne, headed toward the Crescent City Connection and his home in Belle Chasse, his nephew's screams had completely frayed his nerves. What if the kid was in pain?

Remembering the pacifier he'd jammed in his pocket at the hospital, Max fished the little plastic device from his jeans and picked off the lint that clung to the nipple.

"Easy, little guy," he crooned to the baby. "Here." He twisted toward the backseat and fumbled to find the baby's mouth. Tiny fists hit his hand as Max searched for his target. By now, the child's screams could curdle blood.

He swerved to avoid a pedestrian who seemed more interested in the panhandling saxophone player on the corner than the traffic. Keeping an eye on the bumper in front of him, Max groped blindly across the baby's face until he found his nephew's mouth, opened wide in a deafening howl. The infant latched on to his finger and sucked hard.

"Try this instead." He swapped the pacifier for his finger, and a blessed silence filled the car.

For about thirty seconds.

He heard the soft clunk when the pacifier fell out of the baby's mouth, and Max braced himself.

His nephew let out an angry wail. Max groaned. Escaping the Rialtos' thug no longer seemed his biggest problem. What if he never got the little banshee to stop crying?

Max could enter a burning house with confidence in his firefighting skill and training, but knowing he was in charge of a tiny, needy, noisy life scared him spitless. What if he did the wrong thing and hurt the kid? What if he didn't get the hang of it the way a new father was supposed to? If he failed this time, he'd let two people down, Emily *and* her son.

Sighing, he turned toward the backseat and fumbled in the car seat for the lost pacifier. When his fingers closed around the cool plastic, relief zinged through his blood.

He stuck the device in the baby's mouth and glanced back to the traffic—just as his Cherokee plowed into the back of a white Camry with a nauseating crunch.

More screeching tires. Then the jarring crunch of another car hitting him from behind.

Max muttered a scorching curse.

The driver of the Camry climbed out and glared at him.

And his nephew lost his pacifier again.

Laura Dalton winced as she watched the black Cherokee ram into the Camry. Right after that, a pickup truck smashed into the back of the Cherokee. The *crunch* of the collisions skittered through her system, shooting adrenaline through her veins. Heart thudding, she pulled onto a side street and climbed from her Honda on shaky legs to see if she could help.

Please don't let anyone be hurt. She could handle all the baby barf and dirty diapers that her job at the day care center doled out, but the sight of blood sent her into a panic.

She scowled, realizing none of the other drivers who'd witnessed the accident had stopped to assist or give their statements to the cops.

But Laura knew too well what it was like to need someone yet have no one to turn to. She couldn't easily turn her back when she saw a chance to help.

The driver of the Camry climbed out and scowled at his crumpled fender, but he seemed unharmed. One down. As she approached the scene, the driver of the Cherokee, a tall, good-looking man with jet black hair, got out and stepped to his back door. While he leaned in the backseat of his car, Laura made her way to the pickup where the driver had yet to emerge.

She knocked on the truck's window, and the blond teenage girl at the wheel rolled down the window.

"Are you all right?" Laura asked, searching the teen's pale face.

"I…yeah. Oh, God…my dad's gonna kill me!" The girl buried her face in her hands and groaned.

"But you're okay physically? You're not hurt?"

"No. I'm fine…thanks." The girl flashed her a weak smile.

Laura returned a relieved grin. "Just remind your dad what's important. You're safe. That's what matters. I have a cell phone in my car if you need to call your parents."

"Okay. Thanks." The girl gave her another timid grin, flashing a set of braces.

The familiar howl of a baby in distress called Laura's attention away from the teenager in the truck.

The Cherokee's driver pulled an infant, still strapped in a baby carrier, out of his backseat and set the carrier on the ground beside the car. Images of an injured child flashed through Laura's mind, chilling her blood. "Oh, no."

She hurried over to the raven-haired man who hunkered over the car seat, fumbling to unfasten the baby from the straps.

"Is she hurt?" Laura asked.

"It's a boy. And he's okay. I think." The man added an obscenity as he struggled with trembling hands to free the infant from the straps.

"Here. Let me." She nudged the man aside and mashed the release button that freed the baby of the seat straps. The infant's cries wrenched her heart. He was tiny, like a newborn, and his face had turned beet red from bawling.

The man raked a hand through his black hair, leaving the thick waves rumpled. Taking his son from her, he awkwardly put the infant on his shoulder and rubbed the baby's back. "Thanks."

"Glad to help."

Deep worry lines etched the man's face as he surveyed his crumpled bumper and scanned the gathering crowd. Obviously shaken by the accident, he patted the baby's back harder and began pacing. "Easy, fella. You'll be all right. Shh."

The baby's howls didn't abate, and the louder the baby cried, the more agitated the father grew.

Laura couldn't blame him. The infant's shrieks had her edgy too. She hated hearing a child in distress. At the day care center, she was always the first worker rushing to soothe an upset child.

She remembered too well what it felt like to be young, scared and all alone. No one to comfort you, no one to dry your tears, no one who even noticed you were there.

She fell in step with the dark-haired father as he strode anxiously back and forth beside his wrecked Cherokee, muttering.

"If you'd like, I'll hold your son while you talk to the police."

The man came to an abrupt halt, and his head snapped up. He pinned her with a dark brown stare. "What?"

"I work with children, and I'm good at calming them down, if you want me to—"

"The cops. Damn!" He squeezed his eyes closed, scrunching his face in frustration.

Laura tipped her head and studied the father, who seemed even more disconcerted now. A thin sheen of perspiration dampened his forehead, and a palpable tension vibrated from his square jaw. His concern seemed ridiculously out of proportion to the circumstances.

"Is there a problem, sir? I'd be happy to help if—"

He spun to her with an abrupt jerk. "Where's your car?"

"Excuse me?"

"Your car. I need it." He tore his dark gaze away and glanced nervously around the accident scene.

"My car? Wh-why?"

The man's odd behavior set her on edge. She backed away from him a step, only to have him grab her arm. His touch sent a strange jolt through her. She couldn't remember the last time a man had touched her. The sensation of his strong, hot hand on her arm was overwhelming. He balanced the baby with one hand while his long fingers tightened around her upper arm. The first inkling of panic fluttered to life in her chest.

"I've gotta get out of here before—" He clamped his mouth shut and sighed. "Where's your car?"

The baby now screamed so hard Laura feared he'd hurt himself. Her stomach bunched with worry for the infant's well-being. "Are you sure you wouldn't like me to hold your baby just for a minute? I really think I could calm him down."

The father gave her a wary look then glanced down at the hollering infant. Finally he released her arm and thrust the tiny boy at her. "I'm sure not having any luck. Go ahead."

Laura cradled the wiggling infant against her chest and rocked him gently. "How old is he? He's so small."

"Huh?" The man pulled out his wallet as he surveyed the area. "Oh, he's...uh, just a couple days old. Listen, I need your help." He seized her arm again and guided her farther away from the bustle of people examining the damage to the vehicles.

She shrugged out of his grip, glowering at him. "Would you stop grabbing me like that? What is your deal?"

The man wiped a palm on the leg of his jeans and took a deep breath. Then, raising a hand and lowering his voice, he explained over the baby's continued howling, "My truck is trapped and probably not driveable. I need wheels. Fast."

She narrowed her gaze on him, eyeing him with suspicion. "Why? What's the hurry?"

He opened his mouth as if to answer but then closed it again. With another sigh, he fished his driver's license and some small cards from his wallet. "It's...the baby. I have to get him home. Quickly." He stepped closer, and his expression reeked of desperation. But desperation over what? His own situation or the baby's?

"Go on," she prodded reluctantly.

"He's…sick." The man's black eyebrows knitted in a frown. He glanced away, huffed then pinned her again with a pleading look. "He needs his medicine. That's why he's crying."

Laura's breath caught. "Medicine? Oh, my God…what—"

"Will you help us?"

"I…of course. But what about your car? The police haven't written up the accident yet and—"

"I can't wait around for the cops to get here. Don't you hear him screaming? He needs his medicine. Now!"

"But the other drivers…" Indecision and apprehension swelled in her chest, making it difficult to breathe. When she hesitated, the man grunted and jabbed his wallet back in his rear pocket. With long-legged strides, he stalked over to the driver of the Camry and shoved a business card in the other man's hand. "I'm sorry. I've gotta get the baby home. I'll be in touch about the insurance. Are you hurt?"

When the Camry driver shook his head, the dark-haired man hustled over to the pickup and poked a card through the window to the teenager, too. He drilled a hard look on Laura as he returned. "No one's hurt, and they have my contact numbers. Now can we go?"

The sounds of the baby's wailing tore at her heart. What if the child really was sick, and he suffered because she wouldn't help? How could she live with herself? Then again, how could she trust that this jittery-acting man was telling her the truth?

The man's gaze froze on someone or something in the crowd, and his expression hardened. "*Oh hell,* he's here! We're outta time. Where is your car?"

His tone brooked no resistance.

"I…the Honda over there." She tipped her head, directing his gaze across the intersection.

"Good. Let's move!" With his fingers wrapped around her wrist, he grabbed the baby seat in his other hand and hustled her toward her Honda.

"Who did you see? Who's here?" She stumbled to keep up with his long strides and struggled to keep a safe hold on the baby.

He cut a sharp glance toward her without

slowing his pace. "Never mind. Just get us out of here!"

"I h-have a phone if you'd rather call your wife to have her bring the medicine here." They reached the passenger side of her Accord, and he opened the back door. "That way you could take care of the paperwork for the accident—"

"No." He put the baby's car seat in the back then faced Laura. "That won't work. My wife…isn't home."

When she made no move to get in, he opened the front door and pushed her toward the seat. "Get in! I'll drive."

"But—" Her legs bumped the frame of the car. She lost her balance, dropping clumsily into the passenger seat while clutching the baby to her chest. In the seconds it took her to gather her wits, the man ran around to the driver's door.

A flash of panic crashed down on her. Everything was happening so fast. Too fast. She needed to think, to reason with him or… *Get out. Take the baby and run.*

But he'd already cranked the engine. With a squeal of her tires, they sped away.

Chapter Two

Laura grabbed the armrest to steady herself as her abductor took a corner too fast.

Abductor. The word rattled through her brain with an ominous ring. Was he really kidnapping her? Had he kidnapped the baby, too?

He didn't seem to have a weapon. He'd never threatened her. But his edginess rattled her. That and his no-questions-asked bullying.

She studied the rigid set of his jaw. "A-aren't you going to put the baby in the car seat?"

"Can't take the time now."

"But it's not safe!"

He silenced her with a dark glare. "Just hold him for now and sit tight."

As he hurtled them around another corner, she spotted her cell phone in the console under the radio. But how could she get it without alerting her abductor?

She felt the man's eyes on her and glanced up just as his gaze shifted to the phone. She held her breath. Prayed.

"Don't get any ideas," he growled. Snatching the phone from the console, he jammed it in the map pocket of the driver's door. Out of her reach.

Her stomach sank to her toes. So much for secretly dialing 911. Swallowing her disappointment and fear, she searched for another option.

She glanced down at the infant, the helpless little baby who still screeched for all he was worth. His tiny fingers had clamped around one of her long blond curls, so she gently worked to free her hair from the baby's fist. When she cuddled him closer to her breast, an eerie prickle crept up her spine.

"This baby's not really sick. Is he?" Her voice trembled, as did her hands, her stomach.

He met her gaze, and the hard determination setting his jaw softened. His coffee

brown eyes held a measure of guilt and remorse, but he turned back to watch the road
without answering.

Her thudding heartbeat counted the tense
seconds. While the baby's cries filled the
dearth of conversation, she studied the man's
profile. Warring emotions played across his
rugged features. A muscle jumped under his
square, stubble-covered jaw. His narrow nose
looked as though it had been broken once,
leaving a slight bump near the bridge. Sweat
trickled from a high forehead, dampening
wisps of his thick black hair and leaving wet
stains at the armpits of the blue golf shirt he
wore with his jeans.

He caught her gaze again, and the intensity
of his dark eyes unnerved her, accelerated her
already rapid breathing.

"No. He's not sick." His tone was flat, grave.

His admission caught her off guard. She
blinked her surprise, uncertain how to respond.

Turning away again, he squeezed the steering wheel.

While his confession spun her thoughts in a
hundred directions, a maternal instinct surged
inside her.

Protect the baby.

She drew the infant even closer to her body and eyed her kidnapper warily.

He gave her another quick look and muttered a curse. "Don't look at me like that. I won't hurt you."

Laura raised one eyebrow skeptically to let him know what she thought of his promise. "Why should I believe you?"

He had the audacity to look offended.

"I wouldn't—" He snapped his mouth shut without finishing.

"Did you kidnap this baby?"

He shot her an exasperated look. "No! Of course not!"

His defensiveness intrigued her. What was he hiding?

She studied the baby's features, looking for similarities. Same dark hair, same narrow nose. But with newborns it was hard to tell.

The infant's screams had tapered to mewling whines. She stroked his small pink face, and her heart melted like ice cream in the sun. She'd trained herself not to grow emotionally attached to the children at the day care, a self-defense mechanism she'd mastered growing up, shuffled from one foster family to another. Yet somehow this tiny life chipped at the walls she kept around her heart.

On the job, she could indulge her love for children without forming deep bonds. Emotional bonds served only to wound her when they were inevitably broken. She'd already suffered a lifetime of shattered relationships, broken promises, lost loved ones. Her aching soul could take no more. Yet that same painful childhood fueled a fierce protectiveness in her, a desire to see no other child suffer the same fear and isolation.

"Look, he belongs with me." The man's statement called her attention back to the problem at hand. His tone said he knew she needed convincing.

"Where's your wife?"

The muscle in his cheek jumped again. "The baby's mother is still in the hospital. She…she's not doing well and—" His voice grew quiet, and his dark expression reflected too much emotion to be faked.

His obvious grief grabbed her and rattled the cage where she'd locked her own grim memories of loss. "I'm sorry."

He acknowledged her sympathy with another lingering gaze and quick nod before turning his attention back to the road.

Laura swallowed hard, shoving down the

painful specter of grief that had shadowed her throughout her childhood, followed her from one foster home to the next.

The car bounced over a large pothole, and she turned her gaze to the scenery out her window. She didn't recognize anything about the cypress-dotted flatlands and the isolated road they traveled.

Apprehension prickled her neck again. "Where are we?"

"Near my house."

"Could you be more specific?"

He started to answer but then seemed to reconsider. "Once you drop me off, you'll just get back on this road and follow it out the way we came, until you reach the highway into town. It's simple."

Laura gaped at him. "You mean you're letting me go?"

"Of course I am." He scowled at her. "I hadn't wanted to involve you at all, hadn't wanted to come back to my house. But with my Jeep trapped at the accident, I didn't have a choice." He exhaled sharply. "I have an old truck at home I can use. Once you drop me off, you'll be free to go. With my gratitude."

The news should have elated her. Instead,

she puzzled over his strange behavior. If the baby wasn't really sick, then why the hurry? "You know that leaving the scene of an accident is against the law, don't you?"

He winced. "Yeah, I know. But I couldn't hang out until—" Again he snapped his mouth closed and frowned.

"Until?"

"Never mind."

"You've already admitted the baby's not sick. So what had you spooked? You said, 'He's here.' Who is *he?*"

"Don't worry about it."

"I think considering that you dragged me into—"

"Hey! Do you hear that?"

Laura paused and listened. For what, she wasn't sure. "I don't hear anything."

"Exactly. He quit crying." The man craned his neck to see the baby better.

Glancing down, she found the infant in her arms sleeping with his thumb in his mouth. Her heart squeezed then expanded. Tears puddled in her eyes. Maternal yearnings clambered over dark memories and defensive walls.

"He's so sweet," she whispered. Her fierce protective instinct reared its head again with a vengeance, plucking at her conscience and warming her soul. The little babe in her arms couldn't do a thing for himself, couldn't be more precious if he were her own child. Painful longing twisted inside her.

Drawing a deep breath, she shook off the bout of sentimentalism. *Don't get attached. In a minute, you'll hand him to his father and be on your way. No looking back. As always.*

"Thank you." The deep male voice roused her from her tangential thoughts.

"Hmm?"

"For your help with the baby. For lending me your car—"

"Lending my car? Is that what I did? Seems to me you gave me no choice."

A sheepish grin tugged the corner of his mouth as he slowed to turn in at a gravel driveway. "Sorry if I bullied you. I really do appreciate your help."

Laura took in the ranch-style house nestled in a copse of cypress trees. The red brick and white siding structure had a hominess about it that appealed to her.

He pulled to the back of the house next to a battered pickup truck loaded with split firewood. Though neatly kept, the lawn lacked much landscaping other than live oak and cypress trees which littered the ground with needles. Rusted wrought-iron lawn chairs sat on his back porch next to a well-used grill.

Certainly the home didn't have the appearance of a criminal hideaway. Was that what she'd been expecting?

"Well, this is home. Thanks again for your help." He gave her another grin, this one more rakish, and her pulse stumbled.

While he climbed out and circled the car to the passenger door, she gazed down at the baby. What would happen to him?

The boy's father opened the door beside her, and she dropped a soft kiss on the baby's head. His sweet baby scent, talcum powder and milk, filled her nose and tangled around her heart. The man reached for the child, and a knot of doubt lodged in her chest.

The day care center where she worked maintained a rigid screening process, assuring a child was never released into the care of the wrong person. But she had no assurance this man had any real claim to the baby.

Panic streaked through her. Her thoughts tumbled over each other. She needed some confirmation the man was who he said he was, that she wasn't negligently turning this poor baby over to a kidnapper, before she could drive away in good conscience.

Asking him for that assurance wouldn't help. His word alone wouldn't convince her he had a right to the child. Perhaps something inside his house? Another person to verify his story, an arrangement of blue flowers congratulating him on his son's birth, a wedding picture of him with the mother?

Something. Anything.

She had a responsibility as a childcare worker to protect this baby's interests. But her own history, her experience as the child needing protection, needing someone to care, made her professional responsibility a personal mandate.

Protect the baby.

"Ma'am, I'm really in a hurry. Can I have the baby now?"

He motioned toward the infant impatiently.

"I, uh—"

Without waiting for her to finish, he scooped the boy out of her arms and stepped back. Laura scrambled for a plan. She had to get inside his house, just for a minute, just to reassure herself the baby would be all right. As the man moved quickly toward his carport door, she climbed from her car and called to him. "Hey, may I…use your bathroom before I go?"

He hesitated as if looking for an excuse to tell her no. "Well, okay…but make it quick. I gotta get going."

Get going? He'd just gotten *home*. Her anxiety cranked another notch. She followed him into the carport where a firefighter's sooty turnout gear hung on a peg by the back door with black boots sitting below. He fished in his jeans pocket for his keys, unlocked the door, then stood back to let her enter first. "Around the corner. First door on the right."

"Thanks." She scanned the interior with curious scrutiny as she made her way to the bathroom. The decor could be summed up with one word. *Masculine.*

Dark colors, wood paneling, hunting trophies. Not a ruffle or frill to be seen. Likewise, she saw no evidence in the bathroom that a woman shared his home. No hairspray or makeup or stockings drying over the shower curtain rod. Laura recalled the way he'd answered her query about his wife.

The baby's mother is still in the hospital.
The baby's mother, not *my wife.*

Did that mean he didn't live with his son's mother, that they weren't married? She knew his private life was not her business, but the oddity of his earlier behavior still bothered her. Something didn't add up.

That *something* didn't register until she found her way back to the living room. Not only did the house lack any signs of a woman's touch, she saw nothing, not the first rattle or diaper, indicating he'd expected to care for a baby tonight.

She watched him bounce the infant, awake now and crying again, while he yanked clothes from the drier and jammed them into a grocery sack. More evidence he planned to leave again as soon as she did.

He spared her a brief glance. "Listen, the baby's seat is still in the back of your car. Could you leave it on the driveway for me when you go?"

On the kitchen counter, his answering machine played his messages. "Jordie won't make Friday's game. He has a dentist appointment. Thanks, coach!"

A beep signaled the end of the current message.

"Are you divorced?" She blurted into the silence before the next message began.

His head came up with a jerk. His expression clearly said her bluntness stunned him. "Uh, yeah. Why?"

"It's obvious no woman lives here."

He gave her a slow nod then went back to grabbing clothes to stuff in the paper sack. "You're sharp."

"You also don't have anything here for a baby."

His chin lifted a notch, his expression guarded. "No."

"Max, it's Cheryl," a woman on the answering machine said. "Where you been hiding, handsome? Call me."

Laura spread her hands. "How are you going to feed him or change his diaper with no supplies?"

Before he could answer, the next message began playing.

"Caldwell, we know you have the baby!" The voice on the machine spat venom. Icy shivers snaked up her spine.

"He belongs with us, and *nothing* you can do will stop—"

The man crossed the floor in two steps and slapped the stop button on the answering machine.

Laura gaped at him, speechless. Her heartbeat drummed in her ears. Acid churned in her stomach.

He turned a hard glare at her, his face drawn and grim. "I'm really in a hurry. I need you to go now."

Chapter Three

Accusation burned in the blond woman's eyes. Deep inside, Max squirmed uncomfortably. Her unspoken disapproval and doubts chafed a raw wound inside him. Jennifer had given him that same look too many times, whether he deserved it or not. And, as with his ex-wife, this woman's glare caused a flicker of guilt, of responsibility, of disappointment.

Max knew he could explain the situation to her, try to make her understand, but that would take valuable time he didn't have. He had to get back on the road. Quickly.

Besides, as she'd put it, why should she believe him? He'd already lied to her—lies that nettled his conscience but which he'd deemed necessary to get results. He glanced down at his charge. Emily's son.

Yes, results were what mattered.

However, if he didn't say something to answer the suspicion blazing from her turquoise eyes, she'd be on her cell phone to the cops the minute she left his driveway.

Max released a breath that hissed through his teeth. "It's…not what you think."

"Oh? And what am I thinking?" She crossed her arms over her chest and furrowed her brow.

The pose emphasized the swell of her breasts, and Max's libido kicked hard. He'd been trying not to let her beautiful figure distract him. But like any red-blooded male, he'd noticed and appreciated her lush curves anyway. If his current circumstances were different…

The baby whimpered louder, and he cringed. The woman had nailed it when she suggested he wasn't prepared to care for a baby. She didn't know how right she was.

He took the woman by the arm and tugged her toward the door. "I really don't have time now to explain, but I'm perfectly within my rights to have this child. His mother knows he's with me. That's how she wants it. Now, if you'd just go—"

She shrugged out of his grip. "And the baby's father? What does he want?" Her incisive gaze dared him to contradict his previous assertion that he was the infant's father.

He thought of the baby's real father, Joe. A man involved with drugs—smuggling, most likely, since his father owned a shipping company. A man who'd put Max's sister in harm's way, whose enemy had murdered him and shot Emily, whose family now tried to usurp custody of Emily's son. What a scum. Anger for what Joe had cost Emily heated Max's blood. The baby was better off without Joe's negative influence.

For all intents and purposes, Max was his nephew's father for the time being.

But Max also knew the Rialtos would show up at his door any minute, and he didn't have time to explain the nuances of the situation, hoping to convince her of the truth. Anthony Rialto's message made it clear his energy was better used getting the baby out of town. Hidden. This unplanned return to his house, thanks to his car being trapped at the accident, was costing him valuable time.

Max decided changing his story concerning the baby's paternity now would be counterproductive. And the woman's suspicions already ran high.

"I'm his father. I don't need anyone's permission to have my son with me, and I don't owe you any explanations beyond that." With a hand at the small of her back, he tried again to hustle the woman toward the door. "Now if you'll excuse me, I have to get moving. I promise to make a trip to the grocery for diapers and baby food, okay?"

He fished in his pocket for her car keys and extended them to her.

She stepped forward and snatched the keys, her gaze darting briefly to his sobbing nephew. "Formula."

He cocked an eyebrow. "What?"

She flipped her mane of golden waves over her shoulder with an impatient huff. She turned her attention to the baby, shifting her weight uneasily, clearly champing at the bit to try her hand again at quieting the squalling baby. "A newborn doesn't eat baby food," she said loud enough to be heard over his nephew's screams. "They *drink* mother's milk or formula. Do you know what brand to buy? Did his doctor say anything about soy?"

Soy? Formula? Damn. She could speak a foreign language, and he'd have a better chance of making sense of it. Frustration and impatience roiled inside him. He didn't have time for this!

"Formula, milk, whatever! I'll figure it out. Lady, I'm in a hurry here—"

"So you've said. Why the hurry? What's going on here?"

The resounding wails of his nephew, letting them know in no uncertain terms what he thought of his uncle's ability to care for him, fed his agitation. A pang of sympathy for the baby, stuck with his inept uncle, jabbed his gut. Bouncing the baby on his arm, Max fell back on what he did best when under stress. Pace.

He needed a plan.

In this case, his goal was simply to get rid of this woman and get out of town before the Rialtos came knocking.

"Don't do that!" The blonde scowled and reached for the baby.

"Don't do *what?*" Feelings of futility sharpened his tone. He hated the sense of helplessness and ignorance that had swamped him the minute he stepped out of the hospital.

"Ever heard of shaken baby syndrome?"

She plucked his nephew from his hands and cuddled the infant to her chest. "You can't bounce him around like that. He's too little and that much shaking can damage his brain."

Hell! Brain damage?

He noted with satisfaction that his nephew didn't calm down for her, either. With a flash of envy, he watched the baby nuzzle his face into her breast. *Lucky kid.*

She shot him an accusing look. "Didn't they tell you at the hospital not to jostle or shake him?"

Obviously, he was *way* out of his element, and if someone didn't help him, he feared he'd hurt Emily's son due to plain ignorance regarding babies.

He ran a hand down his face, sighing his fatigue. "No, they didn't tell me anything about brain damage or soy or where to send him to college. Yeah, I'm new at this. No, I don't know what I'm doing. But I'm trying to get it right, so would you cut me some slack?"

Her expression softened, but her eyes still blazed with conviction. "If we were discussing your new iPod, that would wash. But this is a baby. A helpless, dependent little human being."

"I'm well aware of that!" He raised his

voice to be heard over the volume of his nephew's cries. "For God's sake, can you please quiet him down!"

The pressure that had been building inside him since he received the call about Emily's injuries reached a boiling point. He felt ready to explode. Taking a step back from the woman, he raked both hands through his hair and bit out an expletive that would singe dirt. "Damn it, I don't have time to debate with you! They could be here any minute!"

"Would you stop yelling?" she fussed. "You're not helping matters...."

A movement on his driveway distracted him from the rest of her tirade. Through his front window, he watched two large sedans pull up to his house. Alarm streaked through him, tensing every muscle. He was too late.

A tall, linebacker-sized man climbed from the driver's side of the first car. Reaching under his windbreaker, the linebacker pulled a gun from his shoulder holster and checked the chamber.

Max's mouth went dry. Keeping a close watch out the window, he grabbed the woman's arm and pulled her behind him.

"Hey! Wh—"

"Do exactly what I say. No questions. Got

it?" The gravity of his tone obviously told her something was wrong.

"Who's out there?"

"Remember the nice guy making threats on the answering machine?"

"What!" He heard the concern in her voice. His own disconcertion echoed hers with the thundering of his pulse. Fortunately, he did his best work under pressure. The guys at the station called him the Ice Man for his ability to keep his cool amid the smoke, flames and chaos of a fire call.

The station alarm was sounding. Time to get to work.

"Give me back your keys." He thrust his hand at her.

"Why?"

"I said no questions. You're gonna have to trust me."

"Trust you?" she shrieked.

A loud pounding on the front door blew the whistle on their huddle. Time for action.

Max crouched low behind the kitchen counter, yanking her down with him.

"Quiet!" he whispered harshly. "Go out the back. Take the baby, and get in your car. Don't close your car door until I get there. I don't want the noise to alert them."

"Like this screaming baby won't?"

Max gritted his teeth. She was right. They'd certainly hear the baby.

"Are they cops?" she whispered, the hope in her voice unmistakable.

"Afraid not, sweetheart. These men are dangerous, and they mean business."

Her eyes opened wide with trepidation. "But the baby—"

"Stop talking and go!"

He saw the shudder that shook her, and guilt for placing her in danger wrenched inside him.

She scurried for the back door, clasping the baby close to her chest.

"Stay low!" he called.

Without waiting to make sure she'd followed his orders, Max hustled, crouched low, toward his gun cabinet. Like most native Louisiana men, he'd been raised on hunting. He'd learned to fire a gun before he had his driver's license. Now he was the hunted, and he needed his rifles for self-defense.

The men on his porch must have seen him through the tall, narrow window by the door. He heard a shout from one of the goons informing the others of his position.

"Caldwell, open up! That baby belongs to us!"

Anthony Rialto. So, the patriarch of the drug clan had made a personal appearance.

Max searched the top drawer of the gun cabinet for the key to unlock the display case. Moving with deft, sure speed, he grabbed out his best hunting rifle. Next he removed the 9mm Glock he kept for home protection and shoved it in the waistband of his jeans.

His front door rattled and shook as Rialto's men tried to break it down. Gambling precious time, Max crawled across his living room floor to the front window and raised the rifle. With one swift motion, he broke a hole in the glass and aimed at the tires of the lead car.

His fire drew an answering assault from Rialto's men. The rest of the front window shattered under the barrage of bullets. Glass littered the carpet around him. The jagged shards bit his hands as he scrambled away from the window, leaving a trail of blood. He'd reached his kitchen when the front door burst open.

Bullets whizzed over his head and peppered his cabinets. Over the cracking gunfire, he heard the woman scream. His heart leaped to his throat.

Damning the consequences, he rose to his

full height to beat a quicker retreat. A sharp sting pinched his shoulder, telling him he'd been hit.

Spinning, as he taught the kids on his Pee Wee team to dodge a tackle, he ran for the backyard. When he plowed through the back door, he found Anthony Rialto stalking the blond woman. Rialto backed her away from her car with a gun aimed at her head. She held the baby clutched to her chest in a protective grasp that won Max's admiration. She could easily have handed the baby over to Rialto to save her own skin. The woman had guts.

In three long strides, Max covered the distance between him and Emily's father-in-law. He tackled the man from behind, knocking him to the ground. Rialto fired, sending the bullet into an oak tree at the line of the woods.

"Get in the car!" Max yelled.

The blonde jumped to follow his order.

The gunshot and shouts brought reinforcements around the side of the house. Max landed a hard blow to Anthony's temple with his elbow. The abrupt movement caused pain to streak like lightning through his shoulder and arm.

He left the older man clutching his head and staggering.

Shifting his focus to the men at the side of his house, Max held the thugs at bay with a couple of blasts from his rifle. As soon as the woman reached her car, Max made a dash for the driver's door. His feet slipped as he scrambled through the cypress needles littering his yard.

Bullets pocked the side of the Accord. As he climbed in the Honda, he heard Rialto shouting.

"Damn it, hold your fire! My grandson's in that car! What if you hit the gas tank?"

Max wasted no time cranking the engine and shifting into Reverse. Rialto's men tried to stop the escaping car with their bodies, but Max refused to slow down for any reason. The men jumped out of his path at the last second. When the thugs tried shooting at the Honda's tires, Max swerved left then right, making their target more difficult to hit.

"I said, hold your fire!" Rialto screamed. "Follow them!"

Max peeled across his front yard, around the sedans blocking his driveway. He'd managed to take out the front tire of the lead car, he noticed as they sped past. Good. That meant only one car could pursue them.

He stole a glance at the woman as he

wheeled onto the narrow, two-lane road. Tears streaked her pale face, and a mask of sheer terror molded her delicate features.

His gut knotted as he mashed the accelerator and sped away from the nightmare scene. "Did he hurt you?"

She didn't respond.

"Did he hurt you?" he barked.

She jumped. "No."

Max nodded. "Hang on. We're taking the shortcut."

Squeezing her eyes shut, she hugged the baby closer and slumped down in the seat.

Bouncing across the ditch at the side of the road, he headed down a narrow dirt road. "ATV trail. Kids in the area use it to go four-wheeling."

She didn't acknowledge his explanation, and he worried about her slipping into shock. "Stay with me, darlin'. The worst is over. We're gonna be okay now."

Skeptical turquoise eyes rose to meet his glance. Her look asked, *Why should I believe you?*

Good question. He'd gotten her involved in this mess, lied to her, nearly gotten her killed. He knew he didn't deserve her faith. But he also knew he'd move mountains to see that she got out of this disaster safe and sound.

One more person he couldn't let down.

The stakes in this fiasco kept growing. But he'd never been one to let an obstacle keep him from accomplishing a goal. Results were what mattered. He lived by that mantra as a firefighter and taught it to the kids on his football team. No excuses and no quitters.

Especially since, in this game, they were playing for their lives.

The man's hands and shoulder were bleeding.

Laura gaped at the crimson stains on the steering wheel and on his shirt and battled down a wave of nausea. Considering the armed men on their tail, they couldn't afford any delays. That included any stops for her to be sick at the side of the road, so she averted her gaze from the bloodstains.

Mercifully, the baby had finally worn himself out and fallen asleep. Since the baby's safety was paramount to her, even above her own, Laura unfastened her seat belt and wiggled between the front seats, leaning into the back. As they bumped down the dirt side road, she secured the baby in his car seat then slid back into the front.

When the baby's father checked his side and rearview mirrors for the umpteenth time, clearly watching for the men who could be following them, a chill scraped down her spine.

Small talk, she decided, might help distract her from her swirling nausea. "So what... what's the baby's name?"

"Hmm?" He blinked at her, a confused knit in his brow as if he'd forgotten she was there. As if she'd pulled him from serious deliberations.

She had some major thinking of her own to do. And soon. How did she get herself out of this nightmare? And what kind of mess had she stumbled into?

"Your son. What's his name?"

"Uh, I..."

The man's hesitation piqued her suspicion. "You do know your son's name, don't you?"

"Of course." He scoffed and gave her a what-kind-of-idiot-do-you-think-I-am look. But not a name.

"Well?" She lifted an eyebrow, waiting.

"It's...uh, Elmer."

Laura blinked. Surely she'd misunderstood him.

"Did you say *Elmer?* As in Fudd?"

"Um...yeah."

"Nobody'd name a baby that!"

He scowled at her. "It was my grandfather's name. What's wrong with Elmer?"

"Nothing if you don't mind the poor kid getting picked on his whole life. Please tell me he has a middle name he can use."

"No…not yet." The man looked decidedly uncomfortable with the conversation. Her doubts about him stirred to life again.

Careful to keep her gaze on his face, not his bloody shoulder, she gauged his reaction as she fired more questions. "Who *are* you? Are you in some kind of trouble with the law? And who were those men? Why do they want the baby?"

With his lips pressed in a grim line, he rubbed the back of his neck.

She crossed her arms over her chest and tapped a finger on her arm.

Finally he heaved a deep sigh. "Max Caldwell. I'm a firefighter and volunteer coach for the rec center's kindergarten Pee Wee football team."

When he said no more, she scoffed. "Let me guess. You moonlight as a CIA agent, and those men were Russian spies. You've hidden the plans for a new bomb that could destroy the world in Elmer's diaper. Am I close?"

The corner of his mouth curled up, and

when he cast a sideways glance at her, a spark of humor lit his dark eyes. "You watch too much television."

"I don't watch any television, thank you. It's all far too unrealistic. In real life, people don't get kidnapped and chased by bad guys with guns."

A wry chuckle rumbled from his chest, and a lopsided grin eased the tension in his face. When he smiled, she discovered, Max Caldwell was a devastatingly handsome man. She caught herself staring.

"And you are...?" he prompted.

"The beautiful double agent sent by the enemy to steal the bomb plans, of course." She cracked a smart-alecky grin.

His gaze grew hot and penetrating. "Well, you got the beautiful part right."

When he brushed her hair back from her cheek, she gasped, as much from the electric jolt his touch sent through her as from the shock of his intimate gesture. Trembling, she pulled away from his hand.

"Easy, beautiful. I won't hurt you." The husky baritone of his voice caused a tingle to skitter over her skin.

She forced a short laugh. "Said the spider to the fly?"

The humor on his face faded. He focused on the road, his expression hard and grim.

A pang of regret for the lost joviality left a pit in her stomach. She twisted in her seat to check on Elmer.

Protect the baby, the voice in her head chanted again.

"Tell me something." She pinned a hard stare on Max. "If you're a firefighter as you claim, what's with all the guns? Last time I checked, a firefighter didn't need to own a small arsenal or know how to shoot in order to do his job."

Max lifted a black eyebrow, and his returned glance asked, *Are you serious?* "How long have you lived in Louisiana?"

"Only a couple of years. Why?"

"Ever heard the state called the Sportsman's Paradise?"

"Of course."

He gave a quick nod. "Well, that's a hunting rifle. My dad taught me to hunt and shoot when I was twelve. Like his dad taught him, and his grandfather taught his dad, et cetera. It's tradition around here."

Laura thought of the hunting trophies she'd seen in his living room. Okay, that explained the rifles, but…

"What about that gun?" She nodded toward the weapon resting in his lap. "Surely you don't take handguns hunting."

"Home protection. I bought it for my wife, for the nights I was at the fire station and she was home alone." A flicker of pain crossed his face. "She left it with me when we divorced."

"Oh." Laura shifted in her seat. Knowing the whys behind Max's gun ownership didn't make her any more comfortable being around the things. Her attention shifted to something else Max had said. She checked the ring finger of his left hand.

Bare.

If he was divorced...

A fresh prickle of doubt and concern tickled her neck, and she sat straighter in the seat. "Was your divorce recent?"

"Hmm? No, it's been a few years." He furrowed his expressive black eyebrows again. "Why?"

"I just assumed...because of the baby..."

He grimaced and dragged a hand down his face. "Oh...right. I—"

Max heaved a tired sigh, mumbled something about weaving tangled webs, and stared out the windshield.

The suspicion prickling Laura's neck bit harder with every minute of his silence. "Max, whose baby is—?"

"He's my nephew." The haunted, dark-eyed glance he sent her twisted inside her. "My sister's in the hospital. She might..." His Adam's apple bobbed as he swallowed. "She might die. She asked me to protect her son from the men who just shot at us."

Laura narrowed her eyes warily. "You lied to me earlier. When you said you're his father."

"Well, in a way, I am. A father figure at least. His real dad's out of the picture, and—"

"Semantics! You still misled me. You let me believe he was yours!"

Returning his attention to the road, he blew out a harsh puff of air. "I saw no reason to explain. As soon as we got to my house, you were supposed to take your car and leave. The end. Goodbye. No sticky explanations."

"I knew something was fishy." She crossed her arms over her chest and pursed her mouth. "I'm still not convinced I should trust you."

His head whipped toward her, and pain riddled his eyes for an instant before he hardened his expression and tensed his jaw. "Elmer *is* my nephew. And until Emily gets out of the hospital, I'm his guardian. His protector. That's the plain and simple truth."

"What about the message on your answering machine? That guy thinks the baby belongs with him."

"Elmer's mother wants *me* to have him. That's all you need to know." He held her gaze, his own challenging her to believe him, penetrating to her core and stirring a restlessness in her.

Protect the baby.

She twisted toward the backseat to check on the newborn again. *Elmer.* How could anyone have named a baby so sweet and innocent something as awkward as *Elmer?*

Turning back around, she leaned her head against the seat and closed her eyes. What should she do? Did she dare believe Max? He'd lied to her twice. So how did she trust him now?

Fatigue permeated her to the bone. She longed for the calm and seclusion of her apartment. Even the microwave dinner she'd planned for supper held a certain appeal at this point.

She had decisions to make, but exhaustion numbed her mind too much to think straight.

Her only certainty was she had to do what

was best for Elmer. No matter what. Her day care training, her personal experience with foster homes demanded she find out where this baby *really* belonged, where he would be safe, where he would be loved.

A groan from the driver's seat called her attention to the ruggedly handsome man behind the wheel. He winced and rolled his injured shoulder.

"You need a doctor."

"Naw. I'm all right. It's just stiff."

"You should go to a hospital and let some-one—"

"No! It's not serious." He set his jaw in a stubborn glower. "Besides, a doctor would have to report a gunshot wound to the police. I can't get the police involved."

Another uneasy prick jabbed her. "Why not? Those men shot at us!"

He hesitated, checked his mirrors again and sighed. "Long story. But… I have to keep the baby with me. The police might take him and—" He sent her a sharp look and shook his head. "Forget it. Just trust me on this, okay?"

She grunted, and he scowled.

"Well, someone needs to clean the wound

before it gets infected, and I can't do it." She sighed. "Blood makes me sick."

Taking one hand from the steering wheel, he peeled back his shirt to examine his wound. "It's really only a scratch. I'll live." He paused. "But thanks for your concern."

The smile he gave her shone from his eyes and warmed his face. His crooked grin removed the hard, worried edge that had darkened his face from the moment she'd met him.

But handsome as he was, his desire to avoid the police, even with the dangerous men after them, baffled her. Bothered her. If Elmer was in some kind of danger, why *wouldn't* Max involve the police?

And if the baby *was* at risk, how could she justify walking away? The baby's safety was her utmost concern. Max had admitted he wasn't the baby's real father, had said Elmer's real father was "out of the picture"—whatever *that* meant. The facts of this scenario only seemed to get murkier, more confusing. It seemed the real truth was *she* was Elmer's best chance of being returned to the right hands. She needed to take the baby to the police, let the authorities straighten out the question of custody. But how did she get the infant away from Max?

"There's a little town up ahead."

She faced Max when he spoke.

"I'm going to stop at a car rental agency there. I need you to go in and rent a car for me. I'll give you the cash."

"Me?"

He met her curious look. "I can't very well go in with a bloody shoulder. I'd raise too much suspicion. Once I have a different car, you'll be free to go home."

"That's it? You're dismissing me?"

Her comment earned a confused scowl from Max. "You want to go home, right?"

The promise of home and freedom made her spirits jump for joy. But soon after, her sense of responsibility to the infant reared its head. Her stomach clenched.

Protect the baby.

"Well—"

"I'll pay for repairing your car, if that's the problem."

"No, I…"

"What?"

The sinking sun cast deep shadows across his face. The blood on his shirt had dried, leaving a dark vermilion blotch on his blue knit shirt. Max's handgun lay across his lap, ready for the next brush with death. The man's appearance screamed danger. Violence. Trouble.

Yet a niggling sensation in her gut wouldn't be quieted. She had to look out for the innocent baby she'd cradled in her arms. No one had given her the job. Only her conscience, her love for children, her personal experience with being lost in the foster system prodded her to accept the position as the baby's guardian. Along with her certainty that things with Max Caldwell weren't what they seemed.

Protect the baby.

She'd worry about getting away from Max and sorting through the facts later. Right now, baby Elmer needed her. Spurred by her determination to assure the baby's safety, she made her decision and wouldn't look back.

"I'm not going home. I'm staying with you."

Chapter Four

"What do you mean, you're staying?" Max couldn't deny the surge of relief, the flare of hope that raced through him. He desperately wanted the help with Elmer this woman offered. Her concern for the baby, her sense of humor and her sexy smiles took the edge off a bad situation.

But his reaction to her only made it harder to do what he must—change her mind.

He didn't want the responsibility of one more life hanging in the balance. He had no real idea what extremes the Rialtos might try to get Elmer back. He imagined the raid on his house only scratched the surface. As long as this woman stayed with him, her life was at risk. Involving her had been a desperate and foolish thing to do. He knew that now.

The woman lifted her chin, squared her shoulders. "I won't leave Elmer. You obviously have no experience with infants."

Max pulled into the parking lot of a discount department store in rural Mississippi and cut the car's engine. "I can't allow you to stay and put yourself in harm's way. The sooner you go, the better."

When the blonde turned, kneeling in her seat to reach for the baby, Max had an up close and personal view of the woman's shapely fanny—the kind he'd have loved to sink his fingers into during rowdy sex. Under other circumstances.

Max gritted his teeth and averted his gaze. He had no business thinking of her in those terms, no business thinking of anything except keeping his nephew safe.

She unfastened Elmer from the baby carrier and gingerly lifted him into her arms. Cuddling his nephew close to her chest, she twisted and slid back into her seat. "You don't even know what formula to buy. How could I possibly leave—"

"We'll be just fine. I know I've given you

a bad impression of my abilities so far—" He leaned over to take Elmer from her, and she drew back from his reach. "But I can handle things. Let me have him."

She arched a delicate eyebrow. "No. I'm staying until I'm sure the baby will be all right."

"That could be a while. Don't you have a job waiting for you in the morning? A boyfriend who'll be worried about you?"

"I've earned the time off. All I have to do is call the day care director and tell her I need some personal days."

She ignored his question about the boyfriend, he noticed. Interesting.

"Just the same—" Again he reached for the baby. "I can't ask you to—"

She turned her back, refusing to give Elmer up. Sighing, Max raised his hand to rake his hair. The motion sent a sharp ache through his shoulder. He winced, moaned.

"See! You're in no condition to take care of him."

The self-satisfied look on the woman's face should have annoyed him. Instead, he found the whole impossible situation so absurdly impossible, so unbelievably ironic that he huffed a short laugh.

The woman stared at him as if he'd lost his mind. Maybe he had. He was actually thinking of letting her stay, despite everything wrong with that idea.

He slapped the steering wheel in frustration, and the loud noise woke Elmer. The baby wrinkled his face and sent up a wail to wake the dead.

"Now look what you did!" she fussed.

Elmer's complaints grew steadily in volume and verve. Max really hadn't the foggiest idea what to do with the screaming baby or how to calm him.

He pinched the bridge of his nose then regarded her with a steady gaze. "You understand, don't you, that if you stay, you'll be putting yourself in danger? Those guys that shot up my house won't just give up and go home. They're looking for us even as we speak."

She drew her shoulders back, seemed to consider his warning for a moment, then gave a quick nod.

"I'll do my best to keep you and the baby safe," he assured her. "But in the end, the baby is my first priority. Got that, lady?"

"Laura."

"What?"

"My name is Laura…Dalton. I figure if I'm staying, you can't keep calling me *lady*. And for the record, the baby's welfare is my main concern, too. It's the only thing keeping me here."

Her bright turquoise eyes cut through him like lasers. Her scrutiny left him feeling strangely vulnerable, as if she could see through his pretenses, saw through to his soul, knew his past failures and his deepest secrets.

Yet he also sensed that with Laura, and with Emily's son, he'd been offered a gift. A chance at redemption.

"All right, *Laura,* you can stay. For now." He reached for Elmer once more, and despite her grunted protest, he took his nephew from her. Throwing the baby's blanket over his shoulder to hide his bloody wound, he opened the driver's door. "The first thing we need to do is buy supplies for the baby. And I need to get a change of clothes. I suggest you do the same."

Max tucked the Glock in his waistband, covered it with his shirt. "Don't wander off. If you're staying with me, then you're staying *with* me. Where I can protect you. I'm not letting you or Elmer out of my sight. Got it?"

Without waiting for her to answer, he climbed from the car. They may have escaped the Rialtos this time, but he knew Emily's in-laws were hunting them even now. He had to be ready for trouble.

When they returned to the car, Laura changed Elmer's diaper on the backseat while Max loaded their purchases into the trunk. He paused several times to scan the parking lot, a wary itch tickling his neck. He felt exposed, jumpy. The Rialtos' henchmen could be anywhere.

They needed distance. The farther and faster they traveled that night the better.

He paced to the backseat where Laura had fixed Elmer a bottle of ready-made formula. "We gotta get moving. Can you feed him while I drive?"

Laura glanced up then nervously scanned the parking lot. "Did you see those men?"

"No, but the point is to stay well ahead of them. We're too vulnerable sitting here."

Laura's eyes darkened, and she nodded tightly. "Let's go then. I'll ride back here so I can hold his bottle."

As they pulled back onto the Mississippi highway, Max removed the Glock from his jeans and set it on the front seat next to him. "I think we'll head to North Carolina tomorrow."

"Why North Carolina?"

"I have a friend with a hunting cabin up in the Smokies. We usually make a trip sometime in the fall, but his wife just had surgery, so we'd canceled our trip this year. His cabin would be a good place to lay low for a while. For tonight, we'll find a motel somewhere off the beaten path. Get some rest. Regroup."

Laura didn't answer.

Max glanced in the rearview mirror, checking that no suspicious cars had followed them out of the parking lot, but his gaze drifted to the woman in the backseat. Her hair shone like spun gold as the sinking sun cast a warm glow across the horizon. With effort, he pushed down the desire to feel her golden hair against his skin and trained his thoughts on planning his next move.

"Elmer's going to need to be fed every couple of hours throughout the night," she said evenly. "It'd be easier if I keep him in my room at the motel."

Max snapped out of his pensive thoughts when her words sank in. "Like hell! That baby—"

"Stop cussing! The baby doesn't need to hear that kind of language."

"Wha—? He doesn't understand what I'm saying!"

"Yet. It's never too soon to break a bad habit."

"All right, all right, fine." He raised a hand in concession. "I'll watch my language, but there's no way you're taking the baby out of my sight."

She grunted. "He'll keep you awake all night. You don't know how to feed him or…"

"Maybe so. But rule number one is, the baby stays with me. If you want to help with him, you'll have to bunk in with us." Cocking an eyebrow, he sent her a narrow-eyed look in the rearview mirror, daring her to challenge him on the point.

Her shoulders drooped, and her face fell. "Fine."

Rather than feeling he'd won this battle of wills, Max shifted in his seat, uneasy with the arrangement he'd cornered her into. The idea of sharing a motel room with the beautiful blonde made his blood thick, hot.

They were well into rural Mississippi before he stopped at a tiny gas station to refuel the car. Turning toward the silent backseat, he discovered Laura had fallen asleep sometime after Elmer had. He let her sleep as he paid for and pumped the gas.

Through the back window, he watched Laura sleep, her cheek pillowed on her hands. Her smooth skin rivaled Elmer's, looked as silky-soft as the baby's, and he longed to stroke her face, brush his thumb along her lips. His groin tightened, and he shook off the sensual thoughts. He needed to stay focused.

Didn't he warn the kids on his Pee Wee football team what distractions could cost in a game? He squared his shoulders and firmed his resolve. He couldn't let this woman's sex appeal lead him to screw up his responsibilities to Elmer. Or Emily.

An old pickup backfired as it roared away from the pumps, and Laura startled awake. She cast a wide-eyed glance around the gas station then focused on Max. Opening the back door, she unfolded her sleek legs to climb out of the car.

"Where are we?" she asked as she stretched. Her blouse pulled tight across her breasts, and Max peeled his gaze away from the enticing sight.

"Podunk, Mississippi. Your car was on

empty. If this town has a motel, I vote we stop here for the night."

Laura glanced around at the small town and yawned. "Fine with me."

She moved to the front seat, eyeing the Glock uneasily before she moved it from her seat. "Can't you find a better place for that thing?"

"The best place for it is somewhere I can get it quickly, if I have to." As he settled in the driver's seat, he watched her rub her arms, shudder. "You can change your mind anytime. I'll understand if you want to leave."

Her turquoise eyes blazed. "I'm not leaving as long as Elmer is at risk. I have to be sure he's safe."

The conviction firing her eyes burrowed deep into his core. Her dedication, despite the danger her choice put her in, was remarkable. Rare.

He sent her a grateful grin. "In that case, let's find someplace we can get a good night's sleep."

She scoffed and returned a skeptical scowl. "Sleep? You really don't know newborns, do you?"

"Uh, no. I—" He blew a slow breath through his teeth. "Look, I'm gonna need at least a catnap. I have to mentally regroup before driving to North Carolina in the morning. Nothing about today has gone the way I planned."

Starting with the woman in the passenger's seat.

She scoffed. "Tell me about it."

The dashboard lights cast Laura's profile in a blue-white glow that reminded him of the aura that shone around angels in the movies.

Angelic. The word fit. Her face was a study in understated beauty. A pert nose, a sprinkling of freckles, the subtle curve of her cheeks and a gracefully rounded chin. Even her abundant, wavy blond hair created a halo of gold around her head.

Her lips broke the mold, though. Far from angelic, her lush, pouty lips had been created for sin. His own mouth watered imagining their taste.

She turned and caught him staring. "What?"

"What what?"

"You were looking at me funny. Is something wrong?" She twisted to check the baby in the backseat then glanced at him again.

"No, everything's okay. I just…"

She cocked her head and narrowed a leery gaze. Though he'd not given her much reason to trust him, her continued distrust and suspicion nettled him. Maybe because he had his own doubts about how he was going to get Laura out of this mess, how he would keep the promise he'd made Emily.

Emily.

Max sobered. For his sister's sake, he had to figure out how to care for his nephew. Alone. Maybe then Laura wouldn't feel compelled to stay with them.

He considered himself a quick study. After watching how Laura handled Elmer tonight, he figured he could master the mysteries of baby care in no time. He could fix a bottle, rock Elmer to sleep—gently, no bouncing. He could even change a diaper—the teddy bear picture went in front. No problem. No big deal.

So why was the prospect still so nerve-racking? He managed eighteen five-year-olds three times a week for Pee Wee football practice. Of course, his players were potty trained....

"Max? You're pale. Are you sure everything's all right? Is it your shoulder?" Laura reached toward him but snatched her hand back before she touched him. Her skittish, touch-me-not body language mirrored a vulnerability that ghosted across her face. The haunting flash of loneliness and caution plucked at him, but he didn't dwell on it. He had to stay focused on the job at hand.

Emily had trusted him to protect her son, and that was a mandate he'd fulfill, no matter what.

Laura should have been tired. She'd worked a long shift at the day care center, been shot at by thugs and driven through the Mississippi backwoods with Max for hours. But her nerves jangled, and her senses were on full alert.

Her heart did a tap dance when she thought of her name on Max's lips. Every muscle in her body tensed when she considered sharing close quarters at the hotel with him.

In the darkness, every sound and movement from the driver's side of the car seemed amplified. Each time the headlights of another car approached behind them, Max would tense, and her own pulse would scramble. She found herself holding her breath until the car passed them and headed on down the road.

Any time Max sighed his fatigue or shifted his weight in discomfort, an electric bolt of awareness would zing through her. She couldn't forget the skill he'd displayed firing his rifle at the men who'd attacked them, couldn't ignore the power and strength obvious in his muscled shoulders and chest.

He'd said he was a firefighter, and his impressive build proved he was an athlete, as well. But perhaps his most intimidating feature was his eyes.

A disconcerting tremble stirred deep in her core whenever she met his coffee brown gaze. While she saw heated determination and a grim assessment of their situation in his eyes, she also found compassion.

He'd displayed a similar gentleness when he'd brushed her hair from her cheek. Although his concern contradicted the hard-edged and dangerous man she'd first perceived him to be, she couldn't drop her guard. She couldn't let his kindness confuse her about what she had to do for Elmer's sake. *Protect the baby.*

"Looks like a motel up ahead."

She jerked when he spoke.

"Doesn't look like much, but I'm not picky. I'm exhausted." He glanced at her. "Will this place do for you?"

"Yeah. Whatever."

He stopped the car in front of the motel office and faced her. She turned to meet his gaze and quickly regretted it. A certain weary sadness darkened his expression and tweaked her soft heart.

If he were a dog on the side of the road, she'd take him home and feed him—then find a home for him with someone else, before she had the chance to grow attached.

She sighed. "I really don't care where we spend the night. I don't plan to sleep."

He nodded slowly. "All right. I'll get us a room." The look in his eyes warmed, grew more intense. "But don't tell me you don't care. You wouldn't be here if you didn't care…at least about the baby."

She dropped her gaze to her hands, unsettled by the intimate shift in the conversation, in his voice.

Sure, she cared about the baby. How could she not want to help the sweet newborn? She also cared about saving the rain forest and rooting for the Red Sox in the playoffs. She always championed the underdog. After all, she'd been that underdog once, lost in the foster system. She knew how it felt to have the odds against you.

But caring was where, by necessity, she

drew the line. Any deeper personal commitment or emotional investment ran the risk of
breaking her heart. She'd suffered enough rejection, broken promises and painful losses
to last her a lifetime, thank you. She wouldn't
wish her years of drifting through the foster
system on her worst enemy.

"Is there someone you should call while I
check in?"

His question brought her gaze up.

"Someone at home who might be worried
about where you are? A husband? A boyfriend? Roommate?"

Without answering, she turned and stared
out the window at the moths and gnats buzzing around the motel's security light.

"A neighbor or relative?"

"No."

He grunted. "A cat?"

Whipping her head around, she gave him
an irritated glare. She didn't need his reminder of how empty her life was. It was
necessary. Lonely was better than heartbro-
ken. The succession of foster homes and broken ties she'd endured growing up had taught
her that hard lesson. Let no one close enough
to break your heart when they left.

When they left. Not *if.* They always left her. Alone.

"No. There's no one I need to call, okay?"

She'd hoped her cool tone would push him away. Instead, his expression grew darker, more worried. "There's no one?"

She paused. "No. Except the ladies at the day care center. But I'm a big girl. I can take care of myself. I don't need anyone checking up on me."

He made no response for a long time then sighed and rubbed his face. "I guess that's something we have in common. No one's waiting at home for me, either."

The deep rumble of his voice, the regret in his tone made her stomach tighten. She didn't want anything in common with this man. And she especially didn't want to feel any empathy with his isolation. Their concern for the baby was enough. Too much.

"Except for Emily, of course, and...well—" He leaned his head back on the seat and squeezed his eyes shut. "God, I don't know what I'll do if I lose her," he muttered on an exhaled breath.

"Elmer's mother?"

"Yeah."

Leave it alone. Don't go any further with it,

or you'll be sorry. "You're close to your sister, I guess. I mean, to do all this for her…"

He furrowed his brow. "Yeah. Since my divorce, Em's my only family. I took over raising her when our parents died. I'd do anything for her. No matter what."

She felt a funny catch in her chest, like a pang of longing or disappointment. Maybe sympathy. She refused to examine the emotion too closely. Instead, she shoved it down, pushed it away. *Don't let this get personal.*

She had a duty to the baby, a duty to ensure Elmer was in the right hands, was protected. First chance she had, she'd get away from Max and take the baby to the police. She'd let the cops sort the mess out and keep Elmer safe.

Then she could walk away. No looking back.

Chapter Five

"I told you before not to expect me to help." Laura turned her eyes from Max with a wince.

Max sighed his frustration. He stood in the door of their motel bathroom, a bottle of rubbing alcohol in one hand and his bloody shirt in the other. The wound on his shoulder was worse than he'd thought and in desperate need of cleaning and a bandage. "I can't do it alone. You have to help."

"You should have seen a doctor," she said without looking up from the bottle she held for Elmer.

"I told you why a doctor was out. They'd call the cops."

And he'd promised Emily not to get the cops involved. For good reason.

Laura gave him a dramatic sigh, still avoiding looking at him. "Listen, I'd help if I could. Really. But the thing is…blood…" Her fingers flexed and tightened around Elmer's bottle as the baby sucked greedily at his late-night snack. "The sight of blood makes me sick. I'd never get through helping you without throwing up."

Max tossed his bloodstained shirt beside the bag of extra clothes he'd bought earlier. "Swell," he muttered and went back to sit on the edge of the tub. He'd find a way to doctor his wound by himself.

He took one of the washrags provided by the motel and poured a liberal amount of alcohol on it. The alcohol fumes and the stale odor of cigarettes in the motel room turned his own stomach, and he tried to close his nose to the strong scents. He dabbed at the gash on his shoulder, softening the dried blood so he could brush it away. The alcohol burned, firing a sting worse than the original bullet wound.

Grimacing, he growled equally scorching

curses through his clenched teeth. He managed the awkward process of tending his own injury fairly well until he had to wrap the wound with the bandage. Trying to work the cloth strip tight enough to hold the gauze pad securely, he fumbled and dropped the pad. No dice.

"Laura."

"Yes?"

"Please?"

He heard no response, but a moment later, she appeared at the door. Her face looked pale and frightened, the effect heightened by the harsh blue-white glow of the fluorescent lights in the bathroom.

"I can't wrap the bandage tight enough without help."

Her throat convulsed as she swallowed. With a timid nod, she stepped closer, flinching when she looked at the bloody gauze on his shoulder. "Wh-what do I do?"

"I'll hold the end. You wrap, going under my arm then over the wound several times. Okay?"

She nodded again.

He watched her face as she lifted the bandage with trembling hands and tugged to tighten the slack. "That's it. Good. Again."

With her help, he had a neatly bound bandage in no time. "There. Done. Thanks."

She sat back on her heels, pressing a hand to her stomach. When he began gathering the bloody debris from cleaning the wound, she took one look at the crimson-stained rag, and the color drained from her face. She spun toward the toilet and...

Guilt pinched him as she retched. "Hey, you okay?"

She shook her head.

He gathered her long wavy hair in his fist and held it out of the line of fire. The silky strands tickled the small cuts on his palms left by the shards of his broken window as he'd crawled across the floor. The soft caress teased his imagination with how all that hair would feel draped around him during sex. He groaned, forcing the erotic image aside. Tucking her hair inside the neckline of her blouse to keep it back, he searched for a clean washrag and dampened it with cool water. "Here."

She peeked up and accepted the proffered cloth. Sitting back on her haunches, she wiped her mouth and pressed the moist cloth to her throat. "Happens every time."

He offered an apologetic grin. "Can I get you a soft drink from the vending machine?"

She shook her head. "I'm okay. Just embarrassed."

"Don't be. You warned me." He rose to his feet and gave her another long, sympathetic gaze. "Thanks, Laura. I owe you one. Tell me if I can get you anything, okay?"

She flashed a quick, shaky smile. When she struggled to her feet, he put a hand under her elbow to help, but she batted his hand away. "No, I'm good."

Laura left the bathroom on wobbly legs then stopped at the vanity sink to swish a dab of toothpaste in her mouth.

It struck Max that the incident said a lot about Laura. Despite knowing how it would affect her, despite what it cost her, she'd helped him when he really needed her. Just like she'd stuck with him out of concern for Elmer, despite the known risk.

He was forming a picture of a generous and caring woman, one who put others' needs before her own. He respected that.

He picked out a fresh shirt from his new clothes, a button-down he could easily slip his arms into, and carried it into the main room.

Laura sat on the bed with Elmer. Her color was back, and she seemed steadier.

Max propped against a stack of pillows

at the head of one double bed while Laura played with Elmer on the other. He couldn't help staring. Her face glowed with an inner joy as she tickled and cooed at the baby. His own skin shivered with imagined pleasure watching her slim fingers trace circles on Elmer's chest and legs. The baby's gaze riveted on her face with a curious fascination, much the way Max's did.

His nephew had good taste. Laura was easy on the eyes.

And she had a natural ability with Elmer. Sure, she'd said she worked at a day care center, but her skill went beyond knowing how to burp him after his bottle or her lightning-fast diaper changes. It was in the glow.

Jennifer had had that glow. Once. His ex-wife's face had shone with excitement, love and desire when she'd talked about motherhood—the babies she'd wanted, the nursery she'd planned, the dreams she'd cherished. Jennifer would have been a wonderful mother.

If not for him.

Max swung his legs off the bed with a groan and started pacing. He hadn't wanted to dig up the past, but it had been inevitable. The irony that he was now responsible for a baby hadn't escaped him. In fact, the paradox wrestled inside him, reviving the pain of three years he'd rather not remember.

"I thought you were going to sleep," Laura said.

"So did I." As he stalked past her bed for the third time, he cast a quick glance at Laura. The warmth that had filled her face while she played with the baby was gone. The instant she looked at him, her expression became closed, guarded. Her continued wariness and touch-me-not manner rankled.

"I'm sure Elmer will be back to sleep in just a little while." She picked the baby up and put him on her shoulder. "Newborns don't usually stay up for long stretches."

"Elmer's not what's keeping me awake." He dragged a hand over his face. "It's this whole insane mess. Anthony Rialto is a maniac. He sent gun-toting goons after me, for God's sake!"

Laura shot him a peculiar expression he couldn't interpret.

"What's that look for?"

"If I remember correctly, you had your own guns and returned fire." She gave the Glock on the nightstand a meaningful glance.

He huffed. "That's different."

"How?"

Propping his hands on his hips, he stopped pacing and faced her. "I was defending myself and protecting the baby. And you!"

She stared at the bedspread, a serious, thoughtful knit in her brow. "Who were they? What am I involved in?"

Fair questions. He sighed and started pacing again. How much should he tell her?

The less Laura knew about the Rialtos, the better. For her own safety. Firsthand knowledge of a drug smuggler's activity was not good for one's health. If she did leave him and go to the cops spouting her eyewitness account of Rialto's strong-arm tactics, she'd set herself up as the egomaniac's next target.

"Max, on your answering machine, in your driveway, that man said the baby belonged with him. Why? Who is he?"

Max latched on to her last question, a way to give her at least part of the truth. "The man was Anthony Rialto. He's my sister's father-in-law. They want custody of Elmer, but Emily gave him to me. She wants me to have him, to protect him. You saw the kind of people they are, how they use violence to get their way. I promised Emily to keep her son away from those goons."

"If you have Emily's permission, a legal

right to have Elmer, than why not call the police on these guys?"

Max scrubbed a hand over his face as he stalked the small room with restless energy gnawing at him. "It's not as black and white as that. It's not just about legal rights, and involving the police will make things even more complicated."

If Laura dragged the police into this scenario, the cops could easily put Elmer in protective custody where the Rialtos could find him, use their paid contacts inside the police department and stake their claim to the baby. The courts would get involved. It'd be a nightmare.

He'd promised not to let Elmer out of his sight for a minute. Anything could happen. As Emily said, the Rialtos could even take Elmer out of the country.

When he raised his head to meet her gaze, her blue-green eyes drilled into him. For a moment, he simply lost himself in the sharp intelligence, the depth of emotion reflected in their vivid color. A man could drown in those eyes. He fought the magnetic pull of her bright gaze and dragged his thoughts back to the problem at hand.

He needed to focus. Stick to the game plan.

"All you need to know is that the Rialtos, despite their relationship to the baby, can't get their hands on Elmer. They're not nice people. It's in Elmer's best interests that he stays with me. I know that doesn't tell you much, but it's really all I can say."

She grunted.

He gritted his teeth and started pacing again. "You're just going to have to trust me on this."

"You've said that before. But I think I'll reserve judgment on that. Nothing personal. I'd just hate to be wrong about you, and let this little baby fall into the wrong hands."

He sighed in exasperation. "I'm the *right* hands. At least for now. When his mother gets better—"

"*If* his mother gets better."

Max stiffened and swung around to face her. "No! *When.* I refuse to accept that Emily could die. She swore to me to fight, to get well."

Emotion clogged his throat.

Laura stood and blocked his path, carrying Elmer on her shoulder. His nephew now sucked on his fist, but his eyelids drooped.

"You have to face reality, Max. You could

end up in charge of this baby forever. And you can't even change a diaper."

The truth socked him in the gut like a fist, and he tensed in response to the blow. He didn't do helpless well. He much preferred being in control.

"I can learn. I *will* learn." He rubbed the back of his neck. Asking for help went against his grain, but for Elmer, for Emily...

"I... I need you to teach me what to do with him."

She blinked and gaped for a moment. "I... I can do that."

Sucking in a deep breath, he spread his hands. "All right. Shoot. What do I do first?"

A lopsided grin tugged the corner of her mouth. "You're serious?"

"Of course I'm serious. I don't want to... cause him brain damage or something! I need you to show me what to do."

The joyful glow returned to her eyes. This time *he* was the recipient of the warmth, the smile. His body went a little haywire, bathed in her radiance, her approval. His senses sharpened. His adrenaline surged. His skin tingled. Except for the distinct tightening in his groin, the feeling was comparable to the exhilaration of a long jog with the guys at the fire station or the rush of containing a forest fire after battling flames and smoke through a long night.

"I think the best place to start would be for you to get more comfortable with him." She lifted Elmer from her shoulder, placing a hand behind his head, and held the baby out to him.

The exhilaration evaporated, replaced with a pounding anxiety. *Hell.* He hated this sense of inadequacy. "I—"

"Just support his head." She placed Elmer in his arms. "That's right." Grinning her encouragement, she stepped back.

Max sat on the edge of the bed and frowned. "Now what?"

"Look at him. Just look at him. Talk to him maybe. Get to know him."

He arched an eyebrow and sent her a skeptical look. "Like introduce myself?"

"Sure." She chuckled. "Why not?"

With a grunt, he looked down at Elmer. Elmer! Sheesh, what a name.

Why hadn't his indecisive sister chosen a name before her child was born? And why couldn't Grandpa Harding have come to mind when Laura pressed him about a name rather than Grandpa Caldwell? *Jake* would have been much better than *Elmer.* If he survived this undertaking, *Emily* would kill him for giving her child such an awkward name.

The bed sagged as Laura sat next to him. Her arm brushed his, and he tried hard to focus on Elmer's soft skin instead of Laura's.

He stared at the baby, wondering how to proceed. A stir of panic gripped his gut. He couldn't fail, couldn't let Emily down. But the baby might as well have been a pair of knitting needles for all he knew to do next. He was in totally uncharted territory.

Laura leaned closer, looking at Elmer with him, and he caught a whiff of her shampoo. Fruit. Strawberries, maybe?

"He has your mouth," she said.

Her assessment caught him off guard. "What?"

"Elmer has your mouth." She glanced at his mouth then back at the baby's.

"You think so?" Curious, Max studied Elmer's tiny pink lips, wondering what she saw that he'd missed.

"Mmm-hmm." She reached out and stroked Elmer's mouth with her fingertip.

His own lips tingled imagining her touch, and he swallowed a moan. *Get a grip!*

Elmer opened his mouth and suckled her finger.

Max pushed down any number of erotic images, ideas he had for suckling her himself, and cleared his throat. "Do you think he's hungry?"

"Naw. I just fed him. Babies just like to suck. It's comforting to them." She pulled her hand away. "Give him your finger."

He cut a sideways glance to her. "Huh?"

"Go on. He doesn't bite. At least, not hard." She gave him a teasing grin.

Trying to ignore the erratic beating her smile caused in his chest, he poked a finger at Elmer's mouth.

"Gently. Don't force it," she whispered.

Her breath tickled his neck as she huddled close to watch. A prickly heat scampered down his spine, puddled in the core of his body.

Focus. Think about the baby, not the woman.

Max stared hard at Elmer, considered the baby's mouth. Like his? More like Emily's, really.

His breath caught.

Emily's son.

His nephew. This baby was more than just a baby. He was a part of his sister. A part of him.

Family.

His heart kicked up a frenzied cadence, thumping wildly against his ribs. He devoured the sight of the baby with fresh eyes.

Laura was right. He'd been so preoccupied with the threat the Rialtos posed, he hadn't really *looked* at Elmer before.

"Oh, my God," he whispered.

"What?"

He raised his gaze to Laura's, knowing full well he had moisture in his eyes. "He's beautiful."

Laura's chest squeezed painfully at the awed, lovestruck expression on Max's face. His dark eyes glistened with wonder and affection, making her own eyes tear. Had her father been this enamored with her when she was a baby? She'd never know. Oh, how she wished she had even one memory of her father smiling at her in love.

But he'd died while she was an infant.

Max blinked rapidly and cleared his throat as he turned his attention back to Elmer. "He, ah...looks like his mother."

The sudden lump in her throat prevented her from responding.

Max's fingers roamed over Elmer, along

with his gaze. A full range of emotions played across Max's face. He stroked Elmer's fuzzy black hair, the curve of his tiny ear, his delicate cheeks. He studied Elmer with a rapt attention to the smallest detail.

Max's fascination with the baby touched Laura, but the poignancy had a sharp edge that sliced through her. She'd missed so much in her life, not having her father then losing her mother at a tender age. Usually she could keep her emotions in check. She had to in order to protect her heart.

But the day's tumult and her fatigue left her vulnerable. The honesty of the emotions that filled Max's eyes blindsided her. The desperate yearning for her own baby, a desire she'd suppressed for years, blossomed inside her and left a hollow ache in her soul. How could she ever have children of her own when she was scared to death of forming a relationship with a man? She'd heard too many sob stories from her coworkers about boyfriends that cheated, fiancés who changed their mind, marriages that failed. She could never risk that sort of betrayal and abandonment. Hadn't the difficult years, bouncing between foster homes, left enough scars?

"He has fingernails." Max rubbed Elmer's

thin fingers. The warmth in his voice speared through her chest.

She bolted from the bedside, needing air, needing distance. She wrapped her arms around herself as if she could physically hold her breaking heart together. She drew and slowly released a deep, cleansing breath.

Max looked up at her with a puzzled frown denting his forehead. "You okay?"

She nodded. "Just tired, I guess."

"You can catch a nap if you want. I think I can handle this little guy for a while."

"Naw. I have too much on my mind. I'd never get to sleep."

He turned back to Elmer. "Then if you're staying up, how about showing me the trick to changing a diaper? I think I smell something rotten in Denmark."

Laura rubbed her eyes with the heels of her hands and took one more deep breath. Reminding herself how much she'd suffer later if she let herself get too close to this man and child, she fought down the swell of emotions that had escaped in her moment of weakness. Mentally she locked the door on the longings that could only lead to heartache. Families were for other people. She was better off on her own.

"I'll get a clean diaper. You put him on the bed and take off the dirty one." She rummaged in the shopping bag for the package of diapers they'd bought earlier.

She pulled a clean diaper from the pack and turned in time to see Elmer baptize Max in the first lesson regarding baby boys.

"But keep him covered. Boys will squirt you." She chuckled when Max scowled at her.

"Now you tell me." He swiped ineffectually at the wet spots on his shirt. "Thanks a lot, Elmer."

Laura carried the dry diaper over to the bed and demonstrated how to wipe the baby clean, tuck the fresh diaper snugly around his waist and secure the tape. "There. Easy."

Max didn't look convinced. He scooped the baby up, holding Elmer under his arms.

"The head! Support his head." She hurried forward putting her own hand behind Elmer's lolling head.

"Damn. I forgot." Max grimaced. He shoved Elmer toward her with a sigh. "Here. You take him while I put on a dry shirt."

Laura obliged and moved with the baby onto the bed. Elmer whined a bit, and she fished around under his blanket for the pacifier. "Want this, sweetie?"

When she heard a grunt, she glanced up. Max held his injured shoulder, his eyes squeezed shut in pain.

"Are you all right?"

"I've been better. But I'll live." He gave her a weary, frustrated glance. "Can you help me get this thing on? My shoulder's still stiff."

When she hesitated, he added with a grin, "No blood this time. I promise."

Laura settled Elmer on the bed, wrapped in his blanket, and crossed the room to Max. She stood in front of him for a moment trying to decide how best to help. She knew what she'd do if this were a four-year-old boy at the day care, but how did one help a grown man dress?

A nervous flutter started in her stomach at the prospect.

Awkwardly she moved closer and raised trembling hands to take the clean T-shirt from him. She managed to get the shirt on his good shoulder without touching him. But in order to guide the sleeve on his other arm without hurting him, she had to be more careful. The back of her hand skimmed his chest as she worked the shirt down his arm.

The contact shocked her system. The warmth of his skin made her body hum and vibrate with suppressed energy. She jerked her gaze up to his, and his dark eyes locked on hers, held her in a spell.

She'd never been this close to a man before, close enough to touch him and watch his pupils dilate with desire. In her sheltered life, she'd certainly never assisted a grown man with anything as intimate as dressing. By her own choice, she was completely inexperienced in matters of men.

The crisp, woodsy scent that clung to him filled her nose and left her light-headed. Standing this close to him, she could feel his body heat wrap around her like a hug. The air surrounding them crackled and sparked. The fire in his gaze consumed her oxygen, made it difficult for her to breathe.

Something powerful and foreign to her zinged between them. Something that mesmerized her. Something that made her bones melt.

Laura needed all her willpower to tear her gaze from the intensity in his hot stare. She paused a moment, gathering herself, before she continued her task. As she fumbled to ease the shirt over his head, his thick hair tickled her fingers. When she saw how rumpled her clumsy attempt left his hair, she squelched the sudden urge to smooth the waves back into place.

"Thank you."

His deep, husky timbre made the two simple words sound like an intimacy whispered between lovers. The sound shimmied down her spine like a sensual caress.

"S-sure." Laura shivered and stepped back, praying that he wouldn't ask her help in changing his jeans.

Max had never known a simple touch to cause such a riot in his body. More than her touch, her eyes and the way she looked at him sent his senses into a tailspin.

He couldn't promise he'd be a gentleman if she looked at him that way again. Hunger shaded her aqua eyes, eyes that could seduce him without the added invitation to devour her on the spot. The subtle brush of her hand on his chest had rocked his control more than he imagined possible. He was no stranger to women, yet this lush-lipped angel had his body reacting like a hormonal schoolboy's.

Tamping his arousal took a sheer act of will, but he did it. He had no business entertaining any of the lustful thoughts that flickered through his mind. Not while he had drug smugglers breathing down his neck and a hell of a lot to learn about caring for a baby.

Laura returned to the bed where she'd settled Elmer. "The baby's fallen asleep again."

"Mmm," he hummed by way of acknowledgment.

She lay down on her side, keeping her back to him, and curled her body around the baby. The unspoken message in her body language said it all. Stay away. He'd received the same message every time he'd touched her and she'd pulled away. She wanted to keep her distance.

Yet the look in her eyes only moments ago had said something entirely different. These conflicting messages intrigued him. Which was the real Laura?

"Warm enough?" he asked as he strode over to the door and double-checked that the dead bolt was on and the security chain latched.

This time Laura hummed an affirmative reply. "Say, uh…leave the bathroom light on for me. Please?"

"Sure." Max dropped tiredly on his bed. He leaned up against his pillows and rolled his head back to stare at the ceiling. If he inhaled deeply, he could still smell the sweet strawberry scent of Laura's hair. His body vibrated again with the electric current of desire. Why was he torturing himself this way?

Searching for some distraction, he turned his thoughts to Emily. Pulling from his pocket a slip of paper on which he'd jotted the hospital phone number, Max picked up the hotel phone and dialed. When the nurse on Emily's floor answered, he told her who he was and asked about his sister's progress.

No change.

Max thanked the woman and hung up, a mix of relief and disappointment tangling in his chest. He pictured Emily, alone in her hospital room, and gritted his teeth in frustration. No doubt the Rialtos would harass her for information about where he'd taken the baby. Or try to strong-arm her into signing those damn custody papers. He prayed for her courage and strength in the face of such menacing opposition, hating that he wasn't with her, defending her, guarding her hospital door. But she'd chosen her son's welfare over her own, and he could do no less in keeping his promise to her.

He shifted his thoughts to his job. Like Laura, he had some personal days saved up, and he knew the guys at the fire station would cover for him under the circumstances.

His Pee Wee football team was another matter. The kids counted on him, and he hated not being there. Frustration roiled, and Max rubbed his gritty eyes with his fingers.

The sound of voices near their door intruded in his reverie, and he tensed. Snatching the Glock from the nightstand, he hurried over to the front window and nudged the curtain aside. His heart thundered against his ribs as he scanned the parking lot. The dark shapes of two men moved slowly from the shadows and under a streetlight. The flash of light reflecting off metal drew Max's attention to their hands. He squinted.

Cans. Probably beer, judging from the way the two men staggered. On closer inspection, he realized the men were, in fact, teenagers, and he released the breath he held. Carousing teens, not drug-dealing thugs. Jeez, he was jumpy.

He let the curtain fall back in place, wondering if those teens' parents knew where they were and what they were doing. He'd made a point of knowing everything Emily was involved in during her rebellious teen years, even though she'd complained he was too controlling. He furrowed his brow. Maybe if he hadn't been so strict with Emily, she wouldn't have defied him and jumped rashly into her marriage with Joe Rialto.

Another failure on his head.

He glanced to the bed where Laura rested with Elmer. His dramatics hadn't drawn so much as a peep from her. Curious, he walked around to the opposite side of her bed and peered down. Both she and Elmer were sound asleep.

"I thought you said you weren't going to sleep," he whispered, a grin tugging his mouth to the side.

He studied her peaceful expression, void now of the subtle tension that had shadowed her all day. In sleep, even more than earlier that evening, her face had an ethereal quality.

He recalled her guts, her grit and determination to guard Elmer in the face of Anthony Rialto's gun. Even now, she curled an arm around his nephew, snuggling the infant in the curve of her body. He admired her willingness to sacrifice her own safety to stay with Elmer. Maybe a little crazy, but admirable. He guessed she'd be the kind of parent who'd stay involved with her teenager. Without smothering and controlling.

Courage, compassion and selflessness all wrapped in a damn fine package. Laura Dalton was a piece of work.

Max angled his head to watch his nephew sleep. When he was quiet, the little tyke was pretty angelic himself. Dark eyelashes fanned across his delicate baby cheeks. He was so tiny, so perfect, so innocent.

A tidal wave of emotion crashed down on Max. If he'd thought he'd gotten the sentimentality out of his system earlier in the evening when he'd held Elmer, he was wrong. Just looking at Emily's son filled his chest with a tender ache that squeezed the air from his lungs.

If only he and Jennifer had had the baby she wanted....

Guilt and disappointment crept over him. If only. How many times had he considered the *if onlys?*

He huffed and refocused his thoughts. No point living in the past. He couldn't go back and change things for Jennifer, couldn't change the way his marriage had ended. And yet, somehow, this baby might be his chance to redeem himself.

Even if he couldn't give his wife a baby, he

could make sure that his sister had a chance to mother her son.

This time he wouldn't fail.

Chapter Six

Laura had a plan.

Not an elaborate one, but a plan nonetheless. In fact, the beauty of her plan was its simplicity.

As she carried her small bag of clothes and toiletries to the car, she weighed the merits of her idea to get Elmer away from Max. It could work if she kept her cool.

But was it the right thing to do?

Before last night, she'd have said undeniably *yes*. Yet she'd witnessed Max's affection and dedication to Elmer firsthand now, and she'd begun doubting the wisdom of her plan. The idea of betraying Max bothered her, too. Throughout the night as they'd tended to Elmer, Max had considered her needs first. For sleep, for room temperature, for extra pillows to prop on while she gave the baby his bottle. He'd insisted she rest in the early morning hours, when Elmer was particularly cranky, and he'd stayed up, pacing the floor with the fussy baby on his shoulder.

He'd been attentive both to her and Elmer, though she could tell he'd needed the sleep just as much as she did. Guilt plucked at Laura, even as she made her plan to take Elmer to the police.

But considering the danger Elmer could be in if the gun-toting crazies caught up with them, didn't she have a responsibility to take the baby to the cops? She had to trust the professionals to sort out who had custody rights. Maybe Max was Elmer's rightful guardian, but she'd leave that decision to the authorities. What mattered was that she honor her responsibility to Elmer, first and foremost.

Protect the baby.

She headed back into the room. When she'd left, Max was calling the hospital to check on Emily.

"I've got her baby," he said quietly into the receiver. "And I've got to lay low for a while.

I don't want his family to find us. I thought I'd use your cabin, if that was okay."

Laura paused at the door and focused on what Max mumbled into the phone. Clearly he was no longer talking to the nurse about Emily.

"No, he's dead." Max paused, grunted.

Who was dead? A numbing chill settled over her.

"You don't know the half of it, man. It's one hell of a mess. I don't know when I'll be back." Max jerked his head up as if he'd just noticed her standing in the doorway. "Listen, I gotta go. I'll check in with you when I can. Thanks, buddy." He set the receiver in the cradle with a soft click. "Ready to go?"

"Who's dead?"

Silently, he began gathering his possessions into a plastic bag.

She leveled a cool glare at him. *"Who is dead?"*

His returned stare was just as stony. He hesitated. "Elmer's father."

A fresh prickle of suspicion crept up her spine. She glanced to the car seat where Elmer was sleeping. "How did his father die?"

"He was shot."

Ice filled her veins. "Wh-who shot him? Did...you?"

"*No*, not me." Max raked fingers through his inky hair. "It's really better for you if you don't know too much. If you want out, now's a good time to go. I'm not stopping you."

She chafed her arms and shook her head. "If the baby is in danger, I can't leave him with you."

"Then I guess we're still at an impasse. Shall we get moving?" Max picked up the car seat and headed outside.

Without answering the other half of her question.

Laura quashed the jittery twinge in her belly and followed Max to her car. When she pulled the car to the door of the motel lobby to check out, Max took the key from the ignition.

"What are you doing?"

"Nothing personal. I'd just hate to be wrong about you and have this little baby fall into the wrong hands," he said with a forced grin that fell short of its mark.

She scowled, knowing she'd used those exact words last night. But did his distrust bother her more or did the fact he had a reason not to trust her?

While he darted inside with the key, she closed her eyes and firmed her resolve. She had to act. Soon. The snippets of conversation she'd overheard and new doubts she had about the situation made her decision easier.

Protect the baby.

When he returned, Max had a small bag in his hand. He handed the sack to her along with the keys as he climbed in the car.

"What's this?" She unrolled the top of the bag and peeked inside.

"Breakfast. Comes with the price of the room. I grabbed a few things off the buffet. Thought you might be hungry."

While he buckled his seat belt, she pulled items out of the bag. An apple, two bagels, packs of jelly and cream cheese and a blueberry muffin.

A warm, fuzzy feeling puddled inside her, clashing with the cold suspicion. "That was… sweet of you."

"You're welcome. Now let's hit the road. We've got ten hours of driving before nightfall."

Laura pulled the wrapper off a bagel and took a bite, mentally psyching herself for what she knew she had to do. She glanced over to the passenger's side of her Honda where Max leaned the seat back to nap.

"Did you call the hospital?" she asked.

"Mmm-hmm."

"How is Emily?"

"Same. I'd hoped by now she'd be improving, but…at least she's no worse." Max sighed. "Follow this road to I-20 then head east. Wake me up when we hit Birmingham. Okay?" He covered his mouth as he yawned.

"Sure."

Within minutes of hitting the road, Max's deep, even breathing told her he was asleep, and she used the opportunity to study him. His cheeks and chin were covered with black stubble that gave him a dangerous look. His rumpled hair and fatigue-lined face added to his menacing appearance.

Still, memories of his awestruck expression, the tenderness of his touch as he'd held Elmer the night before shattered any illusion that this man would ever hurt the baby in his care. In the wee hours of the morning, as he'd struggled to master the art of feeding and burping a cranky baby, she'd been even more certain Max had this baby's best interests at heart. His dedication couldn't have been faked. His love for the child was written in his eyes.

But that didn't mean he had a legal right to the child.

I've got her baby.

What if he *wasn't* the baby's uncle? What if Elmer's mother was desperately searching for her kidnapped child?

And who had killed Elmer's father? She thought of the men with guns who'd shot at them yesterday and shivered.

Shoving the questions aside, she focused on the matter at hand. Escaping from Max. With the baby.

For the next hour, she prepared herself for action. She played the scenario in her head and examined her plan for flaws. The only hitch she saw lay with the man next to her. She hadn't wanted to like him, to feel any sympathy or gratitude toward him. She, of all people, knew how emotional attachments to people only confused matters and made things more difficult, more painful. Distancing herself from Max was the only way to do this and keep her heart intact.

"Max?" Her voice quaked, and she cleared her throat to try again. "Max, wake up."

He grunted but didn't open his eyes.

"I heard a noise, Max. Something's wrong with the car."

Nothing.

Reaching over, she jostled his arm.

"Ow! Watch the shoulder," he grumbled.

She winced. "Oops. Sorry."

He dragged a hand down his face, his bristly beard making a scratching sound on his palm that skittered through her.

"What kind of noise?" His craggy voice matched his sleep-hazed face when he glowered at her.

"A thumping noise." Springing this on him while he napped nettled her conscience, but she knew the plan had a better chance of working if he was less alert.

Her nerves danced with uneasy anticipation. She had to make him believe her. *Stay cool.*

"I don't hear anything."

"Well, it doesn't do it all the time." She cringed inwardly, when she saw suspicion flicker across his face.

"It's probably nothing. Don't sweat it." He stretched his arms and got comfortable again.

"There! Did you hear that!" She gave him her most convincing I-told-you-so look.

"No," he returned, his face impassive.

She pulled the car over on the shoulder of the two-lane road and stopped. "Well, I did, and I think you should take a look under the hood. I don't want the engine to blow up or something."

He gave her a weary, withering glance. A why-are-women-so-stupid-about-cars look. "The engine's not going to blow up."

She crossed her arms over her chest. She'd debate her knowledge of engines later. "How do you know? How do we know a bullet didn't damage something in the engine yesterday when those thugs shot at us?"

"If there was a problem with the engine, we'd have discovered it last night. Now, drive, would you? I want to make the cabin by dark." He closed his eyes and sighed.

"We won't make the cabin by dark if we break down somewhere."

He looked at her through narrowed eyes and growled. "You're not going to drop this until I look under the hood, are you?"

She met his disgruntled glower without blinking.

Protect the baby.

Focusing on the good she was doing for Elmer, rather than the injustice she planned for Max, she shook her head. "Please? I just want to be sure nothing's wrong."

Max glanced to the backseat where Elmer slept peacefully, then scowled at her as he opened the car door. He grumbled something about women and brick walls and climbed out.

Her stomach clenched, and her heart thudded as he walked a step or two away from the door.

He'd be all right. He was more than capable of fending for himself. Just do it.

Max lifted the hood, and for a couple of minutes, she waited while he examined her idling engine. When he closed the hood with a bang, Laura jumped, her nerves drawn tight. He stepped around to the side of the car, smug satisfaction on his face.

Drawing a deep breath, Laura moved her foot off the brake. He must have read her intent in her expression, because his own face hardened, paled with panic. He lunged for the door.

But not fast enough.

Laura punched the accelerator, and the car rocketed forward.

"No!" His roar mingled with the clunking spray of gravel.

She sped down the road. Her pulse pounded in her ears. The bitter taste of anxiety rose in her throat.

Don't look back. Don't look.

But she did.

Her gaze flicked up to the rearview mirror.

Max stood bent over, his hands on his knees, his head down.

While she watched, his head came up and, even with the growing distance between them, she read the anguish, the horror in his face. And anger.

Squeezing the steering wheel tighter, she sucked in a shaky breath. And drove on.

Max would be all right. She'd send the police to pick him up—after she turned Elmer over to the authorities and the baby was on his way back to his rightful guardian.

Max watched the plume of dust settling around his feet. A fist of despair clutched his chest. He'd known she might try something like this. So why, *why* did he play into her hands like such an idiot? Fatigue was no excuse. Not when so much was at stake.

She'd taken Elmer, damn it. *Damn it!*

He'd screwed up. Lost his nephew. After

less than twenty-four hours. That had to be some kind of record.

How did he tell Emily he'd lost her baby? He'd sworn to protect her son. Instead, he'd let an interfering do-gooder snatch Elmer right from under his nose.

Anger swelled inside him to match his disgust with his own failure. That sneaky, nosy, conniving little…

He huffed and kicked the gravel with the toe of his running shoe. Where would Laura take Elmer, and how did he get the baby back?

Rolling his shoulder to loosen the stiffness, he started walking in the direction she'd driven. For all his fury with her, he knew at some deeper level that Laura would never hurt Elmer. The woman who'd stayed up with him all night, rocking his squalling nephew and cooing endearments, wouldn't hurt a flea. Not intentionally.

But her ignorance of the whole situation, her good intentions could easily ruin everything.

He had to find her, find Elmer before she blew everything. The Rialtos were still out there looking for them. The police would take Elmer away while they sorted out the mess. No good could come of this latest debacle.

Max muttered a curse under his breath as he strode down the side of the road, fuming. He'd fumbled the ball big-time, but he wasn't about to concede the game. He'd find Ms. Laura Dalton, one way or another.

And heaven help her when he did.

The Greasy Spoon Diner appeared much as the name of the establishment implied. Laura sat in her car considering her options before deciding the diner was as good as any place to stop. She'd already tried to call 911 on her cell phone, but this far out in the boonies, she had no signal.

Through the restaurant's plate-glass window, she saw a pay phone. The sooner she called the police, the sooner she could quit worrying. Once the authorities took custody of Elmer, her responsibility to the infant would end. She could head home and put this troublesome event behind her. She needed to cut her ties with the baby before she grew too attached, so attached that leaving him would shatter her fragile soul. This was for the best.

So why did her lungs feel like lead? Why wasn't she racing to make that call? Hadn't the past thirty minutes of agonizing guiltily over Max proven why deeper personal involvement would be a mistake?

She didn't need the grief, the heartache of worrying over Elmer's and Max's fates. She'd done her part, gone above and beyond the call of duty already, hadn't she? When she rescued stray animals, she managed to turn the critters over to the capable hands of a new owner without this much consternation.

Of course, Elmer was a baby, not a dog.

Laura's shoulders sagged. Despite her warnings to herself, she'd let his pitiful wails permeate her soul. When his tiny fingers grabbed her pinky, he might as well have grabbed her heart. She'd tried to keep an emotional distance, but she wasn't sure that was possible with a tiny, helpless baby like Elmer. Despite the inevitable pain, her responsibility was clear-cut. She had to turn him in. Mustering her courage and convictions, she climbed out of the car.

After unloading Elmer in his baby carrier from the backseat, she made her way inside the small restaurant some thirty-odd miles from where she'd ditched Max. The tangy scent of the bacon sizzling on the grill greeted her. Patsy Cline crooned from a neon jukebox in a front corner of the diner, and a thin haze of cigarette smoke hung in the air.

"Mornin', honey," the stout, apron-clad woman behind the counter called when Laura walked in.

"Hello. I need to use the phone. Can I get change for a dollar?" She set Elmer's baby seat on the counter then fished in her purse for a dollar bill.

"Ain't he a doll!" The woman behind the counter, her gray-streaked brown hair slicked back in a limp ponytail, flashed Elmer a toothy grin.

Laura smiled politely. "Thank you."

A strange combination of pride, as if Elmer were her own baby, and longing, since he wasn't, tangled around each other and knotted in her throat.

The waitress punched a button on the cash register, which popped open with a ding, and traded Laura's bill for coins.

"Phone's back that way." The woman directed her with a hitch of her gnarled thumb.

"Could I impose on you to heat this bottle for me?" Laura handed the woman a bottle of formula she had fixed earlier that morning.

"Sure thing, hon." The woman ambled off with the bottle, and Laura made her way to the back of the diner, lugging Elmer in his car seat to a booth beside the phone.

Jingling the coins in her hand, she drew a deep breath.

You're doing the right thing.

She paged to the front of the worn phone book that dangled from a chain and found the number for the sheriff's department. Fishing out a quarter from her change, she dropped it in the slot.

He's beautiful.

The unbidden memory of Max's wonder-filled expression sent an arrow of doubt through her resolve. Last night, his love for Elmer had been obvious.

With trembling hands, she picked a dime from the coins in her palm.

He has fingernails.

The dime missed the slot. She squeezed her eyes shut, forcefully blocking Max's husky voice from her mind.

"You're doing the right thing," she muttered to herself.

By now her hand shook so badly she missed the coin slot with her second and third attempts, too.

Nothing personal. I'd just hate to be wrong

about you and have this little baby fall into the wrong hands.

The dime hit its mark and clanked as it fell into the pay phone. She jabbed the first button with determination.

Whose hands would Elmer go to if she called the sheriff? Most likely, some undetermined foster home until his custody could be sorted out. Laura's stomach pitched.

She wouldn't wish her years of drifting through the foster system on her worst enemy.

She pushed the next button with less conviction.

She'd been in foster homes for more than ten years after her mother died. She knew some kids got lucky, found loving people to care for them and nurture them.

But she hadn't.

Well, the Powells had been wonderful, but she'd been ripped from that home within six months. Heartbreak number one in a long line.

"Here's your bottle, hon." The waitress's voice shook her from the memories of her childhood.

Clutching the receiver with both hands, she turned to offer the woman a smile, but her lips only trembled.

"You all right, ma'am?"

Laura huffed her frustration with herself. "I'm fine, thanks. Could I have a glass of milk?"

Maybe milk would settle the bite of acid in her swirling stomach.

"Sure. Be right back." The lady set Elmer's bottle on the table next to the car seat.

"If you'd like to make a call, please hang up and dial again," the canned voice of an operator instructed from the receiver.

Protect the baby.

Laura pressed the receiver hook, and her money clattered into the change hole. She started over.

"You're doing the right thing."

But she was less convinced now.

Quarter. Dime. Dial—5-5-5-6-3-0-0.

How could she send Elmer to a foster home, let him get lost in the system, when she knew Max loved him?

Her heart contracted. Pain sliced her chest, stole her breath.

Max might be inept and awkward with the baby, might not even be Elmer's real family, but he *cared*. He cared enough to risk his life to save him from the men with guns. He cared enough to learn to change a diaper. He cared enough to go into hiding in order to protect him.

And dadgummit, *she* cared, too!

Protect the baby! She knew what the voice in her head was telling her now. She couldn't send Elmer to the police, to an unknown foster home. Not when *she* wanted to take care of him, not when *she* wanted to guard him and nurture him until he was returned to his rightful home.

The phone rang once. "Sheriff's operator. Can I help you?"

She jerked the phone away from her ear and stared at it as though it were a snake, coiled and ready to strike.

Elmer whined, and the sound of his whimper speared through her. She slammed down the receiver, her whole body now shaking convulsively. She'd done it. She'd grown attached to this baby and couldn't break her tie to him. Not yet.

How could she hand him over to a stranger when she *knew* in her own care Elmer would be protected and cherished? When she knew firsthand how it felt to be alone and adrift in an overwhelmed foster system?

She'd already gotten in too deep. Her conscience, her heart wouldn't let her turn her back now. She knew what it meant to be lost in the bureaucratic shuffle, and she wouldn't do that to Elmer.

Protect the baby. This baby needed *her,* and she wouldn't let him down.

With wobbly legs, Laura made her way to the booth and sat down. Elmer cranked his whine to a full cry, and she hurriedly unfastened him from his seat. She cuddled him to her chest, and his wails quieted as he rooted for food against her shoulder.

Rubbing her cheek against his downy head, she swayed slowly, taking solace in his delicate baby powder scent. If this were her baby, she'd want someone like herself to stay with him, to be his advocate and defender. She could do no less for Elmer's mother.

The affection for Elmer she'd tried, and failed, to squash bloomed inside her, filling her chest with unbelievable sweetness. Though she knew how much she'd suffer when the time came to separate from him, she'd treasure every minute she had with the baby until then.

Already she felt better about her decision, and her nagging conscience eased its grip on her gut.

Until she remembered Max.

"Max." She sighed, guilt twisting inside her. Clearly he, too, had made it his personal mandate to protect and care for Elmer despite the odds against him, despite his inexperience with babies. Max cared, just as she did. The baby was a bond they shared, a common goal.

"Here's your milk." The stout waitress set the glass on the table. "Let me know when you're ready to order."

Thanking the older woman for her assistance, Laura settled into the booth and poked the bottle in Elmer's mouth. While he eagerly sucked down his second meal of the day, Laura stewed over what to do next.

Leaning her head against the plate-glass window, she gazed out at the parking lot and watched a sparrow hop across the pavement, pecking at trash for his breakfast.

Elmer made a sweet cooing sound as he drank and, dropping her gaze to the baby, Laura smiled. "Don't worry, sweetie. We'll figure this out and get you back to your mommy."

Outside the sparrow took flight, and the flurry of motion caught Laura's attention. Turning back to the window, she saw a large sedan pull into the diner parking lot. The driver climbed out and yanked off a pair of dark sunglasses.

The man was huge. His imposing height and wide, muscular shoulders normally wouldn't make an impression on her. But combined with his surly expression, which boded ill, something about him reminded her of the older man who'd stalked her with a gun in Max's backyard. A chill of apprehension slithered up her spine, made her neck prickle with fear.

He sauntered over to her car, examined the bullet holes on the driver's door and looked inside.

Her heart thudded a frantic cadence. Gut instinct told her the man was one of the thugs who'd shot up Max's house. This giant's manner screamed danger.

She hugged Elmer closer, her nerves jumping as the man stepped in the front door of the diner and scanned the room. His gaze found her.

And stopped.

Chapter Seven

Why, oh why, had she ditched Max? Laura realized, in the absence of his reassuring presence, how much she'd appreciated Max's solid strength and protection last night. Without Max, facing the threat this thug posed, her vulnerability hit home, left a hollow pit in her stomach.

Don't tip him off by panicking.

Holding her breath, Laura turned back to the window. She tried to act natural, not stare, despite every impulse she had to gape at him in horror.

She had to get Elmer out of here, away from the goon. But how? Even if she could sneak to her car, buckling Elmer into the backseat would take precious time.

She felt his menacing stare like a gathering storm blocking the sun. She hazarded a quick glance as the man moved to a booth. He caught her looking and gave a subtle nod, his expression stony. Without a word, he said, "I have you now."

"Can I get you anything else?"

She gasped and jerked nervously when the waitress spoke. Fighting to calm her ragged breathing, Laura made some quick calculations.

"I—I need…" She swallowed hard to clear the hoarse sound from her voice. "I need a favor."

"Yeah?"

The waitress was grinning at Elmer, and Laura waited until she had the woman's attention before she spoke. Could the goon read lips?

Taking the woman's order pad from her, Laura scribbled,

The man at the next booth is following me. Meet me in restroom.

She forced herself to smile as she handed the waitress the pad. "And a small orange juice. Thanks."

To the woman's credit, the waitress didn't gawk at the man and give Laura away. Instead, she smiled and said, "I'll have your order in just a minute."

When the waitress left the table, Laura sucked in a deep breath and slid out of the booth. She gathered Elmer's bottle, blanket and car seat together on top of the table so she could grab them quickly when the time came. The thug's gaze drilled into Laura, but the waitress—bless her—stepped between them and poked an open menu in front of him, blocking his view.

Laura took her cue. Cradling Elmer close, she darted into the ladies' room. She didn't draw an easy breath until the restroom door swung closed. Laura knew the thug was smart enough not to hurt her or snatch the baby here at the restaurant with so many people around, so many witnesses. He'd wait her out. Follow her. Run her off the road or attack her when she was alone.

She squelched the urge to panic, to fly apart at the seams. These men—Max had called them the Rialtos—had been willing to kill Max to get the baby. She knew she stood little chance of surviving if they tried to take Elmer from her.

She drew a deep breath and counted to ten. Elmer needed her to think rationally, to stay calm. She had to think of a way to leave the restaurant undetected.

Again she wished she had Max beside her. Why hadn't she considered the dangerous men chasing them when she'd dumped him at the side of the road?

Her heartbeat tripped. Max was alone, unarmed, along the side of the highway. What if the Rialtos found *him?* If they killed him, it would be her fault. She'd stranded him, left him vulnerable and at their mercy.

Dear God, what had she been thinking? She had to go back for Max before the thugs who'd threatened his life found him.

If they hadn't already.

Swallowing the bile and self-reproach that rose in her throat, she battled for composure.

The bathroom door swung open, and the waitress barreled in. "You all right, honey? What's all this about that man following you?"

"He's dangerous. I have to get out of here without him following me. And when he does come after me, 'cause I know he will, I need something to slow him down." She sucked in quick, shallow breaths, knowing she was about to hyperventilate but not sure how to prevent it.

"Okay, hon. Take it easy. We'll get you outta here. Now let's put our heads together."

Laura lifted Elmer to her shoulder and rubbed the baby's back while she thought.

The waitress twirled her limp ponytail around her finger while chewing her bottom lip. "I have it. Leave everything to me. You just be ready to get when the gettin' is good. Ya hear?"

"How will I know when that is?"

"Keep an eye out from here. Peek out the door without lettin' him see you. Then go out through the kitchen to the back door. Okay?"

"Right. Oh, and here..." Laura balanced Elmer while she dug in her pocket and pulled out a few bills. "For the milk and your help."

The waitress winked. "My pleasure, hon."

With that, the older woman breezed out of the restroom like a soldier with a mission.

While she waited in the bathroom, nervous tension coiled tightly in her stomach.

Laura's thoughts turned to Max again. He had to be all right. *Had to be*. She couldn't bear the thought that, because of her, he might have been gunned down or dragged off and beaten or...

Blinking back tears, she tried to shove those thoughts aside with happier ones. Burying her face in Elmer's soft pajamas, she recalled the way Max's hair had tickled her hand when she'd helped him with his shirt. She hugged Elmer closer and remembered the warmth in Max's eyes as he'd looked deeply into hers. She recalled the firm determination that set Max's lips and wondered how it might feel to kiss that hard, stubborn mouth.

If for no other reason, she wanted to live long enough to find out how Max Caldwell kissed a woman. If the consideration he'd showed her and his gentleness with Elmer were any indication, Max's kisses would be sweet, passionate, earth-shaking. The flutter that stirred inside her now couldn't be blamed on nervous tension.

Max, please be all right.

Opening the door a crack, she peered out. She watched the waitress pick up a pot of coffee and approach the table where the menacing-looking man sat. He lifted his gaze to the woman and spoke to her, shaking his head. But the waitress didn't give up. She leaned forward, as if reaching for something on the table, and tipped the pot of coffee. The hot drink poured into the man's lap, and he shouted a curse.

During the flurry of attention to the spill, Laura whipped the bathroom door open and hurried to grab Elmer's car seat. Without looking back, she fled for the kitchen. Darting past the startled kitchen help, she ran out the back door and rushed around the building to her car. Hands shaking, she fumbled to buckle Elmer in then hopped behind the wheel.

The Rialtos' thug appeared at the front door as she cranked the engine. His angry gaze narrowed on her.

Panic exploding in her chest, she stomped the accelerator. The car rocketed backward.

The man scurried for his sedan, but a large pickup truck had been parked squarely behind him, blocking him.

Laura whispered her thanks to the ingenious waitress and sped down the highway in the direction she'd just come. She had precious little time to find Max before the Rialtos' goon freed his car and came after her.

He wasn't in the desert, so the white Honda pulling off the road in front of him couldn't be a mirage.

The kidnapping little wench had second thoughts, huh?

Max balled his fists and marched toward the car with long, stiff strides. Fury was a living beast inside him. Both with Laura and with himself.

Laura stopped the car and climbed out. Her wide-eyed, worried expression was probably intended to soften him up.

Yeah, lady, you better worry. 'Cause when I'm through with you…

"Max!" she cried, running toward him and flinging her arms around his neck. She clung to him as if her life depended on it. "Thank God you're all right!"

Not the greeting he'd expected.

He was learning, however, that Laura Dalton was nothing if not unpredictable. He also learned now that the press of her body against his could make certain parts of his anatomy forget her betrayal. The strawberry scent of her shampoo filled his senses, scattered his thoughts, and the crush of her soft breasts to his chest caused a delicious ache in his groin.

Although her enthusiastic hug caught him off guard, the anger he'd nursed for the past two hours quickly simmered to a boil again. He seized her by the waist and pushed her away.

Turquoise eyes gazed up at him with unshed tears sparkling in the sunlight, but he steeled himself to their effect on him.

"Where's Elmer?" he growled through gritted teeth.

"In the car, of course."

He brushed past her, bumping her shoulder, and stalked to the back door to see for himself. He leaned in and checked the baby, who had found his thumb and was sucking contentedly.

He had Elmer back. *Thank you, God.*

A huge weight lifted from Max's shoulders, and his knees buckled in relief. Straightening from the backseat, he spun to face Laura and nailed her with a hard, unforgiving glare. "Do you have *any* idea the *hell* you've put me through in the last two hours?"

"I'm sorry, but I—"

"Sorry?" he roared, and she winced. "Sorry! I— You kidnapped Elmer!"

"No!" she shrieked.

"I will *not* let you screw this up for me." He jabbed a finger at her as he railed. "Do you understand? That baby is Emily's reason to live. I won't let you or anyone else take that reason from her!"

"Max, we can argue about this later. We

have to go now!" She grabbed his arm, tugged him toward the front door.

He shook her off. "No, we'll have it out now. You had *no right* to take him from me!"

"But I—"

"I don't give a damn what your reasons were. That baby belongs with me." He punctuated this statement by slapping his palm to his chest. "He's *my* responsibility, damn it!"

Her eyes pleaded with him. "We don't have time for this now. He's coming! Get in the car!"

"I promised Emily to protect her son, and, by God, I'll *die* before I break that promise." He stuck his nose in her face to drive home that point.

She pressed her lips in a thin line, and fire flashed in her aqua eyes. "If you don't quit arguing and get your butt in the car, you may do just that!"

"Are you threatening me?" It was almost laughable. Almost. "You took my nephew, and you're threatening *me?*"

"No! Max, listen to me!"

"No, you listen, lady! That kid *is* my flesh and blood. I don't care what noble intentions you have for him. I'm all he has until Emily gets well—"

"Max!" she screeched, her body trembling.

"What!" He paused, his chest heaving as he sucked in one irate breath after another.

"They found us." Tears puddled in her eyes, and he braced himself for one to fall and land a sucker punch to his soul.

"The Riantos or whatever their name—"

"The Rialtos." His gut pitched. Iciness washed over him as his anger drained away in a heartbeat. He grabbed her by the arms, his gaze sweeping over her. "Dear God, are you all right? Did they hurt you?"

She shook her head, and the first tear fell. "It was just one man. A big, mean-looking guy. He saw the car and—" She drew a shaky breath. "We have to go! He saw me get away and came after me. I don't know how much time we have before he catches up."

She tugged on his arm again, pulling him to the front seat. Max turned the tables on her, shoving her into the seat instead. "I'll drive this time."

Slamming her door, he ran around to the driver's side, a tight fist of anxiety squeezing his chest. The Rialtos' thug had tracked them this far. He'd known Anthony Rialto wouldn't give up.

Even as secluded as his friend's cabin was,

would it be enough? And for how long? For now, though, the cabin in North Carolina was their best option.

"I *am* sorry." Laura's softly spoken apology broke the tense silence as he drove toward the interstate, taking an obscure side road. "I only wanted what was best for Elmer."

Max clenched his teeth, biting back the ugly response that sprang to mind. He gave her a resentful look. "I *am* what's best for Elmer. At least for now. Get that through your head."

"I know that. Now."

He cast her another sidelong glance. "Meaning?"

"I couldn't do it. I was going to call the police, turn Elmer in, and I couldn't do it."

He didn't want to ask. He wasn't finished being ticked off with her. "Why not?" he said anyway.

"Because it's obvious you love him." She was silent for a moment, staring out her window. "Because *I* care about him. I couldn't turn him over to a stranger. I still don't know if I believe you're his uncle, if you have any real right to have him, but…you care about him. You'd protect him with your own life and that says a lot."

"Damn right," he grumbled.

"I know you're mad at me—"

"I'm more than mad, lady. You stole my nephew! I can't just forget that. If you were a man, you'd be nursing a bashed nose right now."

She sent him an injured look. "I also brought him back. I didn't have to do that. I had planned to take care of him alone until I figured out what's really going on here. But that Rialto henchman showed up and—"

She shivered, and a primitive urge to hold her, comfort her, beat back her enemies with a club swamped him. Max forced his gaze back to the road.

"I got scared," she whispered. "Worried... about you."

He cut another quick, hard glance toward her. "Me?"

"You were vulnerable. Unarmed. A sitting duck out here by yourself."

He didn't like being called vulnerable, but in truth, he had been an easy mark. And she'd been worried about him. His anger eased its stranglehold a fraction more.

"I've never been so frightened." She turned her bright, laserlike eyes to him. "The way he was watching me, the pure evil that surrounded him. I know he intended to kill me and take Elmer. He just couldn't do it there in public."

Cold fingers of terror crawled up Max's spine. Knowing how close he'd come to losing Elmer for good, how close Laura had come to being killed left him chilled to the marrow.

His heart seized, and his anger cooled another degree. Not only had Laura risked her life to guard Elmer, she'd come back for Max himself when she feared for his life. For that, she regained a grudging measure of his respect.

"I'm not asking you to like me, Max. I'm not even asking you to trust me. But the truth is neither of us can do this alone. Those men are ready to kill to get this baby back. That gash in your shoulder proves that much."

His gut tightened. She had a point. "Go on."

"You need to have your full attention on watching out for the Rialtos. You can't be distracted with caring for a newborn. That's a full-time job in its own right. And if we drag the police into this, who knows where Elmer will end up. I don't want him with a stranger."

He sighed. "So what do you propose?"

"A truce. An alliance. We both have Elmer's best interests at heart. We'll take care of him and guard him together. At least until we can figure out something else."

"And I'm supposed to forget that you took off with him once before?"

He saw the pain and guilt that flickered across her face. "I won't keep apologizing for that. If you choose not to trust me, there's nothing I can do about that. But I swear to you on my life, I would never do anything to hurt that little boy. *That* you can believe."

And he did. She'd proven her loyalty to Elmer, if not to him. What she said about the Rialtos made sense. He did need to stay alert. Stay focused. Having her along hadn't been part of his plan, but now it looked like his best move.

"All right. We have a truce. For Elmer's sake. But from now on, I call the shots. You do what I say, no questions asked. Got it?"

Her eyes widened, and she opened her mouth as if to protest.

He forestalled her complaint by poking a finger in her face. "I mean it. I'm in charge. Take it or leave it."

Her shoulders drooped, and her already full lips pouted even more. "Fine."

"Good. It's settled then."

"Actually, there is one other thing I need to know."

"What?"

Laura leaned across the front seat, grabbed his chin.

And planted a kiss on his mouth.

Chapter Eight

Max almost drove off the road in shock. Instead, he stood on the brake, stopping in the middle of the deserted highway. He sank his fingers into Laura's riot of blond waves, anchoring her in place until he'd sated himself on her lips. Heat thickened his blood. Desire streaked through him like a blaze fed by gasoline. His tongue plundered, reveling in the sweet taste of her mouth. The soft caress of her lips, drawing gently on his, was a sensual dream come true.

She pulled away and gazed at him with heavy-lidded eyes. "Hmm. Not bad."

She licked her lips as she settled back in

the passenger seat. Calmly she tucked a tangled wisp of her gold hair behind her ear and turned to look out the window as if she hadn't just blown his socks off.

Not bad? How could she be so blasé about something that still had his senses reeling?

"What was that about?" he asked, hating that his voice sounded stunned, thick with lust.

"Just satisfying my curiosity."

He started to tell her it had been a damn sight better than *not bad,* but he swallowed his argument along with his pride. Maybe it *had* been only *not bad* for her. Maybe he'd lost his touch. Maybe he hadn't shaken her to the core the way she'd shaken him.

It had been three years since he'd slept with a woman. More like six years since he'd made love for the sake of pleasure and sexual gratification.

In the final years of his marriage, sex had been about ovulation and conception and maximizing windows of opportunity. The process had become clinical and rehearsed and devoid of the passion that had marked the early years with Jennifer. Before she'd asked for a baby. Before they couldn't conceive. Before they'd been told his sperm count made the odds of natural conception next to nil.

With a tired sigh, Max worked to push the memories aside, battling the swell of disappointment, the resentment, the humiliation. But Laura's *not bad* assessment lanced a festering wound to his male ego, his pride. Knowing he couldn't get a woman pregnant had struck a massive blow to his sense of masculinity. When sex with Jennifer had grown increasingly goal-oriented and decreasingly fun, he'd even questioned his ability to satisfy her physical needs.

Not bad. Damn it, he wanted her to melt from his touch, to scream with ecstasy and feel her whole world tilt on its axis because of his kiss.

He glanced at Laura, dropped his gaze to her lips, still swollen from their kiss. Need and longing kicked him in the gut.

Hell. He didn't need a distraction from the serious business of protecting them from the Rialtos. But he wanted more than *not bad.* By God, he *could* please a woman, *could* make her scream with passion. And before they were through, Laura Dalton would know it, too.

For the past ten hours, as they'd driven to the Smoky Mountains of North Carolina, Laura had thought of little besides that one kiss. Sure she'd kissed a few boys as a teen-ager—before she'd realized kisses could lead to crushes and then rejection—but Max was a man, not a fumbling boy.

Having no experience with men, nothing had prepared her for the mind-blowing sensation of Max's firm lips possessing hers. He'd taken control of the kiss almost immediately and masterfully demonstrated how passionate that hard mouth of his could be. The memory of his tongue gently invading her mouth turned her insides to mush, and since she couldn't stop thinking about the kiss, her body had quivered like jelly for the last five hundred miles.

Now, as they traveled a twisty mountain road, she wished for something to occupy her and get her mind off Max. She couldn't even use Elmer as an excuse to busy herself, since he snoozed contentedly in his car seat.

When kept in a dry diaper and fed on schedule, Elmer proved to be an even-tempered baby. He'd slept much of the way up to the mountains and only fussed mildly as he settled back to sleep after a diaper change.

They hadn't made it to the cabin before night fell as Max had hoped, and though the shifting shadows and darkness stretched Laura's taut nerves even further, at least the cover of night hid her body's reaction to Max. She didn't want him to know that every time he sighed or cleared his throat or glanced her way, her pulse jumped and her limbs trembled. She wanted to appear cool and detached, even if her traitorous body longed to be close to Max. Very close.

"This is it." He turned onto a narrow dirt road, and they bounced over the ruts that pocked the drive. Like the other mountain roads they'd traveled for the last hour, the driveway to the cabin cut through a dense forest. Low-hanging branches scraped the car like hands grabbing at her from the blackness. "Damn. I forgot the place has no phone, or I'd have stopped earlier to check on Emily." Max sighed. "I'll have to drive down the mountain in the morning."

Laura scrunched down deeper in her seat and tried to think of something besides the menacing stare of the goon at the diner. "So no phone. Does this place at least have indoor plumbing?"

"Yep. Indoor plumbing. As for electricity, well…"

"It doesn't have electricity?" she asked, aghast.

"Sort of. Not exactly."

"What *exactly* does it have if not electricity?" She tried to infuse her tone with humor. Or irritation. Anything but the panic that choked her.

No electricity meant no lights.

"Don't freak. The place has a generator. A big enough one to power the place and all the appliances."

She released the breath she'd been holding. "Then what's the problem?"

"I won't be able to start the generator until tomorrow."

"Why?"

"It's dark."

Tell me about it! "So?"

He huffed and gave her a sideways glance. Even in the dim car, she saw the unsettling intensity of his mahogany eyes.

"Have you ever tried to start an engine, like a lawn mower or chainsaw, after months of nonuse?"

"No. Can't say that I have. I use my chainsaw year-round."

His scowl, illuminated by the dashboard lights, told her he'd heard the sarcasm in her tone.

"Well, they need work. Priming, tuning,

call it what you want. I can't see to fix the generator until morning."

"Great. So you're telling me there'll be no lights."

"That's what I'm telling you. And since the water pump is electric, we won't have water until morning, either."

Laura shuddered. An isolated cabin. Killers after them. In the dark. Could it be any worse?

"Max?"

"Hmm?"

"I'mafraidofthedark."

"What?"

She sighed and turned to face him as he cut the engine in front of a shadowy building.

"Ever since I was a little kid, I—I've been…afraid of the dark."

He was silent for a minute, then he gave a short, disbelieving laugh. "You're kidding, right?"

"No, I'm not. I—" She sighed heavily and dropped her gaze while she fidgeted with her fingers in her lap. "When I was five, my best friend's brother died of SIDS. He was fine when her mom put him to bed, and in the morning, he was dead."

"How horrible."

"After that, I was afraid to go to bed at night, especially in the dark, because I thought I would die, too."

"But you're an adult now, and you know—"

"Then...when I was seven," she interrupted, and he turned in his seat to face her more fully. "My babysitter woke me up to tell me that my mom, who'd been in the hospital for a simple procedure, had died of an allergic reaction to a medicine they'd given her. She died in her sleep. In the middle of the night."

"Laura, I—I'm sorry."

She avoided his gaze. Telling him the truth was one thing; facing his sympathy was another. She didn't want to lean on him, count on his comfort. She had to be strong and take care of herself. As she'd had to do since she was seven. "After that I went into foster homes. Not only was I coping with the loss of my mom, I was in a different bedroom about every six months for the first three years. A total of twelve different homes by the time I left the system at eighteen."

He was silent, staring at her across the front seat with an eerie stillness.

"So, yeah, I'm an adult now. My head knows it's a silly fear. But...there it is. I sleep with a light on in my bathroom."

He covered her fidgeting fingers with one large, warm hand, and her breath hung in her lungs. Gently he squeezed, his fingers curling around hers to still her nervous fumbling. "I'm sorry."

His comforting hand felt incredibly good in her lap. A slow warmth spread through her, chasing away the chill of fear.

But she pulled her hands from his. Depending on him for support would be a mistake, one she'd already made too many times before as a kid. The problem with depending on any one person for comfort or encouragement or affection was that people left. Or sent you away. Or got lost in the system.

"I'll be all right." She turned to open her door. "I don't know why I even told you that. I... Forget it."

As she climbed out, gravel crunched under the thin-soled tennis shoes she'd bought at the discount store the night before. A stiff, frosty wind cut through her thin blouse, and she chafed her arms to fight the surprisingly brisk temperature. "Brr. Dadgum, it's cold up here."

"Yep. It's the elevation. It'll get even colder tonight. I've been up here before when it snowed in October."

She pivoted to look at Max across the hood of the car. "No way."

"Oh, yeah." He ducked his head into the backseat to get Elmer out of the car.

Laura peered through the window and watched Max cover the baby with both a soft blanket and the thick jacket he'd bought himself at the discount store.

"Why didn't you warn me how cold it would be up here?"

"Didn't know you'd be with me."

She sighed. "I told you last night, I—"

"I know what you said. But I figured by now you'd have changed your mind."

"Well, you figured wrong." She jogged a few steps to keep up with Max's long strides as he headed to the front porch of the cabin. "This isn't just a lark for me. I'm here because I care about Elmer."

"That makes two of us." He thrust the baby carrier into her arms then jangled his keys as he searched by feel for the one that fit the front door.

"And I'm not leaving him until I can be certain he's where he belongs, because I don't want to see him bounced from one foster home to another while his custody is decided."

"There's nothing to decide. Emily's his mother, and she'll raise him as soon as she gets out of the hospital. My job is just to keep Elmer safe until Emily can take over." Once Max had unlocked the door, he shoved it open and stood back. "After you."

He reached for Elmer's carrier, and she pulled it away. "I've got him."

After taking a few tentative steps into the dark cabin, she stopped short. Max collided with her, his hard, wide chest bumping her from behind. "Would you move?"

"But I can't see anything. I don't want to—"

A crash and a mumbled curse from Max interrupted her.

"—trip over something," she finished, chuckling.

"Ha ha. Will you help me find a flashlight? There's a bed to the right where you can put the baby seat. Next to the bed is a small nightstand. Check the drawer."

She scanned the dark room, hoping to make out some vague outline of the interior as she took shuffling, baby steps to the right. A dank, musty smell pervaded the interior, along with the mellow scent of cut wood. When her knees bumped a mattress, she groped in front of her before setting the baby seat on the bed. Then, feeling her way hand over hand, she moved toward the head of the bed and found the nightstand, the drawer and a flashlight.

Flipping on the light, she swept the beam around the room to find Max. The cabin appeared more spacious from the inside than from her impressions of the exterior.

"Now what?"

"Give me the flashlight." Max extended his hand. "I'll go try the generator and see if by some miracle it will crank. If not, maybe there's some wood already cut for a fire." Taking the light from her, he left her in a totally black room.

She listened to the thud of his footsteps on the wooden porch and waited for him to return. Her pulse pounded, and her senses went on full alert. The night sounds—crickets chirping, the hoot of an owl, the wind rustling the leaves—seeped in from outdoors, joining the sound of her own harsh breathing.

Dang, it was cold. Better to concentrate on the cold than on the dark. And the men with guns who could be lurking—

Elmer whimpered, and she started. Taking a deep breath to calm herself, she fumbled through the darkness to find him. The bed gave a protesting creak when she sat down beside the baby carrier to unbuckle him. "Shh, sweetie. I'm here."

Remembering the tiny penlight in her purse, she shuffled across the floor to the front door and made her way back to the car to retrieve her purse and Elmer's diaper bag. The moon was full and bright and provided enough light to make her way across the lawn.

When she returned to the cabin, she held the penlight in her teeth while she checked Elmer's diaper.

Wet.

Fishing out a clean diaper, she started the process of changing him, grateful for the distraction to keep her busy until Max returned.

She had nearly finished when she heard him bump through the front door and sigh. "Nothing. No wood and no luck with the generator. Looks like we're in the cold and dark until morning."

The floor shook slightly as he walked toward her and shone his bigger flashlight on Elmer.

"Is he okay?"

"Mrwr."

His fingers brushed her lips as he took the penlight from her mouth. A warm tingle chased over her skin from the brief contact.

"Say that again."

"Elmer's fine. Just getting dry pants."

"Dress him warmly. As many clothes as will fit on him. It's gonna get frigid in here tonight." The flashlight beam reflected the thin white cloud that formed when Max spoke, echoing his statement.

"Who has a fireplace but no wood?"

"Charles doesn't keep extra wood around 'cause it rots over the summer, and he doesn't want termites getting near the cabin." Max sighed. "That's why I wanted to be here before dark."

Laura felt chill bumps rise on her skin, and she shivered. "Are there blankets for the beds?"

"There should be. In the closet. And it's not beds. It's bed."

"Pardon?" She finished diapering Elmer and dug in his bag for a warm pair of pajamas to put over what he already wore.

"There's only one bed."

"One!"

"That's right. And for tonight, anyway, we'll be sharing."

Chapter Nine

Heart thumping, Laura swung her gaze toward Max, though in the darkness, she couldn't see his face. "Whoa. Think again, hotshot."

He grunted. "No arguments. I'm in charge, remember? We'll huddle together and surround Elmer to keep him and ourselves warm. Share body heat."

Max turned, taking the flashlight, and headed for the closet.

Hugging Elmer against her chest, she scoffed. "And I suppose you think we should be *naked* to get the most benefit from each other's body heat?"

In the dim glow of the flashlight, she saw him pause as he tugged a blanket from the closet shelf. "Now there's an idea worth exploring."

The seductive timbre of his voice fired a slow burn deep inside her. Memories of his kiss flickered though her thoughts again. She bit her lip, recalling the possessive heat of his mouth, the light scrape of his stubbled chin and the alluring taste of his lips. In her belly, an unwelcome desire coiled, and she cleared the tension from her throat before answering. "Get real, Caldwell. I'd sooner eat raw squid."

"Some people consider squid a delicacy."

"And I'm sure you have legions of women who'd love to cuddle naked under the sheets with you, but I'm not one of them." She hoped her tone sounded convincing. Even as she denied her interest in him, an image of his naked body, welcoming her into his bed, flashed through her mind. A shot of pure lust streaked through her on its heels, leaving her trembling from more than the chilly draft that burrowed to the bone.

"Fine. Keep your clothes on. But we will share the bed, and we will get close. I, for one, have no intention of freezing my butt off because you're squeamish about getting close to a man."

"I'm not—" No sense denying it. She *was* nervous about snuggling up to Max, even if her reasons weren't the ones that he thought. As much as a physical relationship with a hunk like Max appealed to her, she couldn't be casual about sex. She was no prude, but for her, sex meant emotion, love…vulnerability. And that was exactly where her association with Max *couldn't* go. She had no use for a broken heart when Elmer's custody mess was resolved.

Elmer whimpered and wiggled against her. The poor fella had to be as cold as she was. Setting him back in his carrier, she tucked the thin blanket around him then draped Max's coat on top, covering him up to his chin.

She blew in her hands to warm them, cupped her palms around the baby's ears, then repeated the process.

Max dropped the blanket on the bed and turned toward her.

"Want first dibs on the bathroom?"

He pointed with the flashlight beam to the door on the far wall. She considered his offer, but also considered all sorts of crawly things that could be in there, in the dark, lurking.

She shuddered. "Why don't you go first and make sure it's…safe. I'll be fixing Elmer his bedtime bottle."

In the beam of the flashlight, she saw Max shrug as he headed off to the bathroom. After tucking the blanket around Elmer, she dug in his diaper bag for some formula. "Are you hungry, sweetie? How about a yummy bottle?"

While she poured Elmer's formula, her penlight in her teeth again, she listened to Max getting ready for bed. She heard him brushing his teeth, an occasional bump or clatter. Typical sounds in an atypical situation.

To a bystander, they probably looked like a family—husband, wife and baby. That impression could serve them well for cover. Who would suspect anything out of the ordinary about their happy little family unit?

Their happy little family….

She suppressed the pang that thought unleashed. She hadn't been part of a family, a real family, in years. Twenty years.

"Okay." Max's voice made her jump.

"On oo at."

He plucked the penlight from her lips. His fingers touched her lips again. More heated prickles. She groaned. How would she make it through a whole night huddled close to him?

"Did you say something?" His voice held a note of humor.

"I said, don't do that! You scared me silly sneaking up on me like that!"

"I wasn't sneaking. And the bathroom is safe. All clear. No monsters or bogeymen. And I saved our only flush for you."

"Pardon?"

"No water tonight. Remember? The water in the toilet's tank will give us only one flush, so I saved it for you. I didn't really need to go, so I'll wait 'til morning."

"Oh, uh…thanks." She screwed the top on Elmer's bottle and handed it to Max. "Here. You start him eating. Good luck with it, too. He's not likely to enjoy his dinner cold."

He handed her the bigger flashlight, and she excused herself to the bathroom. Door closed, she shone the light around, examining the fixtures. Nothing fancy, but nice nonetheless. An old-fashioned claw-footed tub sat off to one side, renovated to include a showerhead and wraparound shower curtain. The toilet and pedestal sink were modern and in good condition. Plush dark green towels hung neatly on the rack, and she wondered if they'd been left out or whether Max had hung them up. She finished her business in short order and made her way to the bed again through the dark.

Max handed her Elmer, who fussed between sips of his cold bottle. She leaned over to give the baby's head a soft kiss. The heavenly, unique scent of baby filled her nose, and she smiled. When she glanced up, Max stared at her with a peculiar expression.

"What?"

He shook his head. "Nothing. I...nothing."

Turning toward the bed, he spread the extra blanket and folded back the covers. He sat on the edge of the bed to take off his shoes then padded in sock feet over to the door where he locked them in for the night. From beside the door, he picked up his rifle, presumably the one he'd brought from his house, and carried it over to the side of the bed.

The gun served as a stark reminder that, even at this remote cabin, the Rialto henchmen could find them. And then what? Laura hated even to consider the possibility. She wasn't ready to die.

"When did you bring that in?" she asked as he checked that the rifle was loaded. She shivered again, but not from the cold. The pop of gunfire, smell of gunpowder and heat of flying bullets were too fresh in her memory.

"I got them from the car after I checked on the generator. Would you hand me the diaper bag?"

She did, and from a front pocket, he pulled out the handgun and set it on the nightstand.

With a short, humorless laugh, she shook her head. "You must love this. Getting to be Mr. Macho Action Hero…playing with your guns, the car chases…like in the he-man movies."

He raised his head slowly, and even in the dim glow of the flashlight, his dark gaze cut through her. His face was set in hard, stern lines. "I assure you that none of this is fun for me. Someone I love is lying in a hospital in New Orleans, fighting for her life, and I'm not there for her. I'm in charge of a baby, without a clue how to take care of him. I've got men from the wrong side of the law after me, trying to take the baby. It's the middle of Pee Wee football season, and I've disappeared without a word to my team. I've imposed on the guys at the fire station to cover for me without warning. And I'm stuck in a cold cabin with a woman who has a big mouth and a mountain of attitude. Trust me, sweetheart, this is far from my fantasy."

He stared at her mutely, his jaw tight for a moment before huffing and dropping his gaze to the gun.

"I… I'm sorry," she whispered hoarsely. "I only meant…never mind." Why did she keep baiting him like that? He'd shown her kindness, tolerance and selflessness, even under the difficult circumstances. She'd returned suspicion, sarcasm. Desertion. He didn't deserve it.

She made a silent pledge to herself, to Max, to try to do better, to lose the "attitude." She could keep him at arm's length without being sarcastic, couldn't she?

Sighing, she carried Elmer to the other side of the bed and crawled under the covers. The sheets were crisp and cold and held the faint scent of laundry detergent. Turning on her side, with her back to Max, she settled Elmer in the crook of her arm, holding his bottle so he could finish drinking. The bed shifted, squeaked as Max climbed under the covers.

"Laura."

The intimacy of her name from his lips, spoken in the still darkness, drifted over her, warmed her like a favorite old bathrobe. It felt good, comfortable.

"Yes?"

"I…shouldn't have laid into you like that. I apologize."

"No. Don't apologize. Everything you said was the truth. You were being honest and—"

The creak of the bed gave the only warning before he slid his arm around her. She jumped when he touched her and tensed her body.

Touching was so…personal. As much as she liked touching Max, keeping certain boundaries was more important. Dangerous emotions followed too closely on the heels of touching.

"Easy," he crooned into her ear and pressed his long, muscled frame close behind her. "Just relax."

Relax? Yeah, right!

"This would probably work better for Elmer's sake if you put him between us."

Yes. Between them was good. Very good.

"Right." She scooted a hand under Elmer, who whined when his dinner was taken from him. With some maneuvering and Max's help with the baby, she rolled to face Max. They repositioned Elmer on the bed between them, and she gave the infant his bottle once more. Elmer gave a tiny, contented sigh as he latched on.

The bed dipped slightly as Max moved closer. He wound his arm around her waist again, anchoring her body close, and tugged the covers over their heads.

The darkness wrapped around her like a shroud, and she fought down a swell of panic. Though she couldn't see him, she felt Max's breath as a warm caress on her cheek. His presence gave her a measure of comfort. She sensed his presence deep in her marrow, in a way she couldn't describe. Just as she'd felt a void without him, a vulnerability, when she'd seen the Rialto goon at the diner, she knew a certain completion, a security with him beside her.

She focused on him, rather than on the dark. She smelled his toothpaste, a lingering hint of his cologne, and what she could only call his *man* scent. Sweat. Testosterone. Sex appeal.

For all that sharing the bed with him created an awkwardness, it also seemed…right. Destined.

Stop it.

She huffed her frustration with herself. Imagining any connection or kindred relationship with Max was pure craziness, a sure setup for a big letdown later. He'd made his feelings about her clear. She was an intruder, unwelcome on his mission to save Elmer. Untrustworthy. Inconvenient. With an attitude.

"Warmer?" His hand rubbed her arm.

"Mmm. Better."

"You have another bottle ready for when he wakes up?"

"Um. No. I'll fix a couple when Elmer gets his midnight snack."

He grunted. "Hope they sell formula at the general store at the foot of the mountain. Next closest grocery store is probably twenty miles."

She remained silent for several minutes, listening to Max breathe and Elmer suckle his bottle, while her thoughts tumbled over each other. She tried to focus on the sounds and scents that were Elmer's rather than Max's. The baby powder smell of the clean diaper, the milky-sweet aroma of the formula and the tiny, contented sighs that were so precious she had to smile.

Then a demon doubt stole into her mind. "Max?"

"Hmm."

"He will be all right. Won't he?"

"Who?"

"Elmer." She swallowed the emotion that clogged her throat. "Promise me that he's going to be okay. That all this isn't for nothing."

His hand glided over her shoulder, along the curve of her throat and settled on her cheek. His warm touch both comforted her and stirred a wild flutter in her chest. An odd combination, yet unmistakable.

"He'll be fine. With both of us defending him, caring for him, how could he lose?"

Sunlight filtered through the cabin's shuttered windows, rousing Max from a light sleep. The twittering of birds heralded the morning, and the warm, curvy body snuggled under his arm reminded him of the night just past.

Sleeping beside Laura had been an exercise of pure frustration. Most of the night, while she and Elmer had slept, Max had lain awake, his nerves stretched tight, unbearably aware of her every breath and the fresh, soap-scrubbed scent of her skin. He'd gritted his teeth to endure the soft tickle when her unruly gold mane had brushed his arm, his cheek. Even now the thick riot of whiskey-colored curls spread across her pillow, spilled over her face and teased his cheek. The aroma of strawberries taunted him. Her wild hair intrigued him, and seeing it rumpled from sleep was a powerful turn-on.

But then, having her feminine body snuggled against his had kept him aroused all night. He'd thought sharing the bed was a good idea. For Elmer's sake. He'd thought having Elmer between them would serve as a sufficient buffer.

He'd been wrong.

The long, sleepless hours of the night had been torture.

He had a new appreciation for mules goaded to walk by a carrot dangled before them. For the child allowed only to window-shop at a candy store and for the quarterback whose fourth down sneak play falls inches shy of the goal line.

The taunting memory of her unexpected kiss in the car only deepened his frustration.

Not bad.

Man oh man, how he ached to kiss her senseless, to blot any hint of *not bad* from her mind with a heavy dose of *damn good,* of *mind-numbing,* of *incredibly satisfying.*

Elmer wiggled, grunted and, like an attentive mother, Laura immediately stirred. Her eyelids fluttered open, and she peered down at the baby. But with a snuffle and a sigh, Elmer nestled in, drifting back to sleep.

Elmer had only wakened twice in the night. Each time he'd drunk a full bottle of formula, had gotten a dry diaper, and had easily returned to sleep. Lucky kid.

Laura's gaze rose slowly from the baby to Max's face. When she found him watching her, a sexy pink blush stained her cheeks. Her lush lips twitched, pulled into a groggy smile. Desire, as thick and sweet as syrup on pancakes, flowed through his veins. Her mouth begged to be kissed.

"Good mornin'." The sleepy, provocative rasp in her voice was his undoing. He'd show her a good morning!

Sweeping wisps of wavy, gold hair behind her ear, he captured her chin with his fingers and seized her mouth with his. She gasped her surprise but made no attempt to break free. Her capitulation encouraged him, fanned his arousal. Slowly, her lips came to life under his, responding with an equal enthusiasm and shattering hunger.

Careful not to squash Elmer, he shifted his body onto hers, pressing her into the mattress with his weight. He angled his mouth to more fully possess hers, and she looped her arms around his neck.

Their teeth clicked. Their tongues parried and lunged. Their lips ravaged and plundered. He felt himself sinking into a mindless abyss of pure sensation. His body throbbed with need and drowned in a scorching, sweet oblivion.

He savored the intoxicating taste of her lips, reveled in the gentle suction of her mouth and lost himself in the erotic grinding of her hips against his rock-hard groin.

When he covered her breast with his hand, her nipple beaded and thrust against his palm. A fresh, fiery surge of lust streaked through him, and he groaned. He wouldn't be satisfied until he was buried deep inside her. With his tongue, he imitated the primitive coupling his body ached for. Then, gentling the kiss, he traced her lips with featherlight strokes.

Laura sighed her pleasure, and he sealed their mouths again. She flirted with his lips, giving him nibbling kisses until he caught her lip in his teeth and tugged lightly. She moaned and surrendered to him with an openmouthed kiss, full of heat and wanting.

His body was on fire. His hunger for her consumed him with hot, licking flames.

Until Elmer released a piercing wail.

The baby's cry brought Max crashing down to earth, dousing his overheated desire with cold reality.

What the hell was he doing?

He rolled off Laura faster than a guilty teenager caught necking in his parents' living room. Had they somehow crushed Elmer in their frenzy? He leaned across Laura and discovered that Elmer wasn't squashed, but only awake, wet and hungry.

She lifted the baby onto her chest, and his whimpers subsided as he snuggled against her. Laura cuddled him close while sucking in deep breaths that told him she hadn't quite regained her composure. When she licked her lips, Max's gaze flew to the swollen evidence of his rough kisses.

Propping up on one arm, he raked his free hand through his hair and sighed. "Sorry about that. I...lost my head for a little while."

Her turquoise gaze darted up to meet his.

"You just looked so beautiful...all rumpled and sleepy and—"

"No, don't apologize. I wasn't thinking

clearly, either." She flashed him a sheepish grin. "Just got carried away for a minute."

He bit the inside of his cheek. He couldn't kiss her again, no matter how much he wanted her. He had to keep his focus on Elmer. Still, an urgent need for her approval battered his soul.

He struggled to keep his expression bland— for his pride's sake. "Just the same, it was... not bad."

"Mmm-hmm, not bad." She sat up, holding Elmer against her chest and patting the baby's back.

She'd slipped into the maternal role like changing shoes. Her loving concern for Elmer seemed always at the ready. That was good. Elmer needed, deserved that attention. And he wasn't, *wasn't* jealous of his nephew.

Max sat up, swinging his legs to the floor, and he scrubbed a hand down his face. *Not bad.*

Hell.

Try *fantastic. Incredible. Earth-shaking.* Her greedy kisses hadn't said *not bad.* Her beaded nipples hadn't said *not bad.* Who was she kidding with her—

"Max?" The edge of concern in her tone cut through his reverie.

He turned toward her. "Yeah?"

Laura bit her lip and furrowed her brow as she stared intently at the bed. "I think…it would be wise…if we didn't…" She paused, obviously searching for the most tactful word. But he knew what she was going to say.

They had no business fooling around, not with the threat of danger hovering over them. He couldn't allow himself the distraction. He needed to concentrate on keeping Elmer safe, staying alert and defending them. He needed a long-range plan now that they'd reached the mountain hideout.

If he'd been thinking with his brain instead of another part of his anatomy, he'd have already posed the same warning to her. Hell, he'd never have kissed her at all if he'd been using his head. "I know. You're right. Absolutely right."

A sexual fling was not in his game plan, not with so much at stake. The fact that Laura had been the one to sober to that reality first stung his conscience. He had to do better. He couldn't let Emily or Elmer down.

Her eyes glittered as she raised her gaze to him. "It's just that I can't—"

He lifted his hand to cut her off. "Say no

more. I understand. We need to stick to a strictly hands-off policy. Agreed?"

Her gaze lingered a moment longer, and he felt it all the way to his bones. Was that regret he saw in her eyes?

"Agreed." She stood and crossed the room to get a diaper from Elmer's bag.

Hands off. Period. End of discussion.

So why did he still feel so tense and unsettled about it? As though he'd lost an argument rather than winning her agreement?

Restless, Max got up and began rummaging the shelves in the kitchenette area of the large room. He'd passed hungry hours ago and bordered now on famished. Canned vegetables, tuna, a jar of peanuts, probably rancid by now. Nothing for breakfast, but he wouldn't be choosy. Selecting a can of sliced carrots, he dug through a drawer of utensils until he found a handheld can opener.

"Whatcha got?" she asked, looking up from her diapering duties.

"Carrots. Want some?"

She wrinkled her nose. "For breakfast?"

"We also have peas and corn."

"You're not even going to heat it up?"

"How? No power yet." Max took another large bite.

She nodded. "Oh, right. But cold?"

"A man's gotta eat."

Walking to the kitchenette area, she glanced over his shoulder into the open cabinet. "Cold vegetables is all we have?"

"There's tuna, too."

"Ugh. I'd say a trip to that little store you mentioned last night is our first order of business today. Even before power."

As if he understood what she'd said, Elmer voiced his complaint. Long and loud.

"Aw, sweetie, you can have breakfast. It's just us big people who need food." Laura hurried over to the bed, scooped Elmer into her arms, then dug in the diaper bag for more formula.

Max shoved away from the counter where he was propped, setting the carrots aside. "How soon can you be ready?"

Laura glanced down at her day-old, sleep-wrinkled clothes. "Let me change. I'll be back in a flash."

Stepping up to him, she handed Elmer off. "Can you fix his formula?"

"Of course." Being passed to his uncle seemed to upset Elmer even more. He crumpled his face and shrieked his displeasure. Max sighed. "But hurry just the same."

* * *

After retrieving from the car the grocery sack with the only clean clothes she had left—an inexpensive sweat suit she'd purchased the first night—Laura headed into the bathroom to change. She'd found a hair band in the console between the seats and used it to pull her hair back into a ponytail. Conditioner to tame her hair topped her list for the general store.

When she walked out of the bathroom, she discovered Max had put Elmer, still crying, into his car seat and had lathered his face to shave. Using a shiny pot as a mirror, he'd finished half his face with a disposable razor and was already bleeding from several nicks.

"The bathroom is free if you want that mirror."

"What I want is my electric razor. But thanks." He shoved the pot out of the way and stalked toward the bathroom. He hitched a thumb toward Elmer. "See if you can calm him down. Nothing I've tried works."

"Come here, darlin'," she cooed as she lifted Elmer from his seat. "Did he burp for you? He could have air in his tummy."

Max scowled. "No. Damn it, how am I gonna remember all this stuff?"

She smiled at him. "Practice." Putting

the baby on her shoulder, she walked slowly around the main room, rubbing Elmer's back, and took in the details that had been hidden by the darkness when they arrived.

Everything but the bathroom and a walk-in closet was encompassed in the one large room. She took particular note of the wooden rocking chair with a dark green fringed afghan draped over the back. It looked about as uncomfortable as the wood-framed sofa with thin green cushions, but it would be useful in taking care of Elmer. The chair and couch faced a large natural stone fireplace, an asset if every night turned out to be as cold as last night. Assuming they found some firewood.

The decor was overwhelmingly masculine, but a few feminine touches graced the room, as well. The navy and green plaid curtains looked to be handmade, the quilt on the bed had a blue floral design, and the dried willow stems in a large vase on the hearth seemed an item a woman—his friend's wife, perhaps?—had added for a more homey atmosphere.

"When we get down the mountain, I'll need to find a phone."

She pivoted on the hardwood floor to face Max when he spoke. He stood in the door of the bathroom dabbing his face with a hand towel. She sucked in a sharp breath at the sight of his clean-shaven face. Free of his stubble, he looked even more handsome, more civilized, as if he could put on a red power tie and blend in at a corporate boardroom. Yet his coffee-colored eyes still had a savage intensity that said no office could contain him. She could easily picture him storming into a blazing building, decked out in his firefighting gear, his eyes alive with drive and determination, the challenge of the battle.

She'd tasted the same intensity in his kiss this morning. Dark, dangerous and oh-so-sexy. Her body grew warm just thinking of the way his lips had commanded hers to respond, the rasp of his two-day beard, the velvety heat of his invading tongue. She'd been crazy to let things get out of hand, but his kiss had been so powerfully seductive, so completely mesmerizing. Ignoring the whisper of her conscience had been easy with her body screaming for more of the ecstasy he offered.

"I need to call the hospital to check on Emily's condition."

His voice brought her out of her introspection. She nodded. "Okay. Want to use my cell phone?"

He smiled but shook his head. "Thanks for

the offer, but I've never been able to get a cell phone signal up here. I'll just find a pay phone when we go to the store."

Max glanced at Elmer, squalling pitifully on Laura's shoulder, and she knew from the softening of his expression that he was remembering why he was going to so much trouble. For his sister.

At that moment, Elmer belched loudly. Max arched an eyebrow and grinned. "Was that the kid?"

Laura giggled. "It sure wasn't me!"

"Attaboy!" he said, laughing. The humor that lit Max's eyes was startling, breathtaking.

"Well, I'm ready to go if you are. I think that belch means Elmer's ready now, too." She poked her arm through the straps of the diaper bag.

Max strode across the floor to the nightstand, where he picked up the handgun.

Laura shuddered.

He tucked the gun in the waist of his jeans, the humor gone from his eyes. "Now I'm ready."

Chapter Ten

Parson's General Store could have starred in an old Western movie, except that it was nestled in a forested valley of the Smoky Mountains instead of a dusty desert town. Max had frequented the small, family-operated general store on previous trips and was familiar with the owners and their wares. The clapboard house served as the Parson family residence as well as the mercantile.

As they climbed out of the car and headed up the front steps, a cat napping in the sunshine got up and trotted over to meet them. Laura tucked Elmer close to her chest with one arm and crouched down to scratch the black-and-white feline's head.

"Aren't you friendly?" she cooed to the cat, who rubbed against her legs and responded with a chirplike meow. "See the kitty, Elmer? Nice kitty."

Max smiled, not at all surprised that Laura's soft heart extended to animals, as well.

The elderly store owner appeared at the door and greeted Max. "That's our resident mouser. Name's Ajax. In human years, he's got me beat by a good five years, but he still acts like a kitten."

Laura tipped a grin to the man as she stood. "He makes a fine welcoming committee, too."

The older gentleman laughed. "That he does! Please come in."

Max and Laura entered to the accompaniment of a jingling bell, and the man's wife added her warm welcome. The bluegrass twang of a dulcimer, the stringed instrument indigenous to the Smoky Mountains, wafted from a radio at the front counter.

Mrs. Parson's attention immediately went to the baby.

"Oh, gracious! What have we here?" The woman's face lit with a thousand-gigawatt smile. "May I?" she asked, holding her arms out to take the baby from Laura.

Laura's gaze flicked to Max, the question in her eyes obvious. He nodded, and she reluctantly passed the baby into the older woman's arms. "We need formula. Do you carry any?"

"Certainly, dear. Aisle two. Diapers and lotion are there, too." The older woman clucked over Elmer like a mother hen, and while Laura headed down aisle two for the formula, Max began filling a basket with other essentials.

The hardwood floorboards creaked as he made his way up and down the rows of canned vegetables and boxed cereal. The mellow scent of fresh coffee filled the air, along with the musty smell of old wood and mildew. Dust motes danced in the rays of early morning sunshine that streamed in though the large front window as he meandered through the cozy store. When he reached the back aisle, he found a display of hunting supplies and hesitated. He hadn't brought from his house any extra cartridges for his rifle or the Glock. There hadn't been time.

Grabbing a couple of boxes of the right cartridges for his rifle, he moved on down the row. Better safe than sorry.

When he took his items to the front counter, a boy in his late teens met him at the register. "Will this be all, sir?"

Max sized the teen up. The kid was the Parsons' grandson, if he remembered correctly. With weeks of heavy labor, moving stock for his grandparents, along with the normal teenage flood of hormones, the kid's legs and shoulders had grown man-sized since Max's last visit. And Max liked his manners.

"No, I'm paying for Laura's things, too." He nodded toward the shelf where Laura studied the different flavors of homemade jellies, apple cider and the Indian crafts made in the nearby Cherokee settlement.

"I just can't believe how quickly your wife got back her pretty figure." Mrs. Parson's voice drew his attention.

"Pardon?"

"Well, your baby couldn't be more than a couple of weeks old, but look how trim and beautiful she looks already!"

The older woman handed Elmer to him. "Why, when I had my babies, it took me months to lose those unsightly pounds, and with the last one, well, I never did." She chuckled and clucked her tongue again.

Max looked over at Laura. The blue sweat suit she'd donned that morning did little to disguise her womanly curves. The material hugged her full breasts, slender waist, and subtly rounded hips. Oh, yeah, trim and beautiful. He remembered the feel of those lush curves pressed against him, and his body pulsed. Her breasts filled his hands perfectly, and the memory of her nipples' response to his touch pushed him to the edge.

Easy, Caldwell!

The boy behind the register cut an interested look toward Laura, too, and his eyebrows rose.

Max tensed, seeing the male interest in the kid's expression as his gaze raked over Laura. He didn't like the notion of the kid, or any man for that matter, ogling Laura. He nailed the teen with a glare. He had no use for a punk drooling over his woman. He didn't stop to consider why he thought of Laura as *his woman.*

Max cleared his throat, and when the boy met his hard stare, the teen blushed and looked away.

"When my *wife* is finished shopping, you

can add her things to my bill." His unspoken message was clearly received. By the teenager and by Laura. Laura was *his,* and any man who trespassed on his domain had better look out.

The boy nodded nervously and gulped, "Yes, sir."

Laura turned and opened her mouth as if to deny being married to him but seemed to think better of it. She locked gazes with Max, and he knew from the fire that lit her eyes, the slight tremor that shook her, that she was remembering their encounter that morning, as well. He could think of little else himself, though he'd tried.

Tearing his gaze away, he turned to Mrs. Parson. "Is there a pay phone nearby that I can use?"

"Surely is, dear." She ambled to the front window and aimed a finger down the street. "Right at the corner there, by the gas station."

"Thank you."

Laura put her basket of items on the counter, and when she reached for her purse, Max whisked out his wallet.

He handed her the baby and gave her a conspiratorial grin. "I've got it, honey. Did you find everything you needed?"

She blinked at him and hesitated before answering. "Uh, yeah, sugar bear, I think so."

Sugar bear?

Heat crept to Max's cheeks, and he scowled at her.

With a sassy grin, she flounced out of the store, twitching her hips as she waltzed out the door. "Bye, Ajax," she called to the cat now perched on the steps.

Sugar bear. Sheesh.

Max chuckled to himself as he paid their bill. The little devil. He'd get her back for that one.

Max seemed solemn as they drove back to the cabin. Laura sat in the backseat so she could hold Elmer's bottle for him as they rode. Max had been fine earlier, even giving her a sly smile when he came out of the store. Then he'd made his phone call to check on Emily, and he'd returned to the car with a worried face. He'd brooded ever since.

She didn't want to care about his bad mood, even warned herself of the emotional cost of getting involved with his problems. But she *was* involved, had been from the moment she'd appointed herself Elmer's guardian.

And if the situation was getting worse, she needed to know.

After several minutes of his silence, she mustered the nerve to breach the quiet. "You seem upset. Did you get bad news about Emily?"

"Hmm? Oh, uh…no. Not exactly bad news. Just not good news, either. She's not making any progress." He scowled and pinched the bridge of his nose. "I should be there. I hate not being there for her."

She admired his devotion to Emily and couldn't deny the spark of jealousy toward the sister who had Max's loyalty and dedication. She hadn't had that kind of family bond since her mother had died.

Turning her gaze toward the baby, she studied the way his eager mouth tugged at the nipple of his bottle. She stroked the black peach fuzz on his head and dabbed at the dribble of formula that leaked from the corner of his mouth.

He has fingernails.

When she lifted his hand for a closer look at his minute fingernails, his tiny fingers squeezed around her thumb. Her heart gave a jolting *ka-thump,* and she suddenly found it difficult to breathe. A smile tugged the corner of her mouth while mist filled her eyes.

Elmer was simply perfect. Perfect innocence. Perfect trust. Perfect heartache waiting to happen. But how could she deny this sweet baby the love he needed? The warmth, protection and security his own mother couldn't give him now?

Laura tugged her finger free and pulled the emptied bottle from his mouth. He smacked his lips and puckered his forehead in a scowl far too serious for an infant. Laura grinned to herself. Elmer had his uncle Max's scowl.

Elmer whimpered, his mouth rooting around like a baby bird searching for more food, and Laura gave him her finger to suckle. "Your nephew has quite an appetite."

Max met her gaze in the rearview mirror, and some of the darkness lurking there dissipated. "He's bulking up to play football. Champion quarterback material there."

A bittersweet smile ghosted over his lips before he looked back at the road, and a warm tug tightened her chest.

Clearing her throat, she prompted, "You mentioned a football team you're involved with earlier...."

"Yeah. A Pee Wee team for the rec center.

It's where I got my start years ago. I played football all the way through high school and wanted to give something back, so I volunteer as coach to the kindergarten team." He gave a lopsided grin and chuckled. "The kind of football a five-year-old plays is a different animal than what you see on television. The kids are still learning the basics—and I mean really basic. But you can't beat their enthusiasm or energy."

The warmth that filled his voice when he talked about his Pee Wee team stirred a tender ache in her middle. She continued to watch Max in the mirror, and the next time their eyes met in the reflection, his gaze held something altogether different. Something uncomfortably intimate. Laura tore her eyes away and stared out the window, fighting to settle the rapid tap-tapping of her heartbeat. *Distance. Keep your distance.*

When they arrived back at the cabin, she carried Elmer and his car seat inside while Max began unloading the groceries. He set the bags on the counter in the kitchenette and began shelving the food.

She settled Elmer on the bed to take a nap, and he whimpered softly. Hoping that with his tummy full, he'd drift to sleep, she walked over to help unpack groceries. The first thing her hand hit in the bag was a small box that rattled slightly as she pulled it out.

"What's this?"

Max glanced over. "Rifle cartridges. I didn't have time to bring any from my house."

"Planning on shooting something?" She widened her eyes in dismay as she stared at him. "Max?"

"I have to be prepared. You saw what the Rialtos did at my house. They could show up here for a repeat performance."

Slapping the box down on the counter, she huffed. "This is ludicrous."

"I agree," he said drily.

"Why would any sane person use violence to try to take custody of a baby? What kind of environment is that to raise a child in?"

The look Max pinned on her drilled straight to the marrow. "Exactly."

She shivered. "Are you saying that shoot-out at your house was standard operating procedure for these Rialtos?"

"The baby's crying." Max tipped his head toward the bed.

"Max, are the Rialtos part of the Mafia or something?" Her mouth grew dry at the prospect.

"I have no proof of any link to organized crime, but their M.O. speaks for itself." He clenched his teeth, and a muscle jumped in his jaw. "Are you going to get the baby or should I?"

Laura stared at him, numbed by the idea of Elmer falling in the hands of mobsters.

Max blew a deep breath through his teeth and marched over to the bed. Scooping Elmer up, he cradled the back of his nephew's head with a wide, strong hand, the way she'd taught him. He looked down at Elmer's face and furrowed his brow.

"Shh. Easy, fella. I've got you," he cooed under his breath.

Laura watched, her heart in her throat, as he placed butterfly kisses on Elmer's head, still murmuring gently to the whimpering infant. He glanced up at her briefly, and her thoughts took a new horrifying direction.

"You said the Rialtos were Emily's in-laws."

Max gave a tight nod. "Yeah."

"Is she one of them? Part of some organized crime ring?" She swallowed hard. "Are *you?*"

Max squared his shoulders, leveled a stony stare. "No. Absolutely not."

Seeing the fire in his eyes, hearing the dark conviction in his assertion peeled back the layers of doubt. She believed Max.

The pressure in her chest eased.

He sighed heavily. "Emily had no idea what she was marrying into. And if I'd known the truth back then, I'd have hog-tied her and sent her to Canada to keep her away from the Rialtos if I'd had to."

He looked down at the tiny life in his hands, and his expression shifted, softened—subtly, but the change flooded her soul with a tender ache. Max gazed at the baby with such love and concern, she thought her heart would split open from the bittersweet pain filling it.

Dear God, how she wanted her own baby to love. And how she wished Max would look at her with the same warmth and melting affection.

Fat chance of either happening.

Angry with herself for her wishful thinking, she started shelving groceries again. "Do you have a plan? What are we supposed to do next?"

"We wait here for now. We're safe in the cabin. Secluded." He walked away, gently rocking his upper body to soothe Elmer.

"Wait for what? How long will we be here?"

He sighed tiredly. "I don't know. Depends."

"On what?"

"On how long it takes Emily to get back on her feet. Just leave the planning to me, okay? You're here to take care of the baby."

"Seems to me you're doing all right with the baby for yourself."

Max looked startled by her comment, as if it hadn't occurred to him he was doing well mastering the fine touch of baby care.

Although he still cried, Elmer's whines were more subdued. When he glanced back down at Elmer, Max's expression was endearingly hopeful.

Until Elmer threw up on him.

Max groaned. Grimaced. "Laura!"

"Chill out. It's not toxic."

"Just the same. I'll let you burp him from now on. That's the job you signed on to do, remember?"

She took a cloth diaper from the bed to wipe Elmer's face then stepped over to take the baby from Max. While Max changed his shirt, she carried Elmer over to the rocking chair and finished cleaning his chin.

When she met the baby's dark blue gaze,

his sweet expression stole her breath. Her job, as Max had reminded her, was to take care of the baby. Perhaps the best way to earn Max's faith back, after she'd ditched him on the highway, was to do her job in spades, to prove her devotion to Elmer. That would be easy enough. The newborn had managed to wrap her around his tiny finger. She'd do anything for the little tyke.

But she *could* do her job with Elmer without getting any more tangled up with Max. On that point, she had to draw the line.

"I'll get started on the generator now." Max strode to the door and glanced back at her.

She nodded.

His gaze stayed locked on hers a second longer than was comfortable. The intensity in his eyes reminded her of a thundercloud, full of power and dark promise. The crackle in the air was unmistakable.

Intuitively, she knew the spark between them was a recipe for disaster in more ways than one. Thankfully he'd understood this, too, and he'd agreed that their careless indulgence that morning had been a mistake. Their mutual hands-off policy would make it easier to keep her emotions in line.

She hoped.

Max had the generator started within a few minutes, and Laura had Elmer asleep soon after. Each having completed their tasks, they were left staring at each other with time on their hands.

When she thought about it, Laura realized how much idle time they were likely to have…alone…together. Two words came to mind. *Oh. No.*

Chapter Eleven

The French maid fantasy finally did it. He had to get out of the cabin and clear his head.

Max grabbed his jacket and headed into the woods for a long walk, hoping the brisk mountain air would cool his lust-heated blood.

Laura had busied herself dusting the furniture and washing the cabin windows, presumably to occupy herself since there was nothing else to do. After she'd rocked Elmer to sleep, they'd found themselves painfully short of things to do. No TV. No radio. Little reading material.

He'd watched her flit around the room,

dusting and scrubbing for all she was worth, even wiping the new cans of food in the cabinet. And while she cleaned, he studied the easy, graceful movement of her slim body, thought of their morning kiss and imagined himself occupying her idle hands in other ways.

Ways that involved getting naked. Ways that included getting sweaty. Ways that left his body thrumming with sexual energy.

Hell! Get a grip, Caldwell!

Max stomped noisily through the dried oak and maple leaves, allowing the chill air to nip his cheeks. He tried to focus on the orange and red fall foliage and the majesty of the mist-shrouded mountain range. But images of Laura stretching to reach the top shelves, her clothes pulling tight across her breasts and derriere, replayed in his mind.

Along with the picture of her in a frilly French maid outfit. Of himself removing that frilly maid uniform and filling his hands with her....

Max huffed his frustration, and his breath clouded in the cold air. He braced a hand on the nearest tree and bent at the waist to suck in a restorative breath. The bite of the crisp fall air stung his lungs, and slowly he reclaimed his control.

He decided his best defense was to stay busy himself. He'd find useful ways to keep his hands and his mind occupied. Wood for the fireplace was a good place to start. The cabin most likely needed some sort of minor maintenance repairs after the summer. Anything, as long as it kept his mind off sex. Better yet, he'd plan his strategy concerning Elmer and the Rialtos.

Do you have a plan?

He couldn't tell her he had no plan, that so far he'd been thinking on his feet, taking the hits as they came. He only intended to have Elmer until Emily recovered enough to care for her son. Once it was clear to the Rialtos that Emily wasn't going to die, they'd see they had no case for assuming custody. Right?

He scoffed at his preposterous assumption. The Rialtos weren't going away. They'd fight Emily for the baby, threaten her, possibly have her killed. They didn't play fair.

The hard truth was Emily would need to go underground. He'd keep Elmer safe in the mountains until she was released from the hospital, then he'd take her and the baby to the FBI or DEA or whoever would listen to them about the Rialtos. Maybe he could get Emily into the Witness Security Program.

His mind set and refocused, he headed back to the cabin—in time to catch a glimpse through the front window as Laura yanked her sweatshirt over her head. Her lacy bra, the living-color version of the woman in his daydream, put the French maid fantasy to shame.

She reached for a T-shirt lying on the bed and pulled it on, and he gulped in a deep breath and averted his gaze. Pressing his back to the rough, unfinished wood siding of the cabin, he dragged a hand down his face.

He was in deep trouble. How was he going to keep his promise not to touch her? How were they supposed to share this small living space without him losing it?

His wife. Mrs. Parson's assumption twisted inside him. He knew that the three of them gave the impression of a family. He couldn't blame the store owner for her conclusion. Yet the irony of his position chafed.

He'd bungled his attempt at marriage and family, but here he was playing house with Laura.

Hell.

In reality, he had no right to claim either the woman or the baby in the cabin. That truth raked through him with sharp tines. The scenario had been specially designed to torture him, he was certain.

He crossed to the door with intentionally heavy steps, his loud approach on the wooden porch serving to warn her of his return.

"Shh," she hushed him, putting a finger to her pursed lips as he came through the door. "You'll wake Elmer."

He avoided her gaze, tried not to look at her as he hunted through the kitchen drawers for the key to the outside storage room. "I'm going to split some wood so we can make a fire tonight."

A cozy, romantic fire in an isolated cabin... *damn!* He pushed that image aside and plucked the silver key out of the drawer.

"Need help?"

"No!" he said quickly. Probably too quickly. "Oh."

He didn't miss the note of disappointment in her voice. She *wanted* to help split wood. She was bored out of her skull, too.

Max cleared his throat. "Sorry. Maybe you could...fix something for lunch?"

"I promise you, I don't need to be in a kitchen, and you wouldn't want anything I cooked."

"I'm not picky. A sandwich would be fine."

Laura nodded. "A sandwich I can manage."

When he turned to leave, she added, "Oh, I was wondering if there was a washing machine up here. I'm down to my last clean outfit, and I know Elmer's helped you dirty several shirts...."

The maid thing again. Frilly, low-cut, black....

Gritting his teeth, he spun toward the door, squeezing the storage room key so hard it dug into his palm. "There's a Laundromat just down from Parson's. We can wash a load tomorrow when I head down the mountain to call Emily again."

"Tomorrow. Right." She heaved a disappointed sigh and cast a glance around the freshly tidied cabin. "You're sure you don't need help chopping—"

"I'm sure. I can do it alone," he said, lifting a hand to cut her off as he backed out the door. He knew she just wanted something to do, a way to kill time. But the hazard of mixing a blond distraction with a sharp ax was a mistake he wouldn't make.

Crossing to the cabin window, Laura watched Max take an ax out of the storage room and approach the pile of logs needing to be split. He positioned the first log, raised the ax...and winced.

Setting the ax down, he grabbed his injured shoulder.

Without hesitating, Laura rushed outside. "Max! Are you all right?"

He cut a glance toward her and picked up the ax again. "I'm fine. I just have to work out the stiffness first."

"I can help with the—"

"I said I'm fine. Go on inside. I can do this." Clenching his teeth, he raised the ax again and slammed it down into the waiting log, grunting at the effort it took.

Darn the stubborn man! What was he trying to prove?

She *could* help him. She *wanted* to help him, needed something to do....

Instead, she stepped back and watched him swing the ax again while grimacing in pain. The muscles just under his soft flannel shirt rippled and strained. The first beads of perspiration popped out on his forehead.

He made an incredibly hot lumberjack.

She studied the tense lines in his rugged jaw and the determined fire in his eyes. Like the heat in his gaze when he'd kissed her this morning.

She swallowed hard and pressed a hand to her stomach as it flip-flopped inside her. If she was going to spend the next several days cooped up with this sexy man and still keep her sanity, she didn't need to spend her time ogling him while he chopped wood.

Laura turned on her heel and tramped back to the house, removing herself from the tempting sight of his muscles toiling, the disconcerting knowledge of the pain he worked through and a better understanding of why he'd bolted from the cabin that morning for "fresh air."

She marched into the kitchen and opened the refrigerator. He'd be hungry when he came in, and she had to find something to feed him. It was the least she could do.

That night when Max lit the fire in the fireplace, the crackling flames weren't the only source of warmth. Knowing the effort and pain he'd endured to provide them with heat stirred a special glow deep inside her.

She had no doubt this man would move the Smokies to take care of her and Elmer, to keep them safe and comfortable. For years, she'd forced herself to be self-reliant, to be independent and to count on no one but herself.

Knowing that she could depend on Max gave her an odd sensation in the pit of her stomach.

She squelched the funny niggling. Knowing he *could* provide for them didn't mean she *had* to rely on him or put herself in his hands. Just that she could. If she wanted to. Which she didn't.

Max dusted off his hands as he rose from the fireplace, and he glanced her way. Seeking her approval?

A grin tugged the corner of her mouth. "Thank you."

He straightened. "For what?"

"The fire. It feels good."

His gaze lingered as if assessing her. Then his countenance eased, and his posture relaxed. His eyes took on the dark intensity with which she was quickly becoming familiar. "You're welcome."

He took a seat, dropping wearily on the old couch, and they passed the rest of the evening with quiet conversation.

As conversations went, theirs was awkward, strained, even forced at times. But their discussion of mundane things passed the time. And they built the first bonds of an affable partnership.

It was a step in the right direction.

* * *

"Hey, look what I found."

Max glanced up from the stick he'd spent the last two hours whittling down to a worthless nub.

Laura held out the deck of cards she'd removed from a drawer in the nightstand.

Ordinarily, he wouldn't consider a deck of playing cards any reason to get excited. But after four tedious days with little to occupy himself, except a concentrated effort to keep his hands off Laura, the deck of cards promised relief from the nerve-racking boredom. That, and a distraction from his disconcerting preoccupation with Laura.

He'd tried avoidance. Walks in the woods helped break the monotony, but he hated leaving the cabin for long, in case of trouble.

They made daily trips down the twisty mountain road to the pay phone by Parson's General Store so that he could call the hospital and check on Emily. His sister had finally begun to make slow progress, but even that little bit of improvement gave him hope.

Otherwise, he'd chopped enough firewood to last through a nuclear winter. And he'd discovered after hours of whittling that all he could carve was a pile of shavings.

What he *had* made, using a laundry basket and a firm cushion from the sofa, was a makeshift cradle for Elmer. With Elmer in his cradle and him on the couch, Laura now slept alone in the queen-sized bed. She hadn't complained about sharing the bed with Elmer, but the project had given him something to do.

For about ten minutes.

Then he'd gone back to whittling piles of shavings. All the while, Laura skirted his thoughts.

By day, if she so much as walked by him, the fruity scent of her shampoo teased his senses. He easily conjured fantasies of her lathering her hair in the shower, water streaming down her naked skin.

By night, he lay on the lumpy couch, memorizing the knots in the wood beams of the roof, sensitized to every creak from the bed. In his mind, he replayed the night they'd arrived at the cabin, the feel of her body against his, the gentle sough of her breath as she slept.

After four days, lack of sleep and repressed lust made him edgy.

"Wanna play hearts?" she asked, glancing into Elmer's cradle to check on him before sitting down at the opposite end of the couch.

"Real men don't play games called *hearts*."

He reached for the deck in her hand, and his fingers brushed her wrist as he took the cards from her. High-energy sparks raced across his nerves, shooting straight to his groin.

Her blue-green eyes darted up to meet his, and he jerked his hand away, dropping the cards and scattering them in the process.

It was crazy. Just a brief touch sent him through the roof. He had to get a grip.

With shaky hands, she started picking up the cards. Careful not to bump her hands, he helped gather the deck again.

"How about poker? Do real men play poker?" Laura tucked an errant wisp of her hair behind one ear.

"This one does. Five card draw?"

When she nodded, her blond curls caught the dim glow from the fireplace and shone like spun gold. His fingers itched to plow through the soft, unruly waves and simply lose himself in silky tresses.

"A nickel per toothpick?" she asked.

"Make it a dime."

"Whoo-hoo. Last of the big spenders." She flashed him a teasing grin as she got up and brought back the box of toothpicks from the kitchen. The impact of that coy smile spun through him like a twister through a trailer park. It devastated his control.

Taking several seconds to cool his jets before he launched himself at her, he shuffled the cards. "So where'd you learn to play poker?"

"Mr. Powell taught me."

"Who's Mr. Powell?" Max dealt five cards to each of them and arranged his cards in his hand.

She leaned sideways against the back of the sofa, so that she faced him, and tucked one leg beneath her. "One of my foster dads. My first foster dad."

"Mmm," he hummed in acknowledgment. He studied his cards a moment. "So how long were you at the Powells'?"

Her eyebrows snapped together in a frown. "Why?"

It amazed him how prickly she became whenever he inquired about her personal life, her past.

With a shrug that belied his curiosity over her wariness and distance, he took two toothpicks and put them on the couch between them. "Dunno. Just making conversation. Ante up."

"Well, pick another topic. I don't like talking about my past."

So I noticed.

Shadows stole across her face, and he wondered what had happened that was so difficult for her to discuss. Since he was no stranger to painful secrets himself, however, he didn't press her to open up.

She raised him by one toothpick, and he raised her another two toothpicks.

"What *do* you want to talk about then?" He peered up from his cards and watched her face as she studied her own hand. She pouted, bit her bottom lip, sighed. He read her expressions like a book. Nothing. She had nothing. If only he could solve all the mysteries surrounding her as easily as he could guess the cards in her hand.

"Well, you could tell me about your ex-wife. Why did you get divorced?" The tilt of her head and subtle lift of her brow said she was more interested in making a point about some topics being too personal, too taboo, than in hearing about his failed marriage. She dropped another toothpick on the couch from her pile. "Call."

He grunted and laid down two cards. "Touché. Whatcha say we just play cards without any conversation?"

"Fine by me. Give me one." She grinned

smugly as she laid down one card, and he dealt her a new one.

He looked at his new cards and bet two more toothpicks.

Laura studied her hand long and hard without speaking, her face growing darker and more serious.

"Well?" he prodded.

"Call." She put her two toothpicks out on the cushion and laid down her hand. "I have nothing."

"Full house," he said and chuckled. He scooped up the toothpicks and began shuffling the cards again.

"I was the one who found him."

He glanced up at her when she spoke, and seeing the distant, stormy look on her face, his hands stilled on the deck of cards.

"Found who?"

"Mr. Powell," she whispered then grew eerily quiet. The faraway look in her eyes told him her thoughts were back at the Powells' foster home.

She shivered and blinked then glanced up at him. "He'd had a stroke in the backyard while mowing the grass. I found him lying on the lawn when I went out to play on the swing set. He was alive but unable to move."

"Ah, sweetheart," he crooned gently. His heart turned over, and he reached for her trembling hands.

She jerked them away from his touch and launched herself from the couch. Wrapping her arms around herself as if to ward off a sudden chill, she paced to the far side of the room—away from him.

Distance. Physical distance to match the emotional distance she kept between herself and him. She'd pulled away from the comfort he offered before. Thinking back, he saw the pattern.

No one waiting at home for her. No one to worry about her. Her dry wit deflecting questions about herself. Topical conversations instead of getting personal.

Even after they'd kissed, she'd shown little reaction, as if the kiss hadn't moved her at all. Yet when she looked at Elmer, her face always filled with a glow. A glow she turned off when she faced him. With Max, she remained remote.

Emotional and physical isolation. Apparently she kept everyone at arm's length. Except Elmer. And what threat was a baby? Babies gave unconditional love.

Her remoteness twisted inside him. He

hated the idea of this caring, beautiful woman keeping herself isolated. She deserved more. She deserved loved ones surrounding her and affection heaped on her.

"Did he live?" he asked, going back to the topic at hand. Mr. Powell. He was almost afraid to ask. With the loss of her mother and father, the death of her friend's baby brother, she'd had so much to deal with at an early age. Another death would have been adding insult to injury.

She nodded. "But I heard he died a couple months after that."

"You heard?"

She drew a slow deep breath. "Right after his stroke, all of us foster kids were sent to new homes. Mrs. Powell couldn't take care of us and tend to an invalid husband."

He wanted to go to her, put his arms around her, soothe the demons he saw haunting her eyes. But he knew his comfort would be rejected. Again. So he waited, listened. She was beginning to open up to him, and he didn't want to discourage her in any way.

"I hated leaving the Powells. They'd been so good to me, helping me come to grips with my mother's death." She looked up and gave him a weak, sad smile. "Teaching me to play poker."

The grief in her expression knotted his gut. He knew about loss and the toll it took. He understood loneliness.

He wished she'd allow him to shoulder some of the weight burdening her. She seemed so fragile at the moment that he half expected her to crumble under the load. Yet she held her back stiff and soldiered on. She clearly found her strength in nothing more than determination and stubbornness.

"Losing the Powells hurt almost as much as losing my mother." Her voice was little more than a hoarse whisper, her gaze still removed, remote. "That was the first of many moves to come. I figured out pretty quick that I couldn't count on staying in any one place for long."

And that the best way not to get hurt was not to get too attached, he finished silently.

Of course. Why hadn't he realized it sooner? That had to be the reason she held herself apart, had no close relationships even today. Her response to him was self-protection, learned after repeated disappointments, numerous losses.

At least through the hell his own life had

been, he'd always had someone there. The entire community had rallied around his family when his father was killed in the accident on the offshore oil rig where he worked. Jennifer had shared his grief when his mother had died of cancer. Emily had supported him and listened to him when he'd gotten his divorce. He'd been fortunate to have loved ones to count on.

But whom had Laura had? No one, it seemed. He absorbed her loneliness deep in his own soul, a tight, wrenching fist that choked the breath from him.

"The Rodgers were just a spur-of-the-moment, temporary place to stick me when Mr. Powell got sick. Three weeks later it was the Hamptons, then the Jawoliskis for two months, until they decided to drop out of the program. I stayed at the Greenbergs' for three years, though. I hated the Greenbergs. They ran their house like a concentration camp, always yelling at us kids and—" She sighed and closed her eyes, dropped her chin to her chest.

He thought for a minute that she'd finally given in to the tears he heard in her voice. Max couldn't move, didn't know how to respond, how to help.

And he wanted to help her. His deepest,

most basic instinct screamed for him to do something to fix things for her, to make things right, to take care of her. But his help was unwelcome. She'd made that clear.

Shaking her head, she raised a weary but dry-eyed gaze to him. "I shouldn't be dumping all this on you. I'm sorry."

He held her gaze and murmured, "I don't mind. And I think you needed to get it off your chest."

She snorted and turned away. "It's senseless to rehash it. It's all in the past. It's over." She crossed the floor to the kitchenette and started putting away the dishes they'd left by the sink to dry. "I'd be better off leaving it all in the past where it belongs."

He watched her, listened to the clatter of the dishes and utensils as her restless hands worked.

"Why couldn't someone have adopted you?" he asked.

Her hands stilled, and her shoulders drooped. "Someone *could* have adopted me, but..." She raised her gaze to him then, and he saw the tears blossoming in her eyes. "But...no one wanted me."

When her voice cracked, so did his heart. He couldn't have stayed away then to save his life. Max crossed the room in two giant steps and gathered her into his arms. *He* wanted her, damn it! He wanted to hold her and protect her and lose himself in her aqua eyes.

How he could have fallen so hard and so fast for the sassy, rebellious beauty was beyond him. But he had. She'd proven an invaluable help to him with Elmer. She'd made him laugh, made him angry, made his body zing with desire. She challenged him, inspired him, intrigued him. She was one hell of a woman.

That no one had recognized her specialness, her inner beauty as a child and taken her into their family was inconceivable.

She trembled as he hugged her tightly to his chest, and she squirmed, trying to get away. But he didn't let go.

Finally, with a sigh, as if surrendering a fight, she wilted against him. He bent to scoop her up and carried her to the rocking chair. He sat down with her cradled in his arms and rocked her the way he'd watched her rock Elmer the past four nights. She buried her face in his shoulder, clung to his T-shirt. But she didn't cry.

Sucking in deep breaths, she fought the

tears he knew lay just under the surface. Like a soldier, she kept the enemy tears at bay, wouldn't give in. Her determination not to cry broke his heart almost as much as her need to cry. Desperately she fought the emotions, suppressed the pain, denied the tears.

He stroked her hair, kissed the crown of her head. "Don't fight it anymore, baby. Let it out. I've got you."

She clutched his sleeve, her body quaking, but still shed no tears.

"No," she murmured into his chest, her breath heating his skin, even through his shirt. "Crying doesn't help. It doesn't change anything."

"It might make you feel better, though. Relieve the tension." Drawing a comforting hand down her spine, he felt the shudder that shook her, felt her muscles tense as she battled the emotions warring inside her.

Her fingers lightly raked his shoulder as she clutched his shirt in her fist, held on to him like a life preserver. She tucked her head under his chin, and the strawberry scent of her hair assailed his nose, taunted his libido.

Curled on his lap as she was, she fit him perfectly. He circled her with his arms and held her close while she shivered and dragged in a ragged breath.

"I didn't mean to dump on you like that. I shouldn't have bored you with—"

"Am I complaining?"

She sighed and shifted her weight. Her soft bottom pressed into his groin as she huddled on his lap, and, so help him, he was getting aroused. That was the last thing she needed, to know that he'd managed to become aroused while he comforted her.

Gritting his teeth, he repositioned her so that her weight rested largely on one thigh rather than in the middle of his lap.

She tipped her head back, peeked up at him with bright, piercing eyes. "Am I too heavy? I shouldn't have—"

When she made a move to get up, he hauled her back against him. "Sit. I'm fine, and you're still shaking."

"But—"

He put a finger on her lips to silence her.

Mistake. The warm tickle of her breath and the soft velvet of her full lips caressed his skin. His body went ballistic. He dropped his gaze to the slight pout of her mouth, and the urge to kiss her slammed into him, robbing him of oxygen.

Her own eyes grew smoky with desire, and she raised her chin a fraction of an inch, lifting her mouth, ready to receive his. He trailed his finger to her jaw to angle her head, slowly zeroed in on his target until their breath mingled. Her lips parted in anticipation. His body thrummed as a magnetic pull drew him closer to her lips.

In the fireplace, a log popped with a crack like a gunshot.

Laura gasped, and they jerked apart. Adrenaline and unanswered passion pumped through him, making his heart thunder and his nerves jump. Laura scrambled off his lap like a startled kitten.

Hands off. He'd given her his word. Jeez, what had happened to his self-control?

The fact that she'd obviously wanted the kiss as much as he did didn't change anything. He had to stay sharp, alert, ready for trouble.

And he didn't need to take advantage of her at a moment when her guard was clearly down. *Stupid. Stupid!*

Laura hugged herself, her breathing ragged, obviously trying to calm her own jangled nerves. She walked over to the edge of Elmer's cradle and grinned wryly. "He could sleep through a hurricane."

Max sent her an awkward smile in response and shoved himself out of the rocker, his jeans painfully tight with his arousal.

"I, uh…think I'll get a quick shower before bed." A *cold* shower. He nearly laughed aloud at the cliché. Had it come to this?

He avoided her gaze as he headed into the bathroom, closed the door and leaned against it with a heavy sigh.

He'd almost kissed her. They'd been so close. He still wanted to kiss her.

Hell, he wanted to do more than kiss her. But, of course, he couldn't. He'd promised not to touch her, needed to keep his head in case the Rialtos made another appearance. He had to get control of his raging libido.

Stripping out of his clothes, he turned the shower on full blast.

Sure, it had been a long time since he'd been with a woman. More than three years. By choice. After experiencing sex with someone he loved, casual sex just seemed…empty. Still, his long abstinence was no excuse for acting like a randy teenager.

Max stepped under the cool spray, clenching his teeth as the cold water jolted his system. But not even the icy shower could wash away the image of Laura's desire-hazed eyes or erase the memory of her yielding body in his arms. Resisting the lure of her come-hither gaze when she'd looked up at him had been impossible. But he had to do better, try harder. No excuses. He had to focus on the job at hand, to protect them.

He cupped his hands to splash his face then rubbed his palms over his cheeks.

He knew one thing for a fact. After hearing the gut-wrenching truth about her childhood and watching her battle to suppress the emotions that their discussion had unearthed, he couldn't avoid the obvious.

Laura wanted a family. Laura needed a family. Laura deserved a family more than almost anyone he'd ever met.

No one wanted me.

She had so much love to share, yet she fought her nurturing soul constantly. Her battle-scarred heart warred daily with her loving instinct out of learned self-defense. She must have felt like a stray animal, needing a home, wanting to be loved as she drifted from one foster home to another.

The idea sliced through Max with a dull blade, made him ache to wrap her in his arms and never let go. But, damn it, he was the last person she needed to grow attached to.

A family was the one thing he couldn't

give her. He'd be damned before he'd make the same mistakes with Laura that he'd made with Jennifer.

Laura didn't need to be hurt or disappointed again. And with him, the disappointment and pain of *not* having a family was inevitable. He couldn't burden Laura with his low sperm count. If he needed another reason to keep his lustful urges in check as he'd promised her, he had only to think of her vulnerability. He had no business raising her expectations of him by letting their relationship become physical.

No matter how his body ached for her, his honor wouldn't allow him to break Laura's heart with false hope, false intimacy. He couldn't promise things to her with his kiss, with his touch, that he knew he couldn't follow through on. Things like a future together, love and commitment. Children.

His gut pinched, and a fist of regret and disappointment squeezed his chest. Who would have thought his diminished ability to impregnate a woman would hurt so damn much? Certainly not him. Not before he'd learned of his own lack. It was infuriating. It was frustrating. It was…emasculating.

Max balled his fists and cursed. It wasn't fair. It just wasn't fair.

A high-pitched scream ripped him out of his self-pitying thoughts. His head snapped up, and his heart slammed into overdrive.

Laura.

Then a second scream, louder and more frightened sounding, shattered the night. Without turning off the water, he bolted from the shower.

Chapter Twelve

Max rushed toward the bathroom door. His wet feet slipped on the tile floor. Grabbing a towel, he flung it around his waist as he flew to the main room.

Elmer slept soundly in his cradle by the bed.

But Laura was gone.

The front door stood open. The sound of snapping twigs, footsteps, filtered in from outside. His mouth went dry.

"Laura!" Snatching his rifle from beside the bed, he dashed for the door. The cold night air stung his wet body as he ran out on the porch. "Laur—"

His breath whooshed from his lungs as they collided. She screamed again.

With his free hand, he caught her shoulder, shook her gently.

She looked up at him with wide eyes. Her body shook with violent tremors.

"Laura, it's me. What happened? Who's out there?"

Laura panted for a breath, her gaze dropping to take in the sight of Max's long, lean body. His wet body. His muscled, gorgeous, nearly naked body.

She couldn't help it. She gaped. Heat flooded her night-chilled body, collected in her womb, then spread insidious fingers of fire from head to toe. Just the sight of him turned her blood to warm honey, her knees to mush.

Her eyes followed the arrow of dark hair on his chest until it disappeared under the towel he'd loosely tucked around his waist. The towel drooped low on his hips, slipped a bit more even as she watched. *Oh mercy!*

His hand flew down to catch the errant towel.

"Laura, what happened? I heard you scream." The sharp, worried tone of his voice penetrated her fog of desire.

"I—I went to get…uh, w-wood for the fire."

"Yeah? And?"

"I heard something. Something was out there…by the woodpile."

He scowled. "This something wouldn't have been four-legged and furry, by any chance?"

"And beady-eyed. It startled me." She drew a deep breath, shuddering as she recalled her brush with the raccoon. "Then I dropped a log on my toe. Stupid raccoon."

He leaned the rifle he'd brought out against the porch rail and dragged a hand down his face. He'd left his shower and come out with his rifle, ready to defend her, ready to save her from an unknown danger.

Knowing that did crazy things to her composure. His willingness to go to battle for her twisted around a vulnerable part of her heart and spread roots in the dark corners of her soul.

"You nearly gave me a heart attack, woman."

"That raccoon nearly gave *me* a heart attack!"

Tightening his towel and tucking it more securely, he scowled at her. "I'm going back to my shower now—" he picked up the rifle again "—unless there is a roach or a mouse you need exterminated first. I'd rather not be interrupted again."

She grinned at him despite his sarcasm. "No, thank you. I can handle the roaches and mice by myself."

He turned and marched back toward the door, grumbling something about freezing his butt off and the cabin not having mice.

She indulged in the view. The wide span of his shoulders, the way the towel clung damply to his tight rear end, his long, powerful legs and narrow feet. Breathtaking.

"Max?"

He stopped at the door and looked back at her, glowering.

She grinned again. "Thanks anyway."

The tension seemed to drain from him as he stared back at her. He didn't respond at first. But then the corner of his mouth tugged upward and, with a wink, he disappeared inside.

She refused to examine too closely the warm feeling that puddled inside her. Instead, she decided that Max needed to be rewarded for his chivalry. They both needed a release from the tension stretching them as taut as rubber bands. They were both ready to snap. She had an idea of what might help Max's mood. Well, several ideas really, but their hands-off policy ruled out most of them.

Her plan in place, Laura headed back in to warm herself by the fire.

The car was gone.

Max ran from the woods after his daily walk and gaped at the spot where he'd last parked Laura's Honda. He'd only been gone for a few minutes. But the car was most definitely gone.

Elmer.

A wave of icy dread swamped him as he raced into the cabin, throwing the door open with such force that it crashed as it hit the wall.

The baby's car seat was gone. His nephew was nowhere to be seen. Nor was Laura.

Fear swamped him.

Holy hell, had the Rialtos found the cabin? Had they taken Elmer? Kidnapped Laura? Stolen the car to leave him stranded and unable to follow them?

Rage erupted from him in a roar, and he slammed back out of the cabin. He'd let his guard down, left them alone and unprotected, foolishly believing the cabin so remote as to provide all the protection they needed.

Over the last several days, he'd been too preoccupied with the idea of jumping Laura's bones. With trying *not* to jump her bones. He'd allowed his obsession with her to distract him from the danger of the Rialtos. And now Laura and the baby were gone, snatched from under his nose.

Disgust with himself, with his failure, gnawed Max's gut.

He stalked in tight circles, pacing the front lawn of the cabin, deciding his best attack. He'd have to walk down the mountain, find a phone. He'd have to get the police involved, which probably meant they'd put Elmer in protective custody with children's services at least for a while. If the Rialtos hadn't already skipped the country...

Hell. Hell. *Hell!*

He started down the rutted driveway, headed out to the narrow road that led to the foot of the mountain. By the time he reached a phone, they'd be miles from town, maybe out of the state.

And Laura might be dead.

Hell.

He kicked his pace up to a run.

* * *

Laura hummed to herself, enjoying the palette of fall colors dappling the maples and oaks as she drove back up the twisting mountain road. With a glance in the clip-on visor mirror she'd bought today, she checked on Elmer, who blinked sleepily in the backseat. She smiled. He couldn't be any sweeter. He was a good sleeper and content while awake, except at mealtime or when wet. But once his needs were tended to, he'd settle down to nap again or to gaze in wonder at the two adults who cooed over him constantly.

Even Max spoke to the baby with a special inflection in his voice, and hearing Max talk soothingly to the infant filled her with a sentimental warmth she couldn't escape. Seeing him bond with his nephew was endearing. And completely dangerous to her heart. She was getting in too deep.

She'd driven all the way to a small mall in a town past Parson's General Store, and her shopping trip had been a success. Laura had found several things she wanted for Elmer and a few things she needed for herself, as well as her surprise for Max.

But the trip had taken longer than she'd expected, and she hoped Max wouldn't be too worried about them or upset over her late afternoon return. No sooner had the thought crossed her mind than she spotted the tall, broad-shouldered figure of a man jogging along the side of the road. As she approached him, his dark, rugged features became more distinguishable.

Max.

What in the world...? Instantly, a bolt of fear streaked through her. Had there been trouble at the cabin? Had the Rialtos found him? Quickly she pulled to the edge of the road, praying no other car came careening around one of the sharp mountain curves and clipped her.

"Max!" she cried, climbing from the front seat and standing in the open car door. "What happened?"

His head came up, and a full range of emotions played across his face. "Laura! Thank God. Are you all right? Is Elmer with you? I thought the Rialtos—"

He stopped short and released a shuddering sigh.

Compunction bit Laura. "Didn't you...see my note?"

His dark eyebrows snapped together. "What note?"

Max sucked in deep breaths, winded from his jog. A vein on his neck pulsed wildly. She imagined the pleasure it would be to kiss that throbbing pulse, to tease it with her tongue, and had to mentally shake herself in order to answer his question. "I left a note on the kitchen counter for you. I went shopping for a few things. More diapers, a jacket for me, a—"

"Shopping?" His harsh shout must have startled Elmer, because the baby started crying.

Laura winced. "You're upset. You...didn't see the note."

He closed his eyes and ducked his head, clearly struggling to contain his rampaging emotions and catch his breath. "No."

That fact clicked in her head, followed closely by what his assumption regarding her disappearance must have been to have him so rattled.

"You thought the Rialtos had us, didn't you?" Regret for the worry she'd put him through speared her chest.

Raising his head, he met her apologetic gaze with a penetrating, dark brown stare. "I guess I panicked, assumed the worst. But under the circumstances..."

Guilt lanced the bubble of contentment she'd enjoyed moments earlier, the sense of connection she'd felt with Max since their tête-à-tête last night.

Telling him about her time in foster homes had been difficult, like stripping her soul naked for him. But she'd felt compelled to share at least a piece of her history with him. She wanted Max to understand her dedication to Elmer, the reason why she wanted so desperately to ensure that Elmer found a good home, the right home. Because she hadn't had a place to call home.

His compassion and understanding had been a balm to the raw nerve she'd exposed. Incredibly, she'd felt safer, more accepted in the hours since opening herself to him than in all the years since she'd left her last foster home at eighteen. And how had she repaid him? By scaring him to death with her disappearance.

Laura sagged behind the steering wheel, and Max opened the back door to croon to Elmer. "Hey, fella. I'm sorry. Easy does it."

Hearing Max murmur to the crying infant stirred a painful longing deep inside her. He'd soothed her last night the same way, and she missed the seductive lull in his deep voice and gentle hands. The comfort and under-standing he'd given her had awakened some-thing elemental inside her.

Yet succumbing to his soft words and ten-der touch was exactly the kind of mistake, the reckless hope that had crushed her so many times growing up. She couldn't build false hopes around a few moments of kindness and comfort. Why hadn't she learned?

She glanced in her rearview mirror and watched him lightly stroke the baby's cheek with a finger, poke a pacifier in the baby's lips then kiss Elmer's head before ducking back out to close the door.

When he climbed in beside her, he sighed. Tension and anxiety still vibrated from him, and she gave him a guilty glance. "I'm sorry I scared you like that, Max. I should have known how you'd worry. I should have told you where I was going rather than expect you to find my note. I—"

He silenced her with a finger to her lips, his touch sending sizzling sensations through her blood.

"The important thing is you're okay. Elmer's okay. Just...dear God, don't do something like that again."

She winced and shook her head.

Closed in the confines of the car with him, she could smell his sweat, the scent of fall leaves and mountain air that clung to him. The combination of male heat and the crispness of nature tantalized her.

Laura pulled back onto the road, trying to focus on the fall scenery instead of the zing in her blood Max's presence stirred.

After several minutes of riding in silence, Max said, "It's Friday."

"Yeah. So?"

"Friday afternoons are game days in Pee Wee football. My team's playing even as we speak."

She studied the serious countenance of the man beside her, saw in his dark eyes the conflict between his responsibility to his team and to his sister's baby. His frustration, torn between two loyalties, etched lines beside his eyes and plucked at her heart.

"I know that you're thinking you've let your team down by not being there."

He grunted in reply and turned toward his window.

She persevered, determined to offer him a bit of comfort and encouragement as he'd done for her the night before. "But all the time you spent with the team up until now, the practices and encouragement, that all counts for something. They know you'd be there if you could."

Max remained quiet.

"They know you're there in spirit."

With a sigh, he turned to her. "They're five years old. My being there in spirit means nothing to them. All they know is their coach didn't show up for the game."

Laura chewed her bottom lip, reflecting, remembering, then shook her head. "You're wrong. Children understand more than adults give them credit for. Even as young as Elmer is, he knows you love him. He can sense it. After my mom died, I felt her with me, felt her love."

A years-old ache swelled in her chest. Laura paused to draw a deep breath and collect her composure again before continuing. "So don't ever doubt the difference you've made for the kids on your Pee Wee team. Or the importance of what you're doing for Elmer."

She paused and met Max's dark penetrating stare across the front seat. "That's why I came back...the day I ditched you in Mississippi. I knew you cared."

Dropping his gaze, he fisted his hands

in his lap. "Is caring enough, though? All I could think about as I was running down this road was that I'd failed Emily. Failed Elmer. Failed you."

"You haven't failed anyone!"

"We need a backup plan. I have to find us another safe place to stay in case the Rialtos do show up."

She nodded. "Okay. Makes sense. But where?"

"That's what I have to figure out."

"Tell you what." Max bent over Elmer's homemade cradle where his nephew wiggled restlessly and flailed his legs. "When you're older, I'll take you down to my fire station and let you sit behind the wheel of the big ladder truck. What d'ya think?"

Elmer wrinkled his nose and whimpered.

Max glanced to the closed door of the bathroom, wondering how much longer Laura needed to get her evening bath. Wondering how much more of this one-sided conversation with his nephew he needed to keep his thoughts away from Laura and the steamy tub of bubbles in the next room.

Elmer's whimper sharpened to a whine, and Max grimaced. "Come on, buddy. Laura's spent all day taking care of you. She's fed you and bathed you and rocked you and changed your diaper. Give her just a little time to herself, okay?"

His nephew poked out his bottom lip and scrunched his face tighter, tuning up to a wail.

Max rubbed the baby's tummy, stroked his head and cheeks with a finger. "Come on, slugger. It's okay."

Elmer wasn't buying it. He opened his mouth and loosed a loud cry.

"Max? Is he okay?" Laura called from the next room.

"He's fine. I've got him." He scowled at Elmer. "See? She heard you. She's gonna think I can't handle you for five minutes by myself. Pull it together, dude."

He wrapped Elmer's blanket more tightly around him and lifted the baby to the crook of his arm. "What if I told you about your mom? I raised her from the time she was thirteen, ya know."

He jostled Elmer gently as he paced in front of the fireplace.

The bathroom door opened with a click, and Max peeked up from the baby. A cloud of sweet-scented steam followed Laura out of the bathroom. She wore a new, knee-length nightshirt and was combing her wet hair, already curling wildly as it dried.

Nothing about her appearance or her clothing was immodest or intentionally provocative, but the sight of her damp hair, steam-kissed cheeks and bare feet shot liquid heat through Max's body.

Laura set a bottle of lotion on the nightstand and glanced across the room at them. "Need me to take him?"

He ducked his head and cleared the thickness from his throat. "No. You finish—" He waved a hand toward the bed where she sat on the edge of the mattress. "Whatever. We're good. Right, slugger?"

Elmer squawked.

He turned his back to Laura and kept walking the floor and patting Elmer's diapered bottom.

"I bought you something while I was out today," Laura said.

"Something for me?" Max glanced toward the bed. And nearly swallowed his tongue.

Laura had propped one foot on the bed and used both hands to smooth lotion on her sleek, shapely calf. Her nightshirt had crept up to her hip, revealing miles of leg and skin.

Pulse thumping, he yanked his gaze away and paced faster, shifting Elmer to his shoulder.

"A football. I know you've been bored, and I thought maybe you could teach me how to pass and tackle and stuff."

From the corner of his eye, he saw Laura switch legs and start spreading lotion on the next calf.

"Oh. Uh, thanks." He imagined himself tackling Laura *now,* on the bed, and swallowed a groan. When he sucked in a deep breath for composure, the lavender scent of Laura's lotion assailed his senses.

The bedsprings creaked as Laura shifted her weight, and Max gave up pretenses and turned to stare. He drank in the sight of her silky thighs, lush lips and glowing skin. Temptation personified.

Elmer whined again, and his flailing fist caught Max in the chin.

Max let a sigh of frustration hiss through his teeth. He refocused his attention on Elmer, remembering what Laura had said earlier. *Even as young as Elmer is, he knows you love him. He can sense it.*

"You know, kid, your mom, uh…she'd be here if she could. She loves you, little guy.

She loves you, and she wants you to be safe. That's why you're here with me instead of with her. But…you're going to have your mommy back soon."

He stopped pacing and pulled the edge of Elmer's blanket back to peer down at the tiny face so like Emily's. Elmer blinked at him sleepily, a spit bubble clinging to the corner of his bowed mouth. Max dabbed the drool with a corner of the blanket and realized Elmer had quit fussing.

He'd calmed the baby by himself.

A warm sense of satisfaction and affection puddled in his gut. Max bent his head to drop a kiss on his nephew's fuzzy hair. "I love you, too, slugger. We're gonna be all right. I promise."

Max sighed. Keeping that promise meant no more screw-ups like today's. It meant finding another safe place where they could hide if needed. Someplace the Rialtos wouldn't think to look. Someplace random and not linked to any of his friends the way this cabin was. But hotels cost money, and he was running low on cash. Credit cards could be tracked.

And wherever they went, they'd need the facilities to take care of the baby, sterilize bottles, keep the formula chilled. That limited their options.

Crouching by Elmer's bed, he settled the baby in for the night and gave the boy's cheek one last stroke.

He had to come up with a plan. They needed to move.

Soon.

Chapter Thirteen

He was a wreck. Physically and mentally.

As if not knowing Emily's condition weren't enough to drive him nuts, Max fought to repress the coil of lust that wound tighter every day, wreaking havoc on his body, his brain. Erotic images of Laura's long, sleek legs had taunted Max through another sleepless night on the lumpy couch. How would they feel wrapped around him?

He couldn't afford to find out. Max growled and rinsed the traces of shaving cream from his chin.

Hands off.

Restless energy, the need to work off the

sexual tension stringing him tight demanded that he get out of the cabin. The day had dawned bright and sunny, and a crisp, cool breeze rustled the fall leaves. The outdoors beckoned.

But he wouldn't leave Laura alone again. His gut wrenched every time he thought what could have happened yesterday—all because he'd shirked his duty to keep Elmer safe, to protect his nephew and Laura.

Don't let him outta your sight. Emily's raspy plea reverberated in Max's brain.

"I want you to go with me today." Max took a couple of soft drinks, two apples and a bag of potato chips from the kitchen and put them in a sack.

"Go where?" Laura looked up from the baby. She held Elmer, rocking him long past the time he'd fallen asleep for his late morning nap.

"Just get your jacket and follow me. I think we could all use some exercise to battle this cabin fever." Max leaned over her and carefully lifted Elmer out of her arms. He put the sleeping baby on the bed where he began dressing Elmer in warm pajamas.

When Laura tried to help him, he batted her hands away. "I can do this by myself.

You get your coat. And a bottle and diapers for Elmer."

"Don't you dare wake him up," she said as she fetched her new jacket. "He needs his sleep. He had a restless night."

He's not the only one.

Actually, getting up with Elmer four times last night had been a relief. Max had needed the distraction from his circular thoughts. Laura. The need for new lodging. Emily. Laura.

The spring of tension in his gut pulled tighter. He took a deep breath for control. He grimaced, realizing how unsteady his hands were as he eased Elmer's fists through the small sleeves.

"Thanks for taking baby duty last night, by the way." Laura slipped her arms into her jacket and collected the baby's things.

"No problem. I wasn't sleeping anyway."

"Worrying about the Rialtos? Your Pee Wee team?"

"And other things."

"There's always the pay phone outside Parson's. You could call and find out what happened at the Pee Wee game when you call about Emily today." She picked up the sack of food he'd packed and stuck Elmer's things in the bag.

"I will. But later. We could all use some fresh air, a chance to recharge. And I need to clear my head so I can figure out another place we can go that's safe."

Laura raised a worried gaze. "You don't think this cabin is safe enough?"

"It is for now. But eventually the Rialtos will figure out where we are. It may be weeks before they figure it out or it could be tomorrow. But we have to assume they'll talk to my friends, the men at the fire station, my neighbors, or that they'll remember something Emily told them about my hunting trips. Whatever. I'm linked to this cabin because of my friend, because I've come here so many times before." He moved Elmer gently to the baby seat. Glancing down at the baby, he thought about Emily and sighed.

As soon as Emily recovered enough to care for Elmer, the Rialtos wouldn't have any legal grounds to sue for custody. Of course, the threat of them stealing the baby remained. Even if Emily got a restraining order.

The Rialtos operated outside the law. Again he faced the truth that his sister would most likely have to go underground. Whether she

joined the Witness Security Program or simply hid through her own means, Emily would
probably have to cut herself off from him in
order to hide her baby from her drug-smug-
gling in-laws. That truth twisted inside him
with a sharp edge. He didn't want to lose any
more family.

"Ready."

He faced Laura when she spoke. Her new
navy jacket made her eyes look more green
than blue today. He hated to think about how
accustomed he'd grown to seeing those hyp-
notic eyes in the morning. Or how naturally
he'd fallen into the familylike routine they'd
established.

"Let me get a cover for the tyke." Max went
to Elmer's homemade cradle and got a soft
blanket, which he draped over the baby seat
to keep the sun out of Elmer's eyes. "All set."

He picked up the baby carrier, and Laura
followed him out. She walked in front of him
as they headed down the wooded path he used
every day for his hikes.

He shouldn't have tortured himself, thinking about parting company soon with this
blond angel with the tempting lips. Yet that
was where his thoughts traveled.

His lifestyle, determined by the inescapable fact that he couldn't give a woman a family, dictated that he couldn't marry again. At least, he couldn't marry someone who longed for and deserved a family the way Laura obviously did. He had to start considering how to cut his ties with Laura, before he got himself, or her, in any deeper.

When they reached the large rock outcropping he had in mind for their picnic, Laura stepped to the edge of the flat boulder and admired the view.

"Oh, Max, look at it!" Awe filled her voice, and the bright sunlight bathed her radiant face. "You can see for miles!"

Mist-shrouded mountains, mottled with autumn shades of orange, green and red, spread before them like a patchwork quilt. The mountain scenery was almost as breathtaking as the woman enjoying the view. A light breeze lifted her rebellious curls and caused her golden hair to fly in her face.

He couldn't resist the urge to brush stray wisps behind her ear. "I'm kinda partial to what's right in front of me."

She gasped when he touched her and pulled away. The wonder that filled her expression as she gazed out at the vista faded, replaced by the damnable remoteness she got when around him. Knowing the source of her distance didn't make her reserve with him sting any less. Not when he wanted, needed to feel her return the affection, the admiration, the desire he felt for her. Still, he knew it was better this way.

He didn't want her hurt when he sent her away.

Taking a can of soda from the bag, he popped the tab and took a swig. The cola was tepid, but it quenched his thirst. He sat next to the baby carrier and surveyed the horizon for himself. "I've been coming up here for years. But no matter how many times I'm here, the scenery never fails to amaze me."

Laura settled next to him and took an apple from the bag. "Tell me more about Emily. I heard what you were telling Elmer last night and I just wondered what she's like."

Max leaned back, propping on his elbows, his legs stretched out in front of him. "Emily is...bright, outgoing, full of energy." He grinned, thinking of his baby sister. Emily would faint if she heard him talking about her this way. He didn't tell her enough that he was proud of her. He'd remedy that as soon as he got a chance to speak to her again. "She's also sassy, spoiled and stubborn. But I guess I can blame myself for that in large part."

"Why?" Laura listened attentively, her bright eyes focused on him.

"I'm one of the main people who spoiled her, gave her everything she wanted. She was only thirteen when our mom died, so she moved in with me and my wife." He shrugged. "I can see her spoiling Elmer the same way I did her. She has a big heart, without a lot of discipline. I'll have to make sure she doesn't let the kid become a brat."

Laura glanced out to the mountain range and chewed her bottom lip. He watched her rake her teeth over the full lip. The urge to nibble the soft flesh himself kicked him in the gut.

Down, boy! Don't start that again.

"What will you do if...if she doesn't make it?"

Laura's question hit him like ice water. His muscles tensed. "She won't die."

Angling her head, Laura met his gaze with a sympathy and bluntness in her eyes. "I'm sorry. I know you don't want to think about it, but you should consider the possibility."

He turned away, releasing his frustration in a harsh puff of air through his lips. Hard as it was, he *did* have to face that possibility. "I guess I'll file the papers to legally adopt Elmer. I'm not sure if Emily has a will or any documents naming me as his guardian if she dies. That kind of preplanning isn't her style. I might have a legal battle with the Rialtos on my hands."

She took a large bite from her apple and chewed slowly, thoughtfully. "A legal battle with people who've already tried to kill you. Max, how can you think—"

"Let's just hope it doesn't come to that," he said with a smile, hoping to assuage her worry. The Rialtos were his problem. He didn't want Laura worrying unnecessarily. "Hey, look!"

He pointed in the distance to the large bird swooping through the sky. "A red-tailed hawk."

She shifted her attention to the bird of prey, and he silently thanked the hawk for its timing. He'd brought Laura out here because he wanted an escape from the mind-numbing worries that faced him about Emily. He had some ideas about dealing with the Rialtos' threat, which he intended to follow up on when they drove down to Parson's. But not now. Not when he had this precious time with

Laura, the scenic view, the balmy weather, the sun on his face.

He knew Laura wouldn't let go of the topic easily, so he quickly picked a new subject to divert her attention. "I think Elmer smiled at me last night while I was trying to get him back to sleep."

She whipped her gaze back to him, and the toss of her hair wafted the strawberry scent of her shampoo his way. "Newborns can't smile. It was probably gas."

He shook his head. "Nope. I know a smile when I see it. He definitely smiled at me." He gave her a satisfied grin of his own, and she chuckled. "Besides, he's not a newborn any more. He's almost two weeks old now."

"Oh, excuse me!" Laura laughed. "I'd not realized how *old* he was. Gosh, he's practically ready for college."

He pulled the baby carrier closer and peeked under the blanket. "Are you hearing this, Elmer? The lady is doubting your talent and maturity."

"Hogwash. I know talent when I see it. And Elmer's gonna have plenty of it, I'm sure. But I also know the difference between gas and an honest-to-goodness smile."

"You're just jealous 'cause he smiled for me and not you."

She laughed again, and the clear, sweet sound reminded him of the babbling mountain streams that flowed in almost every valley in the area. Her laughter coursed through him, refreshing his weary spirit and easing the tension that tied him in knots. It wouldn't take much to envision himself falling in love with this woman.

Her beauty went all the way to her soul.

"Maybe I *am* jealous. You'll get to see this fella smile and learn to walk and ride a bike, when I won't." She lifted Elmer's tiny hand into hers and rubbed his fist. "But I know Elmer likes me. He's told me so many times."

With a stab of regret, Max wished he were the right man to soothe her aching soul and foster her caring spirit. He could easily lose himself in this woman's warmth and vitality. If only...

"You'll make a great mother someday," he murmured. The warm sun and relaxed mood were making him drowsy, reflective.

When she raised her gaze to him, he saw in her eyes her yearning for a child of her own. Proof positive that he couldn't make her happy, just as he'd failed to make Jennifer happy.

Laura flashed him a melancholy grin. "Maybe. Someday. Elmer sure makes me think about what I'm missing."

Max didn't need Elmer to know what he was missing. The hollowness in his life told him what he lacked. The ache in his chest told him what he needed. But the memory of Jennifer's resentment reminded him of his shortcomings.

"This was a good idea." Laura obviously forced the cheer into her voice. But she'd never admit it. She soldiered on when the chips were down, pushing the disappointment aside as always.

"Come here." He tugged on her arm, urging her to move close to him, and she stiffened. This time, he was determined not to let her pull away. "Just lie here with me. The sun feels good, and as long as we have no place in particular to be, we might as well enjoy it."

He hauled her in, and she landed with an *oof* against his chest, knocking the wind from the protest on her lips. He tightened his arms around her, pressed her head to the pillow of his shoulder with a splayed hand and closed his eyes. She squirmed to get away, but he refused to release her.

"Easy, sweetheart," he said with a yawn. "I won't try anything. I promised, didn't I?"

Her struggles stilled, and eventually she relaxed against him. She fit in the crook of his arm like a custom order.

Exhaustion from his many restless nights and the tranquilizing effects of the sun soon lulled him to sleep.

When he woke, a good while later judging from the position of the sun, Laura was still cuddled against him. Her hand rested lightly on his chest, and her brown eyelashes fanned her cheek as she slept. Elmer, on the other hand, was awake and sucking on his fist. Max knew it wouldn't be long before the fist wasn't good enough and Elmer would whine for his bottle.

Blinking against the bright sun, Max stretched his stiff muscles and gently jostled Laura. "Rise and shine, sweetheart. Elmer's almost ready for his bottle, and I'm about ready to head down to Parson's and make a few phone calls."

Laura's fingers curled into the fabric of his shirt, and she nuzzled his shoulder groggily before an apparent flash of awareness jolted her awake. She tensed and jerked away from him. Immediately he missed the soft crush of her in his arms.

As if he knew his primary caregiver had awakened, Elmer mewled softly, calling Laura to his carrier.

"Hey, pumpkin. Here I am. Don't fuss," she cooed, lifting him from his seat.

Max took the baby's bottle and a can of formula from the sack and fixed Elmer his lunch. "Hand him to me, and I'll feed him."

"I don't mind—"

"Neither do I." He wiggled his fingers in a gesture that said "Come on. Hand him over."

After passing the baby to him, Laura stood and dusted off the seat of her pants.

"I'll be right back."

"You okay?"

"Mmm-hmm. Um…nature calls."

Turning to prop his back against a large rock so that his body shielded Elmer from the glare of the sun, he offered the baby his bottle. With a gurgle and a sigh, his nephew started to suck down his lunch.

Keep his head up and the bottle at an angle. Don't let him suck air. Easy enough. Max looked down at the tiny human in his arms. Emily's son. His chest tightened as it frequently did when he fed the baby. He tried to sort out what he felt and why this little baby seemed to bring everything to the surface.

Maybe because Elmer represented the best and worst aspects of his life. Emily, who was fighting for her life almost a thousand miles away. Jennifer, with whom he'd tried to build a family and failed, leaving them both emotionally depleted. Laura, who'd put her own life on hold to care for a stranger's child, exhibiting a love and sacrifice that staggered him.

And the future. Elmer represented the future. The promise, the potential, the hope. *If* he didn't let the child down. God, he'd do anything to make sure this baby had a promising future.

He lifted one of Elmer's hands and studied the long fingers he'd inherited from his mother. Quarterback hands, for sure.

"You want to play for my team when you grow up, champ?" He brushed his thumb over Elmer's tiny knuckles, and the baby squeezed with a firm grip. As if Elmer had grabbed his windpipe instead of his finger, Max's throat closed. His breath caught in his lungs. The gentle clutch of the miniature hand wrung the last drop of his composure. Moisture burned in his eyes, and he blinked back the sting of tears.

Emily's son.

So fragile. So vulnerable. So indelibly stamped on his heart in so few days.

His sister's reason to live, to fight. *Don't die, Emily. We need you. We both need you.*

Later that afternoon at Parson's General Store, Max handed Laura a box of chocolate cereal for their basket of purchases. "That's all for me. I'm going to call my assistant coach and the hospital. Meet me at the car, okay?"

"Sure." Max left through the front door, pausing long enough to pat Ajax the cat, who napped on the front porch.

As Laura turned her attention back to shopping, she noticed another customer at the counter who pointed toward the door then reached in her purse and pulled out a folded newspaper. The customer seemed agitated.

Curious, Laura took her purchases up front. As she set her cereal and fruit on the counter, she heard Mrs. Parson murmur, "Oh, my. The resemblance is remarkable. I... I don't know what to think."

"Happened down in New Orleans, but I

can't help wonderin'…" the customer whispered loudly as she leaned toward Mrs. Parson.

"Just the same," Mrs. Parson said, "he's been vacationing here and coming into our store for years. It's just a coincidence."

When the older woman looked up, she found Laura staring at her and became flustered. "Oh, dear. I, well…" Mrs. Parson extended the paper in her hand to Laura and smiled weakly. "We were just commenting on the resemblance between your husband and the man in the Charlotte newspaper. What a strange coincidence."

Laura's heart slowed as she warily took the offered newspaper and glanced down at it.

The photo was definitely Max.

"Oh, he…he does look like my h-husband. That is strange." She gave them a nervous smile then read the Associated Press story printed below the photograph.

New Orleans— The newborn son of Emily and Joe Rialto, heir to shipping magnate Anthony Rialto, was kidnapped shortly after the baby was discharged from the hospital last week. The chief suspect in the kidnapping is Max Caldwell, an Orleans Parish firefighter.

The police deny any report has been filed regarding the missing child, but an unofficial source confirms the family has mounted a private search for the baby. A statement released by the family on behalf of Emily Rialto pleaded for the safe return of her child....

Laura couldn't breathe. Her lungs ached for air, but shock rendered her frozen.

Could it be true? She'd suspected in the beginning that Max had kidnapped Elmer. She had no proof Emily wanted Max to have her baby, no proof Emily was even Max's sister. A sharp stab of pain pierced her heart. Had Max lied to her, used her?

She clutched the edge of the counter to steady herself as she swayed dizzily. When she lifted her gaze to Mrs. Parson and the woman who'd produced the article, she found them both eyeing her cautiously.

"Are you all right, dear? You look pale."

"I...uh, since I had the b-baby, I get brief d-dizzy spells every now and then. I'll be fine in a minute."

Great. Max had turned her into a liar as well!

"Would you like to sit down?" Mrs. Parson came around the end of the counter and wrapped an arm around her. "You could lie down upstairs, if—"

"No, I'm fine. I...really. I just want to check out and get home to rest. But thanks."

"Don't you find it a rather...*odd* coincidence that your husband looks like the accused kidnapper *and* that you have a baby of the same age?" the woman with Mrs. Parson pressed, her lips pinched in disapproval.

Laura lifted her chin, though her knees shook and her gut swirled. "Yes. The coincidence is...unsettling. But...that's all it is. An unfortunate coincidence. I—I feel terrible for the poor mother in New Orleans."

Without giving the woman a chance to reply, Laura moved to the end of the counter where Mr. Parson had been entertaining Elmer with a rattle. She needed time to figure things out before she confronted Max. She jammed the newspaper in a pocket of Elmer's diaper bag.

Dread and disappointment left her quaking. She tried to calm her trembling hands by squeezing them into fists.

"He's a fine boy, ma'am. Alert and happy. You've a right to be proud of that one." Mr. Parson handed her the rattle.

"I am." She smiled weakly, her chest pinched by wistful longing and what might have been. "Very proud of him. Thanks."

Did she really think that she and Max would fall deeply in love and live happily ever after, raising Elmer as their own? Real life was not a fairy tale. Her mother's death, her years in foster homes had taught her that. Yet she'd let herself hope that with Max it could be different.

The inevitable heartbreak had caught up with her. She'd been naive to think she could outrun the specter that had haunted her life from the beginning. No happily ever after waited in her future; she was only saving herself while she could, protecting her heart from more abuse.

Quickly Laura paid for her groceries and hurried out to the car. Max was still on the phone, and after she loaded her groceries and buckled Elmer in the backseat, she watched Max.

His tall, muscular body, his rugged face and dark good looks still made her pulse go a little haywire. But if he was who the article said, a kidnapper, a criminal, how could she continue to aid and abet him?

She'd give him one last chance to come

clean. Maybe there was some mistake, some error or another side of the story that he could shed light on and clear things up.

Please, let the article be wrong.

Chapter Fourteen

"How did the kids do?" Max asked, turning his back to the brisk wind that buffeted him. "Did we win?"

"By a touchdown in the final seconds. It was a beautiful thing, Max," his assistant coach replied. "The kids were so excited. I took them out for pizza to celebrate."

Relief and pride swept through him, and he whooped. "That's awesome. Tell the team I'm proud of 'em, okay?"

"When will you be back?"

Max raked his fingers through his hair. "I don't know. A lot depends on Emily's recovery. It's a long story, and I'm not going to go into it now, but…well, it could be another couple of weeks."

He heard Charles sigh. "Well, family's gotta come first. It's just…"

"What?"

"The media has picked up your story. They're saying…"

Max mumbled a swearword. "Forget what they're saying. You know the truth. You know me."

"Yeah, I do. I just thought you should know."

"Thanks." He hesitated. "Uh, Charles, I need a big favor."

"Sure, what."

"I need cash. For reasons I'd rather not go into, I can't use my credit card right now. Could you wire me a few hundred bucks? I'll pay you back with interest when this mess is over."

"I…yeah. Okay. But the bank's closed already and Monday is Columbus Day. It'll be Tuesday, probably late afternoon before I can get the money to you. That good enough?"

Max frowned and rubbed the back of his neck. He hated the delay, would much rather head to a hotel tonight. But without cash, he had little choice. "That's fine. Wire it to the

Western Union at Parson's. You remember the little general store near your cabin, at the foot of the mountain?"

"Right. Parson's. Got it."

"Thanks, man. I appreciate this more than you know." Max disconnected the phone call and waited for the dial tone before calling the hospital.

When the hospital operator answered, he asked to be connected with Emily's room and was put on hold.

"ICU," a woman's voice answered.

"Uh, I'm sorry. I was supposed to be connected to Emily Rialto's room." Max noticed Laura was back at the car, and he appreciated the view of her backside as she leaned in to buckle the baby in the car. Lordy, the woman had a great body.

"Yes, sir. Can I help you?"

"Can you connect me with Emily's room? I'd like to speak to my sister."

"Um, sir, Mrs. Rialto is unable to speak to you."

The hesitation in the woman's voice set off alarm bells. The hair on the back of his neck prickled. "Why not?"

"I can't give out that information, but—"

"Talk to me, damn it! I'm her brother. What's wrong with Emily?" he shouted.

"Let me get her doctor on the line. He's in with her now."

Max squeezed the receiver with a death grip as he waited. His pulse pounded in his ears. *Emily. Oh, God, don't take Emily!*

"This is Dr. Schubert."

"Doc, this is Max Caldwell. I'm Emily's brother."

"Yes, Mr. Caldwell. I remember you."

"I want to know what is happening with her, and don't give me any bull about confidentiality. What's happened with my sister?"

"Apparently something upset your sister this morning. When her heart rate and blood pressure went up, she threw a blood clot to her lungs. She became hypoxic."

"Hypoxic? What does that mean?" Max raked his fingers through his hair, trying to absorb what the doctor was saying.

"That means the oxygen levels in her bloodstream and brain dropped. She lost consciousness and hasn't wakened since."

Max felt his heart rise to his throat. His stomach pitched, and he thought he might be sick. "Will...will she pull through?"

"Well, her heart rate and breathing have

stabilized. Both good signs," the doctor said. "We'll run an EEG soon to see if she's suffered any brain damage. This sort of thing is always a possibility following surgery."

"Oh, God," Max groaned, leaning against the booth for support. "What upset her?"

"I can only assume it had to do with her husband's death or other family business. She crashed during a visit from her father-in-law. Hopefully the tests we run will—"

"Her father-in-law?" Max straightened again, his heart pounding a wild rhythm. "You let Anthony Rialto in to see her?"

"Well, yes. Why?"

Max cursed bitterly and punched the wall of the phone booth with his fist. "Keep him away from her!"

"I don't—"

"Keep the Rialtos away from her!" he ground out.

The line was silent.

Max sucked in a deep, fortifying breath. *If Emily died...*

Hell, he couldn't imagine. The prospect terrified him. He'd helped raise her. She was as much his daughter as his sister. Life without Emily would be...bleak.

"Dr. Schubert?" Max's voice sounded hoarse and strangled.

"Yes?"

"Don't let my sister die."

No one spoke on the trip back to the cabin. Although she didn't know what had upset Max so that he brooded silently, she could only assume he'd had bad news about Emily.

Assumptions, however, were not good. She'd believed Max was Elmer's uncle, that he had the baby with permission from Emily. But the article suggested she'd been wrong to believe Max. Wrong to trust him. Wrong to help him hide a child that didn't belong to him.

She'd been an idiot, following her heart instead of listening to her head.

When he stopped the car in front of the cabin and cut the engine, no one moved. Max squeezed the steering wheel and stared out the windshield with a stricken expression darkening his face. Laura hated the pitter-pat of sympathy in her chest, the pang of longing to comfort him and ease his grief.

What if he'd lied to her, betrayed her trust? How could she feel anything but contempt for someone who'd kidnap someone else's baby?

Somewhere deep inside her, a small voice cried foul. She wanted desperately to believe Max, believe that the love and tenderness she'd witnessed these past several days reflected the true nature of this man.

The information in the Charlotte newspaper had to be wrong.

"Max?" She swallowed and took a deep breath when she heard her voice wobble.

He turned toward her, his eyes bleak, desolate.

Her chest clenched tighter. "Are you really Elmer's uncle?"

Max tensed and narrowed his eyes suspiciously. "Why would you ask that?"

She gritted her teeth in frustration. "Just answer me. Honestly. Did Emily *really* give you custody of Elmer until she recovers or... did you kidnap him?"

Max glared at her, drew his shoulders back defensively. "Emily asked me to protect her son. I've explained this all before. Why would I lie?"

She handed him the article, tears burning her eyes. "Then explain this."

He studied the article, his brow furrowing in consternation. "Laura, I didn't kidnap Elmer. This article is obviously the work of the Rialtos, using their contacts and influence to sway public opinion or flush me out of hiding."

"Can you prove your claims to me? That you have this baby with his mother's permission and blessing?"

When he faced her again, his dark eyes drilled into her without mercy, pleading for her to believe him. "No. I have no proof. Just my word."

Confusion, an internal battle between her conscience and her heart muddled her brain, twisted inside her like tangled vines. "I want to believe you, but—"

"Then do." He seized her shoulders, and the article fluttered to the floor. "You told me the other day that you came back after ditching me because you knew in your heart I cared about Elmer. Has that changed?"

"I don't—" Her voice caught on a sob.

"Have I done anything to make you believe I would hurt this child? Have I done anything to make you believe I'm lying about this situation?" The passion and raw honesty in his eyes raked through her. "The only proof I have is what you've seen, what you know from living with me and my nephew these past days."

He sighed and closed his eyes, gritted his teeth. "What is your heart telling you, Laura? That's the only truth you need."

"I don't know what to believe. I—" Her heart breaking, she pulled out of his grasp and bolted from the car. Ran. She needed time alone, time to think and to untangle the web of her emotions.

Tears blurred her vision as she ran along the narrow path toward the outcropping of rock where they'd picnicked. Low branches and scraggly weeds slapped at her as she hurried through the trees, punishing her for breaking her own cardinal rule.

She'd let Max in. She'd allowed herself to feel something for him, even though experience had proven such trust a risky gamble at best. Now he was asking her to dive into those dark, dangerous waters and believe him based on nothing more than faith.

How could she give Max her blind trust without also giving her heart? How could she risk so much pain for a man with whom she had no future?

Or could Max want the same fairy tale she'd foolishly pinned her hopes on?

Max watched Laura disappear into the woods, remorse hammering him with heavy, painful blows. The disappointment and hurt in her eyes when she'd shown him the article and voiced her doubts clawed through him, left him bleeding inside.

Learning of Emily's setback had been bad enough. He didn't need this confrontation with Laura. His battered soul longed for the kind of unconditional love and acceptance she gave Elmer. He needed her soft touch and soothing voice. He wanted to bury himself inside her, to drown in her soulful eyes and escape the awful grief that hounded him.

He could lose his baby sister, and there wasn't a damn thing he could do about it. He needed Laura's warmth and support more than ever.

Instead she'd zinged him with suspicion and skepticism. The pain he'd seen in her eyes sliced to his marrow, reviving memories of another woman whose lack of faith in him, whose resentment for his failures had ended his marriage. Jennifer's pain and disappointment lived inside him, a malignancy that ate away at him. He couldn't help the fact that he had a low sperm count, couldn't do anything to change it. But it still tore him apart knowing that his deficiency deprived his wife of what she wanted more than anything else. A baby.

His brain told him he couldn't be blamed for the miscarriage when, after visits to the fertility clinic and expensive high-tech procedures, Jennifer had finally gotten pregnant. Yet he blamed himself anyway.

If he'd been a better husband, more supportive or understanding, maybe her grief wouldn't have turned to resentment. If he'd been able to do something for Jennifer, to ease her pain, maybe he could have saved his marriage. But he'd given in, thrown in the towel when she asked for an out. The lingering ache of that failure reverberated in the empty spaces of his heart.

Max gripped the steering wheel and stared out the window without really seeing anything. Another thought filtered through his anguish and sat like a linebacker on his chest. A tremor raced through him.

Laura's doubts could only cut this deeply if he'd done the unthinkable—he'd fallen in love. Somewhere over the course of the last two weeks, Laura had found her way past his defenses, slipped under the radar of his best intentions and past experience. She'd captured his heart.

Knowing how things had ended with Jennifer, why had he let Laura under his skin?

Despite the bleak memories of his failed marriage, he'd fallen for another woman with hopes and desires for a family and children. Hell, he'd gone as far as to ask for her faith in him, knowing he had nothing but broken dreams to offer her in return.

Max ground his teeth until his jaw hurt. Self-reproach dug a pit in his gut. He'd known he had no future with Laura, known he couldn't burden her with his infertility.

So what did he do now?

He refused to drag her or the fragile friendship blossoming between them into the kind of hell that had killed his marriage. He wouldn't repeat the mistakes he'd made with Jennifer. He couldn't relive the agony of watching another relationship, everything he valued, a woman's dreams, wither on the vine.

Because Laura deserved more. Much more.

Laura wiped her cheeks and stared out over the horizon. The mist that hovered over the mountains reflected her gray mood. After hours alone on the rock outcropping, she'd have thought she'd cried herself out, but years' worth of pent-up tears fought their way out.

What is your heart telling you, Laura? That's the only truth you need.

She knew what to believe about Max, about his relationship to Elmer and his right to have the baby. If she were honest with herself, she'd known the truth all along.

Max couldn't hide the honesty of his affection for Elmer.

Her doubts, her fears had more to do with her own dishonesty. She kept Max at arm's length when what she truly wanted was to be held close. She'd pulled away, hiding behind their hands-off agreement, because she was afraid of getting hurt. But the article and Max's challenge to listen to her heart stripped away pretenses and forced her to look the truth in the eye. She was falling in love with Max.

When he'd believed she was in danger a few nights before, he'd valiantly rushed to her aid, towel and all. His loyalty to Emily was heartrending. He'd sacrificed so much to protect Elmer. He'd proven again and again the depth of his commitment to his mission to keep the baby safe. He was gracious, thoughtful and warm.

Over the past several days, she'd seen the

real Max—a man she trusted and cared for, a man who deserved her loyalty and faith.

The quiet voice that had found the newspaper article so unbelievable shouted now. The voice of faith, the part of her that rooted for the underdog, the fiercely optimistic side of her soul.

Her heart seized. It was too late for caution, for distance or defenses. Max had become a part of her soul.

The cautious woman, the little girl who'd been hurt so many times, flinched from the reality. She couldn't put her emotions, her very heart and soul in such obvious jeopardy.

But just as she was certain Max hadn't kidnapped Elmer, she knew Max wouldn't hurt or betray her. He wasn't that kind of man. That truth rattled the protective walls she kept around her soul for years and dared her to take a risk, to place her faith, her heart in Max's hands.

The sun sank low, slipping behind the mountain range. Long shadows danced around her. It would be dark soon. Night fell quickly in the mountains.

She stood and dusted the dirt from the seat of her jeans, suddenly eager to get back to the cabin. Back to Max.

Dried leaves crunched under her feet as she jogged down the path toward the cabin. When she reached the edge of the woods, she caught sight of the cabin and stopped.

In the gathering dark, the soft purple light of dusk cloaked the small wooden house. Max had lit the porch in anticipation of her return, and the yellow light greeted her like an old friend, welcoming her home. Nestled among the vibrant red, orange and gold trees, the cabin reminded her of a Thomas Kinkade painting. The faint scent of burning wood and the curling smoke that rose from the chimney testified to the fire he'd made inside.

The coziness and invitation of the scene stole her breath and centered around the man who'd dragged the rocking chair to the front porch to wait for her. Max held Elmer in the crook of his arm, rocking slowly.

At that moment, something made him look up, and his gaze fixed on hers. A sweet tingling swept through her. The embracing warmth of the cabin, of having someone waiting for her, showed her by stark contrast how empty and cold her life had been. She'd maintained a life of isolation to protect her heart.

But here in the mountains, at this cabin,

with Elmer, with Max, she'd found her home. Her family. Warmth.

Coming home to Max felt right. Felt good. So good.

Tears of joy filled her eyes as she crossed the lawn to the front porch. Max rose from the rocking chair and met her on the steps, his eyes reflecting a certain wariness along with compassion and concern.

"I was beginning to worry. You were gone a long time." The deep, sexy rasp of his voice wrapped her in a hug even before she stepped into the embrace he offered.

Holding Elmer aside with one arm, he pulled her close to his other side and buried his face in her hair. Laura closed her own arms around his broad back, curling her fingers into the soft flannel of his shirt. She inhaled the comforting blend of wood smoke, laundry detergent and sunshine that clung to him. He smelled like the mountains, like man, like home.

"Laura, I don't know what else I can tell you to—"

She pressed her fingers to his lips to silence him. Tipping her head back, she met the question in his dark eyes and smiled. "You don't have to say anything. I shouldn't have doubted you."

His black eyebrows lifted, and hope shone from his eyes.

"The truth has been right under my nose from the beginning," she said. "I see it in the way you look at Elmer, the way you worry about Emily, the way you…take care of me. You have my faith, Max. My trust. One hundred percent." She rubbed her finger slowly along his bottom lip, pressed herself closer to his side.

His breath escaped in a hiss, just before she brushed her lips against his.

"Ah, Laura," he murmured on a sigh. His arm tightened around her, and he skimmed his hand up her spine, sinking his fingers into her hair and pulling her closer.

He angled his head, capturing her mouth with an achingly tender kiss. The moist heat of his tongue traced her lips, and she opened them to accept his gentle probing. She wound her fingers in his thick hair, sealing their mouths with a more aggressive kiss.

He groaned and drew harder on her yielding lips.

Need and desire burst into flame inside her. The fire grew, licking her with more intensity for each stroke of his tongue, each sweet caress of his lips on hers.

Her lungs' demand for oxygen finally tore her away from his kiss. They both panted for breath while their gazes met and sparks of longing arced between them.

"I know what we agreed on, Max. But I want… I need you to make love to me."

He moaned, and she felt the shudder that raced through him. Pressing a kiss to her forehead, he took a step back, pulling out of her arms. "Laura, I…"

A cold shard of ice stabbed her. Was he rejecting her? Panic swirled in her gut. "Please, Max."

A bittersweet smile brightened his face, and his eyes glowed with warmth and promise. "You're sure?"

She nodded, more confident in this decision than any she'd made in years.

He slipped his hand into hers and stepped back. "Let me settle the baby in for his nap."

Relief swamped Laura, and she dropped her gaze to the infant sleeping in the crook of Max's other arm.

They put Elmer into his homemade cradle, careful not to wake the sleeping child. Laura paused only long enough to realize the picture-perfect family the three of them made. She would gladly live out her remaining days offering herself to this man and child. They filled her, completed her. They gave her life purpose and color.

Then Max raised a burning gaze, scorching her with the desire in his eyes, and she melted.

"Come over here, sweetheart," he whispered.

She did.

Chapter Fifteen

Max's arms closed around her, drew her close. When his mouth descended to hers for a voracious kiss, pure pleasure skittered through her veins. Sighing, Laura sank against his solid strength, letting him pull her with him onto the bed. He covered her with his body, and she reveled in the weight and width of him pressing her into the soft mattress.

Max skimmed his hands over her hips, her waist, her breasts, lingering long enough to graze her nipples with his thumbs. Jolts of sensation spiraled inside her, and she shivered with delight. Anticipation made a powerful aphrodisiac, and she'd been waiting for this moment with Max for so long.

Days. Weeks. Years, really.

She'd never felt safe enough with a man to share her body, had never dared to risk her heart. She'd saved herself for this moment. For Max.

He moved his hands along the curve of her throat before sinking his fingers into her hair. He wound his fingers through her curls and buried his face in the unruly waves, inhaling deeply.

"I love your hair," he murmured. "The way it smells, the way it moves, the way it feels against my skin. So silky and soft." He dropped a light kiss on her lips. "It's sexy as hell."

While combing his fingers through her hair, he flashed her a sly grin. "Do you have any idea how many times in the last couple of weeks I've fantasized about doing this, just running my hands through all your gold curls?"

She could only manage a lazy "hmm" in response. The gentle massaging of his fingers on her scalp left her thrumming with a heady lethargy.

He nudged her chin up with his thumbs to gain a better angle to seize her mouth again.

He nipped lightly at first then staked his claim with a deep, searching kiss.

The muscles of his back rippled under her fingers as she stroked her hands over the expanse of his shoulders. The cottony fabric of his shirt felt good to her fingers but didn't satisfy her. She needed to feel Max, heat and skin. Tugging on his shirt, she pulled it free of his jeans and bunched the material in her fingers until she could work her hands beneath. With a yank, he brought the shirt over his head, leaving her hands free to indulge.

She smoothed her palms down his chest, luxuriating in the strength and firmness of his muscles, the warmth of his skin and crispness of his dark hair. When she lightly dragged her fingernails over him, he groaned and caught her hand, kissing her fingers. "My turn."

He tugged on her T-shirt, and her breath caught. Anticipation made her breasts tingle and her nipples peak. Max peeled her shirt and bra out of his way in one pass, and cool air nipped her skin. A husky growl rumbled from his throat as he raked his gaze, his fingers over her. "You are so beautiful."

She gave him a nervous laugh, a shy smile and shook her head. "You don't have to flatter me, Max."

His dark eyes found hers, and a gentle glow lit his gaze. "You *are* beautiful, Laura. All the way to your soul."

His words stirred something deep inside her. Her heart thumped harder, and emotion tightened her throat.

Cupping her breasts, he kneaded her, tweaking the pink tips gently. His dark eyes bored into her, a fire burning in his gaze. His hands, his mouth worked down from her breasts to her stomach. With skilled fingers, he unfastened her jeans and worked them over her hips while his tongue traced lazy patterns around her navel. The moist caress rocketed through her, left her weak and trembling.

His hands roamed her body, his strokes charging every nerve ending until her whole body hummed. She sighed, dizzy with her growing need.

Plowing her fingers through his thick hair, she guided him back up and captured his mouth with hers.

While he reciprocated her kisses, his hand insinuated between her legs. The shock of his fingers against her most intimate spot jolted through her, and she gasped, tensed.

"Easy, sweetheart. You're okay," he murmured against her lips. The deep, velvety voice he used to calm Elmer soothed her, intoxicated her.

She was much better than okay. His fingers worked magic on her, probing, gliding, arousing. The rush of sensation, hot and tingling, hard and fast, stole her breath. "Ma-ax!"

Her climax crashed through her before she could do more than squeeze the sheet in her fists and bite back the moan that burgeoned in her throat. As the waves of pleasure strumming her body crested and receded, she released a slow cleansing breath.

"Not bad, hotshot." She sighed, giving him a drowsy grin.

He levered up to brace on his arms and cast her a dark, irritated look. "Damn it, Laura. You did it again."

She blinked at him, puzzled by his frustration, and more than a little concerned that she'd done something wrong out of inexperience. "What did I do?"

He pushed off the bed and unbuttoned his jeans. Shoving them down his legs, he held her gaze with a hot, hard stare. "A man needs better than 'not bad.' *I* need more."

Despite the intensity in his burning gaze, her eyes shifted to admire his masculine beauty. Max naked was an impressive sight, and a thrill chased down her spine.

"I've had all the cold, boring, clinical sex I can stand in this lifetime." His frustration, his complaints confused her.

Had she been boring and cold? The idea mortified her.

"Max? I—"

"You know what I want, Laura?" His obsidian eyes drilled into her as he climbed onto the bed and hovered over her. She saw more than just his irritation blazing in his gaze. She saw desperation, pleading and a need that reached deep into her soul, even though she didn't understand it. More than anything, she wanted to give him what he sought.

"Tell me, Max. I want to give you what you need...."

"I want sweaty, satisfying, frantic sex," he murmured on a low growl. His raspy voice stirred a tingle of expectation. His tone, his heated stare, the hard set of his jaw hinted danger. But she didn't fear him. Instead, the rough edge, his intensity was provocative, breathtaking. He worked himself between her legs and ground his hardness against her, as if to leave no doubt how aroused he was.

"I want it raw and wild," he muttered

darkly, his lips ghosting over her cheek before he bit gently on her earlobe.

She worked hard to swallow, finding her mouth had gone dry. Just his words, the way he whispered them in her ear, set her on fire. She panted for air, her anticipation allowing her to draw only shallow breaths.

He captured her head between his hands, and his penetrating gaze seemed to ask permission to satisfy the needs he'd spelled out to her in graphic detail.

She couldn't speak; her voice had fled from the first press of his naked body to hers. Instead she answered with a kiss. She fused their mouths, showing him with her ardor, her willingness to give him whatever she could, surrendering herself to his mercy.

He groaned and gathered her closer, squeezing her so tightly in his arms that she could barely breathe. But she didn't care.

Their tongues dueled and danced; their mouths searched and seared. There was an urgency about the way he held her and kissed her that she couldn't quite understand. But she didn't question his need; she only sought to satisfy it, to fill him the way he did her. She'd give him whatever it took to quiet the demons that tortured him and drove him to this frenzy.

His hands explored her restlessly. He moved against her, rubbing himself along the heat between her thighs. She responded, meeting his thrusts with her own, undulating her hips in the rhythm and sway that came naturally. Her body grew damp with perspiration, and his skin became equally slick. She lost herself in the frenetic meshing of their lips, the pulsing pace of their overheated bodies.

He shifted, reached between them, and she felt him poise himself, ready to enter her.

She opened herself to receive him, with her body as well as her heart.

Max groaned and plunged into Laura's welcoming warmth with a long, smooth stroke. She cried out, her body bowing up beneath him, and he muffled her moan with a kiss.

Her body was so tight, so sweet and slick that he, too, could have shouted from the ecstasy. He'd suspected he was her first, but now he had his proof. The lonely woman who'd learned to keep herself emotionally isolated, who had no friends checking up on her, wouldn't have allowed a man close enough to give him her virginity. Bittersweet humility for the gift she'd given him burrowed to his core. He hesitated several excruciating seconds, giving her body time to adjust to him, time to relax.

He'd make her first time special. His pride demanded it. He might not be able to give her a baby, but he damn well could satisfy her in bed. He could, *would* make her first experience memorable.

She stroked his cheek. "I'm all right, Max. Really." The tiny grin that tugged the corner of her mouth, curving her sexy lips, was playful, naughty. "In fact, I'm better than all right." She moved her hips, taking him deeper into her with a sigh. "You'd better finish what you've started, hotshot. Don't hold out on me now."

He kissed her hard, kissed her thoroughly. Then he moved again, slowly at first, stroking her with long, easy motions.

When he teased her nipples, they beaded in his fingers. Her quick response to his touch was deeply satisfying. And a tremendous turn-on.

She whimpered as he nibbled her chin, sighed when he pressed hot, open-mouthed kisses at the pulse point of her throat. The sounds rippled through him like lava, heating his blood. He watched her face, gauging her progress and her reactions. She held his gaze, and the faith he saw reflected in her expression reached deep inside him, turned his heart inside out.

Then she closed her eyes tightly, arched her throat and made a little mewling sound. Her legs gripped him harder. Her fingers dug into his back. Max thrust deeper, harder, his own body shaking from the effort not to shatter before she was ready. Ladies first.

The first pulse of her body contracting around his sent him careening into nirvana. With a roar of sweet release, he pumped into her three years of waiting for the right woman, three years of abstinence.

He clutched her close as she trembled and clung to him, his own body quaking. It had been a long time, granted, but he couldn't remember anything close to the powerful and moving experience he'd just shared with Laura.

He collapsed, rolling her on top so that he didn't crush her. And he held her while they gasped for a steady breath.

"Well, hotshot, I'd say—"

"Don't you dare say that was *not bad*." He opened an eye and quirked a grin.

She laughed. "I was going to say that it's a

good thing your nephew is a sound sleeper. We haven't exactly been quiet."

He caught her fingers and pressed a kiss to her palm. "One thing we Caldwells do well is sleep. Emily was always a bear to get out of bed in the morning."

He thought of his sister, lying in the New Orleans hospital unconscious, and grief twisted inside him.

"Max, what is it?" Laura rolled off him and cuddled under his arm. She flattened her hand on his chest and raised a gentle, searching expression to meet his gaze.

"Emily's worse. She's had a setback."

Laura propped up on an elbow, and her brow puckered in concern. "Oh, no! What happened?"

He explained what the doctor had told him over the phone, and her hold on him tightened.

"Her doctor is hopeful, but..."

She settled under his arm again and sighed. "I could tell you were upset earlier, but I let that dumb article throw me. I should have known it wasn't the whole picture."

"The whole picture, darling, is worse than you think. Don't suppose the article mentioned the Rialtos' connection to drug smuggling?"

Laura bolted upright in the bed. "What?"

He frowned and nodded. "Emily found out after she married Joe. Now the Rialtos want to raise Elmer in their world of drugs and violence." Max drilled Laura with a determined glare. "But I won't let that happen. Emily entrusted her son's life, his protection to me so that he didn't grow up in a crime family."

She nodded. "I believe you."

He absorbed her words, her faith in him like a dry sponge soaking up water. She quenched a part of his soul that thirsted for just the kind of affirmation and respect she gave him. But he sensed something more. Something Laura didn't verbalize, though it shone in her eyes.

She was falling in love with him.

His gut tightened. He hadn't meant for that to happen, but he should have seen it coming. Laura was an all-or-nothing kind of person, devoting all of herself, as she had to Elmer, or giving nothing, as she had earlier with him.

But they'd made love, and she'd crossed the line with him. A heartsick, sinking feeling settled in him. Bitter disappointment clawed his heart. He couldn't give her the future he knew she dreamed of. The family. The commitment.

His infertility made him the wrong man for Laura.

"Sweetheart, there's something else I think you should know." He tipped her chin up. Better to set the record straight now.

"Uh-oh. I don't like that look in your eyes." She tried to smile, but he saw the nervous twitch in her cheek.

"You asked me last week about my divorce, and I put you off, changed the subject. But you need to know the truth."

Her face paled, and he drew a breath to steel himself. "My wife and I divorced because…we couldn't have a baby. We tried for four years, and she never got pregnant…the natural way."

Max rolled onto his side and stroked a hand over Laura's hip.

"What…what was the problem? If I can ask." Her eyes held with his, probed gently for understanding.

He squeezed her hand, knowing he owed her an explanation but hating how raw this conversation left him. Emotionally eviscerated. "I was."

"You?"

He nodded. "Jennifer and I tried everything to work around the problem. But nothing helped. Our sex became clinical and passionless and stressful. Every month that passed with no results, Jennifer grew to resent me more. It was my fault, my low sperm count that kept her from having the baby she wanted. It started affecting every aspect of our life and…"

"I'm sorry," she whispered, lightly caressing his cheek.

"When we used clinical methods to get pregnant, she miscarried. We were completely jinxed. The miscarriage almost destroyed her. She asked for a divorce the next week. She'd had enough."

He wrapped his fingers around Laura's hand, and she squeezed back, lending her support.

"I didn't fight the divorce. I guess I'd had enough, too."

She rolled closer to him, pressed her body against his and lifted her lips to kiss his cheek. "Thank you. For telling me. I know it must be difficult to talk about."

"Besides Jennifer and our doctor, you're the only person who knows. Emily only knew that there was a problem somewhere. I never told her the details."

"What about the women since then? Haven't you dated?"

He threaded his fingers through her hair. He couldn't get enough of her wavy hair. Of her. "Dates. Only dates. You're the first woman I've made love to since Jennifer. I don't believe in casual sex. I just wanted you to know that you were safe with me...that you wouldn't..."

Laura cocked her head to the side and gave him a measuring scrutiny. "It's the wrong time of the month anyway. That's why I didn't say anything before."

She slid her body along his, her breasts grazing his chest and her thigh stroking him. "But since protection's not an issue...and Elmer's still asleep...we could—" She nibbled at his lip, and he growled his pleasure.

He captured her lips and lost himself in the sweetness and trust she offered. Their lovemaking was slower this time and far more intimate. He explored every inch of her body and taught her what touches pleasured him the most. And after they rose together to another startling climax, they slept, wrapped in each other's arms.

Chapter Sixteen

"Thirteen slant blue. Hike!"

Laura tossed the football backward between her legs then jogged across the leaf-strewn yard. She inhaled the cool, woodsy air and smiled. The crisp autumn Sunday was perfect for tag football, even if she and Max were the only two playing. Especially since they were the only two playing.

"Go long!" Max waved Laura farther across the lawn, but she stopped.

"Just throw the ball, hotshot!"

He did. A perfect, arcing pass right to her chest. She closed her arms around the ball and squealed her delight. "I caught it!"

"Good job. Now run," he called to her.

"I don't wanna run. I'm pooped!"

"If you don't run, I'm gonna tackle you." He raised his arms and started jogging toward her.

Flashing him a sultry grin, she tossed her hair over her shoulder. "Maybe I want you to tackle me."

With a long step he reached her, wrapped his strong arms around her and pulled her off her feet. Laura yelped, chuckled.

Max twisted as they fell and took the brunt of the fall, cushioning her as they tumbled to the ground. Then he rolled her to the bottom and pressed her into the soft grass with his warm body.

Images of their lovemaking sprang immediately to mind. *I don't believe in casual sex.*

Did that mean that what had happened between them had meant something important to Max? With every fiber of her being, she wanted to believe that their joining had moved and changed him the way it had her. She'd taken the leap of faith, dived headlong into this physical relationship knowing her heart could never survive unscathed.

Until she could be sure how he felt toward her, however, she tried to keep things simple.

She didn't press him for a commitment, for any pledges of his love.

"Lesson number one in football," he said, "If you ever get the ball, *run*. Even my five-year-olds know that!"

"Right, right. If you get the ball, you run."

"Head for your goal line and don't let anything stop you. You're in the game to win. Got it?" He tweaked her nose.

"I got it, coach."

She raised her lips to his for a light kiss, but Elmer's sleepy cry alerted them that he'd roused from his nap. Max groaned but didn't move.

"Duty calls." She flattened her hands on his chest and shoved.

"I'll get him." He caught her arm and turned her back for a quick kiss. "We might as well get our own dinner now, too. What have we got in the cabinet?"

"How about vegetable soup and grilled cheese sandwiches?"

"Sounds good to me."

She followed Max to the front porch, where they'd moved Elmer's homemade bed while they played football, and watched him carefully lift Elmer out. He supported the baby's head, cradled him lovingly on his shoulder.

He soothed the infant's crying with slow, comforting strokes and murmured reassurances—a far cry from the jerky, anxious way he'd handled the baby when she'd first met him.

Max had learned a lot about caring for a baby in the two weeks plus they'd been together. Like any new father would.

She sighed. He could easily handle Elmer without her help now. So why was she still here?

Easy. She didn't want to leave. She'd grown attached to her faux family. But she had to face reality. Max had never said he loved her, never mentioned a future together. Every day she stayed, she fell deeper into the morass of complicated emotions that would be her undoing when she parted. If she were smart, she'd cut her losses now and head back home.

But not just yet. *Please, just let me have one more day.*

Elmer seemed particularly cranky that night.

"Let me see if I can calm him." Max held out his hands to take the baby from Laura.

As she passed the child to him, he looked into her eyes and saw the same conflicting emotions in her expression that swirled inside him. Concern and compassion for the baby warred with frustration. And with eagerness to get the infant to sleep so that they could pick up where they'd left off that afternoon.

It had only been a matter of hours since he'd last made love to Laura, but his body ached for her as if it had been years.

Elmer quieted down a bit, sucking on his fist.

"Get his binkie for me, will ya?" he said.

"His *binkie?*" Laura smiled, and a wave of hot desire crashed over him.

Jeez, he'd survived three years of abstinence in relatively good form, but just a little bit of Laura had turned him into a sex addict. Correction, a Laura addict. His obsession wasn't just about sex, though their lovemaking could bring a man to his knees. No, he couldn't get his fill of the contentious, affectionate, beautiful angel who had saved him from certain disaster with his nephew.

He lifted his eyebrow. "Isn't that what you call his pacifier?"

"Yeah, but I never heard you call it that. You sound really cute when you talk that way." She waggled her eyebrows at him and curled her mouth in a teasing grin.

The effect she had on him was outrageous. Without trying, she'd touched a place inside him he'd believed long dead, made him truly happy. Yet while he was the happiest he'd been in years, he also knew it wouldn't last.

He had to let Laura go. He had to free her to find the man who could give her the family, children and home she deserved. Exactly what he wanted desperately to do for her but couldn't.

That truth tore him apart, but it was for the best. The best for Laura. He, on the other hand, would go crazy without her.

"You seem to have acquired the magic touch, Mr. Caldwell." Laura's voice called him out of his thoughts. "I don't think the binkie will be necessary."

"The touch?" He could think of several places he'd love to touch her right now, but her gaze was on the baby. She meant something different.

Laura nodded toward Elmer, who'd dozed off on his shoulder. "He seems to prefer you over me today. Should I be jealous?"

"If he's anything like his mother, he'll have changed his mind by morning." Max eased toward the baby's bed, crouched and slowly lifted the sleeping infant off his shoulder. Elmer peeped then found his thumb and drifted back to sleep.

"That's my boy. Give Uncle Max a couple of uninterrupted hours with Aunt Laura, and I'll buy you the NFL team of your choice."

Laura grinned. "A whole football team. I'm impressed. Am I worth that much?"

"Baby, you're worth that and more. Come 'ere, gorgeous."

With a titillating grin, she glided into his arms.

He wouldn't think about having to give her up. Not right now. For the moment, he would fill himself up with her sweet essence, her generous heart, her soul-deep kisses.

But Tuesday was a different matter. Charles's bank would be open, and he'd wire Max the money he'd requested. By Tuesday night, Max planned to be out of the cabin and in a hotel somewhere, possibly in another state.

As much as it would kill him to say goodbye, Tuesday was the logical time to send Laura home. He had one day left with her. He intended to make Monday count.

The first crash woke them. By the second crash, it was too late.

Anthony Rialto's thug splintered the wood

around the dead bolt with the ax Max had left by the firewood and broke the door open.

Max knifed upright in the bed. Early morning sunlight spilled in the yawning hole from the chilly outdoors.

Icy fingers of cold air slipped around Max like the hand of the Grim Reaper. A chilling dread sliced through the cobwebs of sleep and burrowed to his bones.

He tensed as the beefy hitman stepped into the cabin, his gun ready. Laura sat up in the bed with a gasp, and the hitman's weapon swung toward her.

Max's blood ran cold. He had to do something to minimize the risk to Laura. He had to protect her at all costs.

Even his own life.

While Laura clutched the sheet to her chest, her gaze frozen on the thug's weapon, Max dived for his Glock on the nightstand. But the gun lay just beyond his reach.

"I wouldn't if I were you, Caldwell. Theo has orders to shoot if you so much as sniff."

The flinty voice stopped Max. He turned to find Anthony Rialto standing just behind his henchman. Theo now aimed his weapon at Max. With a grave, unflinching glare on

Rialto, Max slowly withdrew his hand, his palm up.

Anthony moved toward the nightstand and picked up the Glock. "That's better. Now, where's my grandson?"

"How did you find us?" Max asked in a low, even tone.

Anthony smirked. "We knew a loyal family man like you would be calling to check up on Emily, check in with friends and work. So we tapped a few key phones—your ex-wife's, your fire station's, your pal Charles's—"

Max gritted his teeth. *Hell. Of course.*

"I see you know where I'm going with this." Anthony grinned smugly. "When you told Charles where to wire you money, the general store near his cabin, it was as simple as searching your house to locate this address book." Rialto waved a small brown leather book Max recognized as his. "We entered the information for 'Charles's hunting cabin' at Mapsearch dot com and bingo. We had directions where to find you. Now, where's the baby?"

Elmer.

The baby was defenseless, and Max would be damned if he'd let Rialto get his hands on Emily's son.

He cursed silently, torn between his loyalty to his nephew and to Laura. Could he possibly protect them both?

Rialto scanned the room, his gaze stopping on the homemade cradle. With a nod, he directed Theo to check for the baby.

Laura gasped. She lunged from the bed toward the baby. "No! Don't touch him!"

Shivering in her nightshirt, she threw her body over the top of the basket where Elmer cried. The glare she gave Theo reflected her fear but also a bold challenge. Like a mama bear protecting her cub.

Emotions swelled in Max's chest. Pride in her valor. Admiration for her fighting spirit. Fear for her life.

Theo glowered at Laura. "Outta the way, blondie."

"No! You can't have him," she growled.

"Get the baby," Rialto repeated tightly.

Theo grabbed Laura around the waist and thrust her aside with a vicious shove. She stumbled and fell against the cast-iron fireplace tools on the hearth with a loud clatter.

Protective rage erupted in Max. The bastard! Nobody treated a woman that way around him. Max charged from the bed toward Theo. He tackled the thug shoulder-first, hitting Theo low and hard the way he taught his players. Together, he and Theo collapsed against the rocking chair, narrowly missing Elmer's bed. In his peripheral vision, he saw the thug's gun skitter across the floor.

Theo's thickly muscled torso twisted under Max, and before Max had recovered his balance, Theo slammed a rocklike fist into his jaw. A strange buzzing filled his ears, along with Laura's scream. Elmer's startled cry followed.

Despite the pain ricocheting through his skull, Max readied himself quickly to stave off another blow. He couldn't fail Emily. Couldn't.

He set his feet wide and shifted his weight to brace himself. A cold draft from the open door reminded him he wore only his boxers and T-shirt, but he refused to let his dishabille be a disadvantage.

When Theo swung his arm at him, Max ducked. Channeling his power to his legs, Max lunged up and kicked at Rialto's thug in the same swift movement. He landed a solid blow to Theo's gut. The henchman grunted and doubled over, holding his ribs.

Max sensed more than saw Laura easing across the floor toward Theo's weapon. A flash of fear crawled up his spine. If Rialto saw her going for the gun...

He had to keep attention away from her. But where was Rialto? The man was too quiet. Max cut a glance across the room toward Emily's father-in-law.

When their eyes met, Rialto gave him a smug smile and raised Max's Glock.

Max's heart stilled. He could go head to head with the beefy thug, but no man could compete with a 9mm bullet.

"Max, look out!" Laura screamed.

He spun back toward Theo—just in time to receive the fist that came rocketing toward him. Again, blinding pain ripped through him. Max blocked the next punch, grabbing Theo's wrist and twisting the man's arm backward. Throwing his weight against his attacker, Max knocked Theo to the floor. The henchman's head hit the stone hearth with a heavy thud.

Following him down, Max hit the ground with a bone-jarring crash. The crack of gunfire boomed through the cabin, and a bullet splintered the wood floor by Max's head.

Quickly, he rolled to his back and found Rialto poised across the room with the Glock aimed at him.

"Theo, I'll handle Caldwell. Get the baby, damn it!" Rialto shouted.

The thug didn't respond, didn't move. One down.

Elmer released a frightened-sounding shriek.

Rialto stalked closer, narrowing a menacing gaze on Max. "I'm sick of your games, Caldwell. The baby belongs to me."

Max tasted something metallic and wiped blood from the corner of his mouth. "The baby belongs with Emily. She's his mother."

Max glimpsed Laura inching across the floor. He didn't dare glance her way for fear of calling attention to her movement. Instead, he held Rialto's hard stare with his own as the man approached. Max waited.

Rialto darted a glance toward the baby's bed where Elmer cried pitifully. And Max seized his chance.

In one fluid motion, he grabbed Theo's gun from the floor and swung it toward Rialto. "Don't touch that boy."

Rialto cast Max a condescending glare. "That boy is Joe's heir. Someday he'll inherit the family business."

Max rose slowly to his feet, holding Rialto at bay with Theo's gun. "Do you really want him raised in your world of drugs and violence? Is that what you want for your grandson?"

Anthony scowled. "I can put the world at his feet."

"Like you did for Joe?" Max crept toward Elmer's bed. "Joe's dead. Murdered."

Rialto stiffened. Color suffused his face.

"Damn you!" the man shouted, raising the Glock.

Laura struck.

With the iron fire poker clutched in her hands, she swung at Rialto's outstretched arm.

Anthony fired.

Max dived for the basket where Elmer cried. He heard a bullet pock the floor.

With an upward swing, Laura struck Rialto in the jaw, and the older man stumbled backward. She scrambled around Rialto and hurried to the baby's bed.

Tossing the fire tool out of Rialto's reach, she scooped Elmer into her arms. Tears filling her own eyes, Laura nestled the crying infant to her breast. "I'm here, sweetie. I've got you. Shh."

Placing himself between Laura and Rialto, Max kept Theo's gun pointed at the drug lord.

"Easy, old man!" He panted for a breath. "I know you'd love to kill me…but I doubt you want to hurt your grandson in the process."

Rialto quivered with rage and growled his frustration. "Give me that baby!"

Max scoffed. "Go to hell."

Rialto waved the Glock at them, his icy control clearly slipping. Max knew they were running out of time.

"Laura," he said quietly. "You've got the ball. You know what to do."

"But—"

"Go. I'll cover you."

"Nobody's going anywhere until I have that baby!" Rialto roared. His hand shook, and the Glock wavered ominously before them.

"Go. Now!" Max repeated.

Laura hesitated only another second before darting for the door.

"Stop!" Rialto shouted. He swung the Glock toward Laura's retreating back.

And fired.

Laura crumpled to the ground.

Icy horror squeezed Max's heart. "Laura!"

Rialto angled the Glock to fire at Laura again. Without hesitation, Max squeezed the trigger of Theo's gun.

Once. Twice.

Rialto jerked as the bullets hit him, then he slumped to the floor.

As the echoes of gunfire faded, Elmer's piercing wail wafted through the eerie stillness. Bitter bile rose in Max's throat as he hurried to Laura's side.

He'd told her to go, and she'd been shot. He'd sworn to protect her and failed. She'd trusted him, and he'd let her down.

Oh, God, let her be all right, and I swear I'll do what I should have done weeks ago— get out of her life.

He dropped to his knees beside her and gently rolled her to her back. A red stain spread at her waist.

"Laura? Can you hear me?" He plucked Elmer from her arms and checked the baby for injury.

She moaned and grimaced. Given the signs of life, Max released a whoosh of air from his lungs.

"Elmer?" she mumbled.

Her concern for the baby, while she lay bleeding, tugged something deep inside him. Even now she put the baby first.

Amazingly, Elmer seemed unharmed, though he screamed his displeasure with the tumble they'd taken. Laura had somehow managed to curl her body around the baby, protecting him as she fell.

"I think he's okay." He set the baby gently on the ground beside her while he tugged her nightshirt up to check her wound.

The bullet had torn an obscene hole in the milky skin at her waist. Skin he'd explored every inch of with his hands and mouth.

His throat tightened. Yanking his own shirt over his head, he balled it up and pressed it against her side, hoping to stem the bleeding.

Weakly she raised a hand and stared at the blood on her fingers. "Blood."

"Hang on, sweetheart. I'm gonna get you to a doctor. You'll be all right."

"Blood...makes me...sick," she whispered.

"Not this time. You have to hold on for me. Understand?"

"I'm sorry... Max." Her eyelids fluttered, and her hand fell limply at her side.

His chest constricted. He framed her face with his hands and looked straight into the fading light in her eyes.

"Listen, Laura, you have to fight. No quitters on my team. No excuses. You have to hold on a little longer."

She gave him the slightest of nods. But it was enough.

He moved Elmer to her chest and scooped both of them in his arms. After strapping both of them in the car, he headed down the twisting mountain road at breakneck speed.

Every mile he drove was anguish, every passing minute an eternity. He castigated himself for all the mistakes he'd made with Laura. She fought for her life now because he'd been too selfish to send her away when he should have.

He'd been wrong to let her stay well after he'd learned to care for Elmer, keeping her in unnecessary danger. Wrong to prolong their time together once he'd realized her deepening attachment to him and the baby. Wrong to let her believe he could give her more than sex. It didn't matter that he cared more about her than his next breath. He couldn't burden her with his infertility.

She deserved more. She deserved the family he couldn't give her, deserved her freedom so she could find a man that could fulfill her needs.

Over and over he repeated his litany.

Let her be all right, and I'll let her go. Please, God, let her live, and I'll get out of her life.

It wasn't much to give a woman who'd risked everything for him, for his nephew. But it was all he had.

Chapter Seventeen

By the time Max finished answering all the sheriff's questions, it was late. He stopped by the small county hospital to check on Laura before going by Parson's to pick up Elmer. The elderly couple had been more than willing to watch the baby while Max settled his business with the sheriff.

He'd explained to the sheriff everything that had happened, who Anthony Rialto was and why Max had shot him. The evidence at the scene and the forensic tests from the cabin supported Max's claim of justifiable homicide. He was free to return home, where the New Orleans police were waiting to question him, as well. The deputies had found Theo at the cabin, still unconscious, and he'd been revived and arrested.

After performing surgery to repair the damage done by the bullet, Laura's doctor had assured Max that she'd pull through in fine form. But Max's concern for her wouldn't be quieted until he checked on her himself. When he reached her hospital room, the attending nurse met him outside her door.

"She's resting now. She woke a moment ago and asked for you, but I think it's better that she sleep right now." The nurse opened the door for Max to peek inside.

He was pleased to see that Laura's color had returned. In fact, other than the IVs hooked to her hand, she looked like the same gutsy angel he'd watched sleep every night for the past several days.

He dragged a hand down his face and sighed his relief.

But his relief was bittersweet. With a sinking remorse, he remembered the bargain he'd made with God, his promise to do what he knew in his heart was best for Laura.

Let her live, and I'll get out of her life.

A knot of frustration and despair clogged

his throat. A clean break was the kindest, the simplest. It was time to move on.

Max cleared the emotion from his throat and faced the nurse. "Will you give her a message for me when she wakes again?"

"Sure. What is it?"

Anguish gripped his chest. What did he tell her?

Thanks for the memories, sweetheart, but I can't give you a baby. Your strength and courage made me fall in love with you, but we have no future? I've never met a woman I wanted to spend my life with more than with you, but you deserve more than I have to give?

Max gritted his teeth, steeling himself to the onslaught of guilt and pain, the sting of tears. "Just…tell her I said thanks."

The nurse blinked. "That's it?"

Leaden regret weighed his lungs. "Yeah. That's all."

"Should I tell her you'll be by in the morning?"

Max shook his head. "I can't stay. There's a police officer from New Orleans waiting in the lobby to escort me back to New Orleans with the baby. I have to answer more questions about this mess for the New Orleans authorities before I'm totally cleared. And I need to check on my sister."

The nurse frowned. "She'll be disappointed she missed seeing you."

Max swallowed hard and glanced back to the bed where Laura slept peacefully. "But it's for the best."

"He left?" Laura struggled to process the news that the night nurse gave her the next evening when she came back on duty. She'd waited all day for Max to come visit.

A sheriff's deputy had stopped by just after lunch, and she'd recounted everything that had happened from the day Max had commandeered her car. When the deputy said her testimony cleared Max of wrongdoing, she'd counted on having a chance to talk to Max herself.

But when he'd come by, he hadn't stayed.

Laura met the nurse's sympathetic gaze. "I... I don't understand."

But deep inside she did understand. Max was gone. Just like so many before him. Searing pain that had nothing to do with her gunshot wound flowed through her body.

"He said to tell you thanks and that a policeman was escorting him and the baby back to New Orleans."

"Did he say...anything else?"

Like "I love you"? Or "I'll be back for you"? Or "I'll call"?

"Sorry. Just 'thanks.'"

Thanks. Just thanks.

For what? Putting her life on hold to help him save his nephew's life? For the hot sex to help pass the hours until he dumped her? For the trust she'd given him, even though experience had taught her the cost?

"But this letter arrived a little while ago along with a bunch of your personal belongings." The nurse's comment interrupted Laura's reverie and sparked hope inside her. The nurse handed Laura a plain envelope from the bedside stand. "Maybe there's more information in it."

Moving her arms to take the envelope sent a wave of sharp pain through her chest, but Laura ignored the discomfort as she ripped open the letter.

Inside the envelope she found a one-way plane ticket to New Orleans, money for a cab to the airport and a short handwritten note.

I've taken your car back to N.O. I knew the doctor wouldn't let you drive for a while after surgery.

I owe you so much, yet I know the

thing you need most is the one thing I can't give you. I'm sorry. Your future is with another man.

Get well soon. Max

Despair doused the spark of hope.

Rather than show the nurse her disappointment and the razor-sharp ache that twisted inside her, Laura gave the woman a short, wry laugh. "He took my car. Again."

The nurse chewed her lip without answering. "Can I get you anything? Do you need another painkiller?"

Laura shook her head. Her worst pain had no remedy.

How did one treat a broken heart?

Four days later, Laura paid the cabdriver who brought her home from the New Orleans airport and shuffled stiffly into her tiny, lonesome apartment.

Home again.

Everything looked the same. Her cluttered kitchen counter, her mystery novel waiting by the sofa, the dim light filtering in from her bathroom night-light. Nothing in her apartment had changed, yet everything about her life had changed. Max had changed her, challenged her, made her feel things she'd never thought she could.

Yet, thinking back, she realized he'd never told her he loved her, never promised her anything beyond the moment. Certainly not a commitment, a future or a white picket fence.

She'd simply let her desperate longing for love and family, a place to belong, override the cruel lessons she'd learned over the years. Love didn't last. People didn't stay in her life long enough to build a family.

Laura stumbled over to her sofa and sank into the cushions. She fought the tears that swelled in her throat, choking the breath from her.

Max hadn't cared enough to stay. The sooner she accepted this truth, the sooner she could move on with her life. Alone. As always.

The idea of facing the next day and the next without Max sent a blinding ache through her. Finally she gave up the battle and let the moisture fill her eyes and stream down her cheeks.

Giving in to her tears made her feel like the helpless and lonely child who'd drifted through the system with no control over her future, no place to call home, no one who truly cared.

She knew crying was an exercise in futility. A waste of energy. All the tears she'd spilled growing up had never changed her circumstances, so why should things be different now?

Laura blew her nose and tried to push the memory of Max from her mind. Memories of quiet nights by a crackling fire, crisp mornings waking in his arms, sunny days playing touch football.

If you ever get the ball, run. Head for the goal line and don't let anything stop you.

Now *there* were words to live by, she thought with a snort. She'd keep that gem in mind the next time she spent a Sunday afternoon with the Kennedys at Hyannisport.

I don't believe in casual sex.

Laura growled in frustration and pressed a throw pillow to her ears as if she could block out the sound of his voice playing in her head.

You have to fight. No quitters on my team.

Laura shivered as Max's command filtered through her mind, along with the terror she'd known that last morning staring down Rialto's gun. Much of what had happened after Anthony Rialto had shot her was hazy. She remembered the blood, the jarring ride down the mountain, Elmer's crying.

And Max's voice. The urgency and fear in his tone.

She'd focused on his voice to keep from slipping into the darkness that beckoned her.

No quitters on my team. No excuses. Hold on....

She had fought for him. She'd held on despite the searing pain as her blood and her strength seeped from her. And for what? She'd awakened in a hospital to find that he'd left her alone.

A fresh flood of tears stung her eyes, and she gritted her teeth in aggravation.

Pushing to her feet, careful not to pull her stitches, she stalked to the kitchen to heat a frozen dinner. She refused to sink into the despondency and sense of helplessness that had shadowed so much of her youth. She'd come too far and struggled too long to put those years behind her for her to lose control now. She wasn't a scared, powerless little girl anymore.

She was a woman with control over her life and her future. Swiping at her damp eyes she drew a slow, cleansing breath.

No quitters on my team. No...quitters.

Laura froze. Her breath hung in her lungs, and her pulse kicked up its pace.

"Oh, my God," she whispered, hope swelling inside her.

When she'd learned Max had left her at the hospital, she'd allowed the resurgence of past pain, the memories of old hurts to paralyze her.

But she *wasn't* a helpless child anymore. She had the power to fight back, to shape her future and fight for her happiness. For a few precious days with Max, she'd shed the manacles of her fear, let him into her heart, and she'd known a joy and hope she'd only dreamed of before.

Laura smiled as determination and purpose flowed through her. "I will fight, Max. For what I want, what I need. For you."

"You named my son what!" Emily shrieked.

Max winced, wishing he'd waited until his head wasn't pounding to tell Emily about Elmer.

As her doctor had predicted, Emily had regained consciousness. Once assured that Max and her son were safe and back in town, she'd made significant progress. Moved back to a regular hospital room, Emily quickly regained her fighting spirit and her strength.

Max rubbed his temples and tried to explain. "I named him after our grandfather. Mom's dad."

Elmer had cried all night, apparently missing Laura as much as he did. The lack of sleep had left Max with a splitting headache. Missing Laura left him aching deeper in his soul.

"Out of all the names on God's green earth, you picked *Elmer?*" His sister covered her face with her hands, and her shoulders shook.

Max groaned. "C'mon, Em. Don't cry. It's not written in stone. Put whatever you want on the birth certificate."

She moved her hands to peer out at him, and he saw that she was laughing, not crying.

"Elmer?" She held her side as she chuckled. "Oo, oh, ouch. It hurts to laugh."

He rolled his eyes and scowled at his sister churlishly. "You're welcome for nearly losing me my job and risking my life and Laura's to save your son. Don't mention it."

Emily bit her bottom lip and gave him a wide, dark-eyed look of remorse. "Oh, Max. You know I appreciate everything you did. Everything you've *always* done for me."

Her expression sobered, and her eyes reflected warmth and love. "That's why *your* name is on my son's birth certificate."

He drew his eyebrows together sharply and frowned. "What?"

"I named my son after you."

Max sat back in his chair, stunned, touched. "You did?"

She nodded. "Maxwell Trey Rialto. I'm going to call him Trey. To avoid confusion."

"Trey. I like it." He smiled.

"But…" Emily said, sobering. "Even though Rialto is on his birth certificate, I don't think I'll use the name for him. Neither of us will. I want to put the Rialtos behind us for good and never look back."

Max nodded, a fresh concern nagging him. "Have you heard from Joe's mother? Is she still pursuing the custody issue?"

Anthony Rialto might be dead, and his henchmen in custody, but Max worried his sister hadn't heard the last from Lydia Rialto.

"My lawyer says Lydia doesn't have a case since I'm Trey's mother. I honestly don't think she was the one behind the custody question to begin with. Her husband totally dominated her, made all the decisions. She knows after everything that's happened, if she wants any chance ever to see her grandson, she has to make amends."

"That's a relief." Max sighed.

"What about the investigation into the drug smuggling?" Emily asked, her eyes dark with concern. "Do you think anyone would try to hurt us in retaliation?"

Max turned up his palms. "The police don't think so. Theo Malone, the thug Anthony brought with him to North Carolina, was still unconscious in the cabin when the cops arrived to secure the scene. He had a pretty bad concussion and a go-directly-to-jail card when he woke up at the hospital. With Rialto dead, Theo decided to save himself and was quite willing to talk. From what I understand, the cops have gotten enough information to close down the drug operation. Apparently the process was pretty cut and dried. They cleared me of wrongdoing once I answered all their questions, so... I think it's over, Em."

"Thank God. Now can we talk about something happier?" Emily's eyes sparkled.

Max narrowed a skeptical gaze on Emily. "Such as?"

"Tell me about this Laura that you mentioned."

Laura. She hadn't been far from his mind since he'd left North Carolina under police escort four days ago. As it did every time he thought of her, his chest tightened with regret and longing. How the hell was he supposed to get over her? "Long story."

"I'm not going anywhere." Grinning, Emily nestled into her pillow as if preparing for a bedtime story. "So spill it, brother. You have something going with her, don't you?"

"Had. It's over, and I'd rather not talk about it."

Emily scowled. "Over? Why?"

"Drop it, Em."

"Do you love her?"

"Does it matter if I do?" Max rose from his chair with an impatient huff to pace. "I loved Jennifer, but I couldn't give her the family she wanted. I won't make the same mistakes with Laura that I did with Jenn."

Emily's gaze followed him back and forth across the room as he paced. "But you already are! You're giving up! You love her, but you're quitting. Is that what you teach your Pee Wee team? When it gets too hard or hurts too much, then quit?"

"Of course not! It's not the same—"

"There were lots of times these past two weeks when I wanted to give up, Max. I hurt. I was weak. I was scared. But I love you. Love my son. So I fought. That's what you have to do if you love Laura, Max. It may be hard, and it may hurt sometimes. But you can't quit."

He dragged a hand down his face and groaned. "Emily..."

Emily aimed a finger at him. "No quitters on *my* team either, Max. Find her and tell her how you feel. Don't you owe her that much?"

The toddler playroom at Happy Camper Day Care Center teemed with enough droopy-diapered rug rats to give the average bachelor a case of hives.

The first thing that Max noticed when he opened the door to the playroom was the volume. The high-pitched squeals of the energetic tykes, the clatter of plastic tea sets and crash of tumbling block towers jangled his already taut nerves.

Yet in the middle of the chaos and noise, Laura sat with the serenity of a butterfly, rolling out blue clay with a table full of children.

He stood and simply watched her for a moment, gathering his thoughts, wondering what he could possibly say to make her understand the tough choices he'd made. Remorse pinched his chest.

Laura smiled at a little girl beside her and tousled the child's hair. Max's stomach somersaulted. Seeing Laura's face brighten when she looked at the child was all the reminder he needed of what he couldn't give her and why he had to let her go.

Reaching in his pocket, he wrapped his fingers around her car keys, but before he could call to her, her gaze snapped up. As if she sensed his presence.

Her easy smile faded, replaced by surprise. Despite the shouts and squeals of the children clambering about the room in frenzied activity, the world narrowed to two people.

He cleared his throat and drew her keys out of his pocket, held them out to her. "I brought you your car. The bullet holes are all fixed up. Good as new."

She nodded. "Thanks." Then tossing her curls over one shoulder she added, "I hope you told them to take care of that funny noise under the hood."

He puckered his brow. "What noise? I drove it home from the mountains and never heard—"

A sly grin tugged the corner of her mouth... and he remembered. A fraction of the tension inside him uncoiled.

"Smarty-pants." He held her gaze. "Can we go somewhere quieter to talk?"

Laura lifted her chin and squared her shoulders, a fiery determination blazing to life in her eyes. "Yes. We definitely need to talk."

As she stood from the child-sized table, she rubbed her hands together to roll the clay off her fingers. "We can use the director's office."

He stood back to let her pass and caught a whiff of strawberry shampoo. The sweet scent slammed into him, conjured images of the hours they'd spent tangled together under the sheets, the silky feel of her curls slipping through his fingers.

"Susan, can you watch the toddlers while I speak to Mr. Caldwell, please?" she called to her coworker as she led him down a short hall decorated with cartoon characters and smiling suns. Stepping into the private office, she closed the door to the children's noise.

He rubbed his sweaty palms on his slacks, drew a deep breath. God, he hated this. "Laura—"

"How's Elmer?"

The baby. Of course, she'd want to know about the baby first. He gave her a quick half grin. "Trey."

She tipped her head and frowned. "Hmm?"

"Emily named him Trey. Maxwell Trey. After me."

Warmth filled her face, and a smile blossomed on her lips. "I know that means a lot to you."

He cleared his throat. "Uh, yeah…it was nice of her." He gritted his teeth, hating the stilted, formal words that came out of his mouth.

Hell, he'd made love to this woman, spent days learning every nuance of her touch, and now he was talking to her as if they were strangers. He didn't want small talk. He didn't want *any* talk. He wanted to press her up against the wall and lose himself in her kiss. Forget the speech he'd prepared. Forget everything but the warmth of her in his arms.

"And Emily?" Laura asked. "Is she better?"

He gave her a jerky nod. "She'll come home today."

Her smile brightened. "Wonderful. I'm so glad."

"How do *you* feel?" He glanced at her right side, even though any evidence of her injury was well hidden under her bulky sweater. "When did you get back?"

"Thursday. And I have to move slowly. I still hurt, but…not as bad as I did last week…

when I woke to find that you'd left without a word to me."

Her bluntness landed a sucker punch in his gut. But he knew he deserved it. Guilt sat in his stomach like a knot, as if he'd swallowed a lump of the clay she'd been molding with the kids.

"That's what I came to explain." He reached for her, but she stepped back, straightening her spine.

"I know I hurt you. I'm sorry."

"Go on." She arched an eyebrow and crossed her arms over her chest. She wore an expression of cool confidence and satisfaction that baffled him. Her manner and appearance had changed dramatically since he'd first met her, and he puzzled over the change in her.

"I couldn't walk away from this without letting you know how I truly felt." He saw the first flicker of apprehension in her eyes and rushed on before he lost his nerve. "I fell in love with you up on that mountain. Deeply in love."

"Max, I—"

"I love you, Laura, but I—"

"But?" Her arms dropped to her sides, her hands balled into fists. She narrowed a hard, challenging gaze on him and scoffed. "You can't say 'I love you' and 'but' in the same sentence."

He groaned. "Laura, listen to me…."

"No! You listen to *me*, hotshot." She jabbed him in the chest with her finger. "I've heard all the *buts* in my life that I can take. 'I'm sorry, *but* your mother died last night.' 'I don't want you to go, *but* Mr. Powell needs all my attention now.'" She aimed a finger at his nose. "If you love me, then you love me. Period."

Guilt twisted in his chest.

"But I can't give you the future…the family and children you deserve." He tried to take her in his arms and soothe her, but she raised her arms and shook loose.

"No buts!"

Hell, why did she have to make this so difficult? But then when had anything, other than falling under her spell, ever been easy with Laura?

"Please, try to understand. It's not what I want, but—"

"But nothing!" she shouted, stubborn determination setting her face, tensing her body. "When I was a child, I had no choice but to suffer through the changes, being ripped from one home and shuffled off to another. I had to live with the shattered bonds and torn relationships inflicted on me. I was defenseless. But I'm an adult now, and I won't lose the man I love without a fight."

"I know this is hard for you. It's hard for me, too. Damn hard." His voice sounded hoarse. "But you know I can't give you children. And I know how empty your life would be without them. You need a family. You deserve a family. I can't give you that. I love you enough to let you go. To find a man who can put babies in you."

Laura shook her head, stirring her strawberry scent. "That's crazy."

"Is it? I watched my marriage to Jennifer crumble because I couldn't give her what her heart desired, what she had every right to have. I couldn't make her happy. Her love turned to resentment and—"

She pressed her hand to his mouth and leaned into him. "I'm not Jennifer."

"I know that."

Her blue-green eyes lifted and pinned him with a steady gaze. "I won't let you go. I won't let you throw our love away as though it means nothing."

"What about children, Laura? We can't

conceive because of me, my low sperm count. Can you honestly say that you'll be happy never having a baby of your own?"

"Yes. Because I know, firsthand, that there are thousands of children waiting in foster homes for people like you and me to give them a family. I know, firsthand, that I can love another woman's baby as well as my own flesh and blood. And I know you can, too. I saw it in your eyes when you looked at Elmer. We can adopt."

Max sucked in a sharp breath and stepped back, staring at her, feeling slightly dazed.

Adoption. Jennifer had rejected the option from the start, selfishly rejecting the idea of raising someone else's child. Why hadn't he known Laura would embrace the idea?

He drew a hand down his cheek, scratched his chin and let the idea percolate in his brain. "Are you sure?"

Laura closed the distance between them and took his hands in hers. "Positive. Max, I need you in my life. I don't want to be alone anymore. I found my home when I met you. I want to build a family with you."

He raised one of her hands to kiss it, but stopped with it inches from his lips. He pulled back to look at her fingers more closely. Blue clay lined her fingernails.

She tried to pull her hands back, blushing.

But he tightened his grip and grinned. Then his smile bloomed to a full laugh. "Only you could make blue clay look sexy."

He kissed her palms then pulled her arms around his neck and wrapped her in a hug. "Come home with me, sweetheart. I need you in my life, too."

"Do you mean it? You really want me?" Tears filled her eyes, and a childlike wistfulness tinged her voice.

He pulled her hips more fully against him. "Oh, yes. I want you, sweetheart. For always." He dropped to one knee. "Laura Dalton, would you do me the honor of becoming my wife and—"

"Yes!" she breathed happily.

He held up a finger. "I'm not finished. And will you make a home with me—"

"Yes!"

He shook his finger. "And will you help me make a family for, say, two or three children who need a home?"

"Five."

"Five?" he gasped.

"Or six."

He laughed and pulled her into his arms. "We'll start our own Pee Wee football team."

"Yes," she whispered and kissed him soundly on the lips.

Epilogue

Max, like the rest of the firefighters at the station, was exhausted. Rising in the night to feed a newborn had nothing on the night he'd just had. He'd gotten no more than two hours of sleep. The department had been called out six times before dawn, and he still smelled like smoke and sweat from his last call.

Still, when Laura appeared at the door to the firemen's living quarters and waved him over, Max perked a bit. The mornings he was on duty at the station, she made a habit of stopping on her way to the day care to say hello and to give him a good-morning kiss.

This morning, she punched his shoulder.

"Ow! What was that for?" Max rubbed the sore spot and frowned at his fiancée.

"We can't get married in June." She scowled at him. "Do you know how long I've dreamed of a June wedding?"

"Why can't we? Is there a conflict at the church?"

"No. The church has us on the calendar. The problem is you!" She stabbed a finger in his chest.

"Me? What did I do?"

"You got me pregnant. By June I'll be too fat to fit in my wedding dress. I don't want to get married looking like a blimp."

Max shook his head as if to clear it. "Whoa! Back up. Run that part about me getting you pregnant by me again."

A spark lit her blue-green eyes, and she tugged her lips in a crooked grin. "You heard me, hotshot. I'm pregnant."

Max struggled for a breath, disbelief and hope warring inside him. "That's impossible. I have—"

"Yeah, yeah, I know. You have a low sperm coun—"

He slapped a hand over her mouth. "A little louder, huh? I don't think the whole station heard you."

He pulled her into the fire marshall's tiny office, where large glass windows looked out to the main living quarters for the firemen. Only then did he take his hand from her mouth.

"That's what I told my doctor. But she said, low sperm doesn't mean *no* sperm." Laura flipped her hair over her shoulder and tipped her head. "And there was your three-year abstinence to build up your reserves, so to speak."

Max drew a slow breath. "I know that, but do you have any idea the odds that my doctor gave me that I'd ever…"

"Then we beat the odds, Max." She stepped close and pressed her body against his. "Because at least one of your little guys had your determination and results-orientation. That one little guy got the job done. He didn't quit till he crossed the goal line."

"You're really pregnant? You're gonna have my baby?" He tried to wrap his brain around the concept. He was stunned.

Laura shot her arms up, grinning broadly. "Touchdown!"

An incredible sense of fulfillment swelled inside him until his chest hurt. He threw his own arms in the air and whooped loud enough for the whole fire station to hear. He grabbed Laura and lifted her in a jubilant hug. "Oh, God, but I love you."

"We'll still adopt, though, right?" she asked.

"Of course. Gotta build that football team."

He smiled then captured her lips for a soul-deep kiss. Catcalls and wolf whistles filtered in from the firefighters in the next room.

Laura broke the kiss and gave him a serious look. "So we move the wedding up to Christmas?"

"Whatever your heart desires, sweetheart. You've already made me the happiest man in the world."

"Done. Christmas it is. Oh, and one more thing…" She quirked an eyebrow.

"Anything."

"*I* name the baby. My children will not bear the names of cartoon characters."

Max laughed and hugged her tightly. "You've got a deal."

* * * * *

HOMETOWN HEARTS ♥

YES! Please send me **The Hometown Hearts Collection** in Larger Print. This collection begins with 3 FREE books and 2 FREE gifts in the first shipment. Along with my 3 free books, I'll also get the next 4 books from the Hometown Hearts Collection, in LARGER PRINT, which I may either return and owe nothing, or keep for the low price of $4.99 U.S./ $5.89 CDN each plus $2.99 for shipping and handling per shipment*. If I decide to continue, about once a month for 8 months I will get 6 or 7 more books, but will only need to pay for 4. That means 2 or 3 books in every shipment will be FREE! If I decide to keep the entire collection, I'll have paid for only 32 books because 19 books are FREE! I understand that accepting the 3 free books and gifts places me under no obligation to buy anything. I can always return a shipment and cancel at any time. My free books and gifts are mine to keep no matter what I decide.

262 HCN 3432 462 HCN 3432

Name	(PLEASE PRINT)	
Address		Apt. #
City	State/Prov.	Zip/Postal Code

Signature (if under 18, a parent or guardian must sign)

Mail to the **Reader Service**:
IN U.S.A.: P.O. Box 1867, Buffalo, NY. 14240-1867
IN CANADA: P.O. Box 609, Fort Erie, Ontario L2A 5X3

* Terms and prices subject to change without notice. Prices do not include applicable taxes. Sales tax applicable in NY. Canadian residents will be charged applicable taxes. This offer is limited to one order per household. All orders subject to approval. Credit or debit balances in a customer's account(s) may be offset by any other outstanding balance owed by or to the customer. Please allow 4 to 6 weeks for delivery. Offer available while quantities last. Offer not available to Quebec residents.

Your Privacy—The Reader Service is committed to protecting your privacy. Our Privacy Policy is available online at www.ReaderService.com or upon request from the Reader Service.

We make a portion of our mailing list available to reputable third parties that offer products we believe may interest you. If you prefer that we not exchange your name with third parties, or if you wish to clarify or modify your communication preferences, please visit us at www.ReaderService.com/consumerschoice or write to us at Reader Service Preference Service, P.O. Box 9062, Buffalo, NY. 14240-9062. Include your complete name and address.

Get 2 Free Books,
Plus 2 Free Gifts—
just for trying the Reader Service!

HRLP17R

Get 2 Free Books,

Plus 2 Free Gifts—
just for trying the Reader Service!

Get 2 Free Books,
Plus 2 Free Gifts—
just for trying the Reader Service!

Get 2 Free Books,
Plus 2 Free Gifts—
just for trying the Reader Service!

YES! Please send me 2 FREE Harlequin® Heartwarming™ Larger-Print novels and my 2 FREE mystery gifts (gifts worth about $10 retail). After receiving them, if I don't wish to receive any more books, I can return the shipping statement marked "cancel." If I don't cancel, I will receive 4 brand-new larger-print novels every month and be billed just $5.49 per book in the U.S. or $6.24 per book in Canada. That's a savings of at least 19% off the cover price. It's quite a bargain! Shipping and handling is just 50¢ per book in the U.S. and 75¢ per book in Canada.* I understand that accepting the 2 free books and gifts places me under no obligation to buy anything. I can always return a shipment and cancel at any time. Even if I never buy another book, the 2 free books and gifts are mine to keep forever.

161/361 IDN GLQL

Name	(PLEASE PRINT)

Address	Apt. #

City	State/Prov.	Zip/Postal Code

Signature (if under 18, a parent or guardian must sign)

Mail to the **Reader Service:**
IN U.S.A.: P.O. Box 1867, Buffalo, NY 14240-1867
IN CANADA: P.O. Box 611, Fort Erie, Ontario L2A 9Z9

Want to try two free books from another line?
Call 1-800-873-8635 today or visit www.ReaderService.com.

* Terms and prices subject to change without notice. Prices do not include applicable taxes. Sales tax applicable in N.Y. Canadian residents will be charged applicable taxes. Offer not valid in Quebec. This offer is limited to one order per household. Books received may not be as shown. Not valid for current subscribers to Harlequin Heartwarming Larger-Print books. All orders subject to credit approval. Credit or debit balances in a customer's account(s) may be offset by any other outstanding balance owed by or to the customer. Please allow 4 to 6 weeks for delivery. Offer available while quantities last.